LACRIMOSA

BY
CHRISTINE FONSECA

LACRIMOSA

THE REQUIEM SERIES
BOOK 1

BY

CHRISTINE FONSECA

Lacrimosa, Requiem #1
Christine Fonseca

Copyright 2012 Christine Fonseca.

All rights reserved. No part of this book may be reproduced by any means, graphic, electronic, or mechanical, including photocopying, taping, or by any information storage system without written permission of the publisher except in the case of brief quotations embodied in critical articles and reviews.

ISBN (hardback): 978-0-9847863-6-7
ISBN (paperback): 978-0-9847863-7-4
ISBN (eBook): 978-0-9847863-8-1

Compass Press books may be ordered through booksellers, Ingram, or by visiting our site and contacting us. http://thecompasspress.blogspot.com

Because of the dynamic nature of the internet, any web address or links contained in this book may have changed since publication and may no longer be valid. The views expressed in this work are solely those of the author and do not necessarily reflect the views of the publisher, and the publisher hereby disclaims any responsibility for them.

Stock imagery provided by Thinkstock. Cover design by CP Design. http://cpdesignandcompasspress.blogspot.com

Compass Press 3/13/2012

Other titles by Christine Fonseca available from Compass Press:

Dies Irae (A Requiem Novella)

Dedicated to Aydan and Nesy ~

It may have taken me longer than I'd wanted, but I've finally given your story to the world. Now all will know of your sacrifices and love.

*"Ah! that day of tears and mourning!
From the dust of earth returning
man for judgment must prepare him;
Spare, O God, in mercy spare him!"*

*~LACRIMOSA, Requiem Mass
English Translation by William Josiah Irons (1849)*

CHAPTER 1 – UNWELCOME FEELING

NESY

I shift in the booth, careful to remain hidden in the shadows. My human form feels foreign, awkward. Nothing about tonight's assignment seems right; not the constant thoughts echoing through my mind or the everpresent feelings I can't seem to shake.

I tighten the muscles across my back, desperate to escape the confinement that comes with this new body. One I never wanted.

My senses register each scent, each sound, adding to the noise of too much mental chatter already ricocheting in my head. Sweat and too-strong perfume from the tangled mix of bodies on the dance floor burn my nostrils. My heart pounds against my ribs and unfamiliar twinges of fear cloud my vision. Feelings I can't decipher crawl through my skin, sending chills throughout my body.

I may have prepared for this task, but nothing could prepare me for being a seventeen-year-old girl.

Again.

LACRIMOSA

I slip further into the booth, surveying the scene. Lights pulse around me, synchronized to the blaring sounds that pound from the speakers. Clubbers sway to the music in intoxicating rhythms, casting a spell throughout the room.

And somewhere in the crowd lurks the one I came for. The UnHoly.

I narrow my eyes, taking in the irony of the church-turned-nightclub. Tall, gothic arches adorn the ceiling. Old stone sculptures of saints and angels watch the hordes of teens gyrating on the dance floor. The altar, once a sanctuary, now houses a stage where up-and-coming bands woo adoring fans. The remaining spaces are punctuated with small alcoves designed to hide the club's true patrons—dark creatures that feed on the lust and fear of the human crowd.

My task is simple enough: find the UnHoly and vanquish him to the Abyss. Just like the countless other assignments I've had over the past few centuries. But something about this task feels wrong. Something that sends fresh shivers cascading down my very human spine.

Little information was given to me about my target, only his name, location, and human age. I'd have to figure out the rest. No problem, since vanquishing the UnHoly is my specialty; whether I'm stuck in a teenage body or not.

I take one last sip of water and recite my plan:

One: Find the UnHoly.

Two: Lure him away from the crowd. Don't want to ruin my perfect record with collateral damage.

Three: Cast him out.

What could go wrong?

Satisfied, I settle my thoughts and prepare for battle. The sooner this is finished, the sooner I can ditch this body and escape the chaos it brings. My human form may look similar to my angelic being, with its familiar blond hair and blue eyes. But I hate feeling trapped in this flesh, stifled by the heaviness of this body. I miss feeling the air move through my wings and play across my skin. More than anything else, I miss the quiet solitude of my mind; no emotions to muddle my thinking, no angst to cloud my judgment. Necessary or not, I'm never masquerading as a teenager again.

I smooth out my clothes—black leather skirt, black tee, leather jacket and boots that stretch up my long legs—and approach the altar-turned-stage.

"Hi there," I say to the stooge blocking my entrance. I lock eyes with him, tipping my head slightly. I may not like being human, but I do know how to use this body to get what I want. "Is Aydan here tonight?"

The would-be guard swallows hard.

Perfect.

His gaze rakes over every inch of me as his lips part slightly. He swallows hard and smirks.

Oh yeah, he's easy. "So? Is he?" I purr.

He fumbles over his words. "Um, yeah. The band performs in a few minutes. Want me to get him for you?"

I think about it for a second, picture my plan in detail. "No, I'll try to find him after his set."

"Oh, I'm sure he'll find you. You're just his type," the guard says.

Of course I am.

The lights dim and I take my position in front of the stage. Four dark shapes emerge from the shadows. The band. I scan each one as the crowd fills in behind me.

Heavy sounds from the bass guitar and drums send the horde into a frenzy. I move with the crowd and continue to search. Which one is he? The drummer? Nope, he's definitely human. The guitarist? Maybe. He's too dark to be fully mortal. Too demonic.

But he's also far too weak to be the UnHoly.

I scrutinize the rest of the band members. He has to be here. I couldn't have made a mistake.

I don't make mistakes. Not ever.

A single spotlight focuses on the lean silhouette of the lead singer; a teenage boy who's definitely more than human.

There you are.

He's taller than I expected, wearing clothes that match my own—black jeans, a black sleeveless shirt open just enough to see his smooth pale skin, and black boots. His chiseled muscles and dye-job-black hair hanging in an unruly mess add to his allure.

But it's his eyes that draw my attention. Amber with flecks of gold.

Mesmerizing, dangerous, and…

Familiar. Too familiar.

I bite my lip, my mind racing. Aydan, the only apprentice to the Dark One. Feared by angel and demon alike. He's rumored to stop at nothing to procure anything and everything his master wants. Judging by the way he hypnotizes the crowd of unsuspecting teens with his voice and eyes, I have no doubt that the rumors are well-earned. More than dangerous, Aydan is lethal.

And just my type.

I check out the club, looking for the best way to lure him outside. He's managed to elude capture for more than four centuries. Clearly he knows how to avoid the likes of the Sentinals, the likes of me. But not tonight. Not with this body.

I focus my attention back on him as he finishes his song. There is no evidence of his true nature reflecting in his features; no fangs or claws to signal danger. No sulfur-scent or bloodlust. No proof of the demon that lurks just under the surface. Nothing except the black bat-like wings curving across his back, hidden from everyone.

Well, almost everyone. *Not expecting* me, *are you?*

His voice intoxicates the crowd. The hunger in his eyes reveals his true intent. Aydan is on the hunt.

Two can play at that game.

LACRIMOSA

I notice a small door at the end of a corridor adjacent to the stage. No doubt it empties to the alley that flanks the church. Perfect. Now, to get him outside before he chooses one of the screaming girls as his prey.

Aydan finishes his song as I make my way around the stage and towards the hall. I watch him turn away from the crowd.

Almost time.

The horde screams for him, begs the band to continue.

Aydan grabs the mic. "Do you want more?" he yells. Their response, a cacophony of *"Yes!"* and *"We love you, Aydan!"* rings through the rafters of the once-holy building.

I watch as he works the mob into a craze. Voices blend away. The scene shifts. All I see, all I hear, is Aydan. An unfamiliar current of electricity streaks through my body, causing my heart to beat wildly against my ribs. The tiny hairs on the back of my neck stiffen with anticipation while anxiety fills my senses.

This can't be happening.

I force my heart to slow and shove aside the silly human reactions.

The guitarist starts to strum a ballad. A light frames Aydan as he begins to sing in slow, rhythmic phrases. He scans the crowd; a predator looking for his prey.

Time stops as he turns to me. Our eyes lock and a smile pulls his lips.

My skin erupts in gooseflesh. My legs begin to wobble. His smile broadens and for a brief moment I forget how to breathe.

Strange sensations inundate my thoughts as I feel my abdomen clench and my body tremble.

His stupid mind tricks are working. On me.

Not acceptable.

CHAPTER 2 — HUNTER

AYDAN

The crowd is wild tonight, hordes of kids desperate for a little action. The perfect hunting grounds. Maybe that's why I stick with the band—the free food.

My senses pick up the distinct scent of vanilla and warm sugar. *My favorite.* I feel the craving start at the back of my throat. I have to find the source of that scent and drink from her soul.

Soon.

The lights drop as I sing a slow melody. The rhythms are smooth, seductive. I watch the girls drop their defenses and feel their lust rise with each word I sing.

Scanning the crowd, I search. My need grows with every passing second. Every girl strains to look at me and through their eyes I see their desire, taste their lust. It floods my senses, nourishing me.

But the feeling is temporary, just enough to awaken the Beast within and force me to continue the hunt.

My eyes settle on a girl near the back of the crowd, sandwiched between the stage and a narrow hallway. She's different from the usual patrons of the club. Beautiful—long blond hair, legs that seem to stretch forever, and curves that make me ache. But it isn't her beauty calling to me, or her distinctive vanilla scent.

It's the mystery.

I can feel her desire. But there's more too. So much more. Something angry, dangerous. Something that fills the very depths of me.

I stare into her eyes, and feel her wave of emotion crest. I sing the lyrics to her and watch our worlds join—just me and her.

Easy prey.

She closes her eyes, obviously trying to break the spell I've cast. But I know it won't work. No one can get away from me. I've had centuries of practice.

I continue to sing, weaving a trap around my target. She stares at me, an almost pained expression on her face, in her eyes.

You're mine now.

A flood of emotions fills me, chaotic and wild, desperate. *Her* emotions, *her* passion. The taste is addictive, and I know I can't resist her. I don't want to.

The song ends as my frenzy grows.

It's time.

CHAPTER 3 - CHAOS FORGOTTEN

NESY

He's coming through the crowd, straight for me. I need to lure him outside; complete this task and get out of this darn form. But my feelings are too erratic, too chaotic. My body is confused. And my mind, lost. Memories that aren't supposed to exist threaten to undo me. I need to think; get this human body under control.

I need to be alone.

I run down the hall, ducking into the bathroom. It is just as I suspect—small, dank, and stuffed with Aydan's would-be victims primping and getting high. I squeeze into their near-vacant thoughts, willing them out of the cramped space. Not exactly within the rules, but a necessity if I'm going to salvage the situation at all.

One by one, the parade of girls spill from the bathroom until, finally, I'm alone. I grab the sink and glare into the human eyes reflecting back at me.

"By the strength of Mikayel, you've got to get it together," I say to my image. "Teenager or not, you're still a warrior. He's your target, nothing more, no matter what you think you feel. He kills humans for sport. He'll kill you tonight if he gets the chance."

I take a quick breath, forcing the nonstop barrage of images from my thoughts. A boy, tall, with amber eyes that stare through me.

He's not Adam. He can't be.

That life ended centuries ago.

I stare back at the human version of myself. "The Council trusted you with this job. No one else. You told them you were ready for it, ready to be human again. Ready for what that might mean. You will not disappoint them. You will not forsake your commitment. You will not *feel*. Period." I stare at myself, half expecting the reflection to answer. Moments click by and the emotional wave passes. The memories clear and my thoughts calm.

I stretch my neck, my spine, my legs, searching for the comfort I once felt in flesh. But it's no use. I feel confined. Out of control. Weak.

I hate being human.

The only way out is to finish the task. Determined, I leave.

"You ran off fast." Aydan leans against the wall in the cramped hallway. "Something scare you?" He moves closer, the warmth of his breath tickling my cheek.

Memories—my memories—pour forward. The smell of pine on his skin, the feel of his arms around my waist, the taste of his lips on mine. I lose myself in his eyes, in my past.

LACRIMOSA

Adam.

Leaning into him, I brush my trembling lips against his.

No! The voice is loud in my head, breaking the UnHoly's spell. I can't breathe. Can't think. I can only...

Run.

The cold night air bites my skin as I burst through the emergency doors, the alarm wailing behind me.

"*Succurre mihi.* Help me." My voice is louder than the shrieking bells. My legs tremble and I grab the stone wall of the church, sliding to the ground. Fear that shouldn't exist, grips the whole of me. "*Succurre mihi,*" I say again. "*Succurre.*" I am overcome by pictures long forgotten. They storm my senses and my mind.

A dark forest...*so cold.*

A hideous monster...*sharp teeth.*

A tall boy, golden. Angry...*my love.*

I touch my lips. The taste of Aydan lingers there, a reminder of things that shouldn't exist.

My heart rips open. "*Succurre,*" I whisper one last time as the images continue and my mind rolls in on itself. I'm lost inside an unwanted fear.

And need.

CHAPTER 4 - TORTURE

AYDAN

I watch as the girl runs from me, intrigued. Her scent, the one I crave, floats in the air, igniting my hunger.

The hunt begins.

Everything about this girl is exactly what I need—enticing looks, desire she can't control, and enough chaos to feed an army of dark creatures.

But it isn't her emotions pouring forward that excite me. It's her confusion, her chaos. Almost like she's never felt so out of control before. It's intoxicating, addicting.

There's a familiarity in her endless blue eyes, a kind of haunting that reminds me of only one other. The one I can't forget. The one I dare not remember.

More than enticing, this girl is dangerous.

"Not going after her? That isn't like you." My master stands behind me, his human form so like my own. Black hair, chiseled features, young in appearance, despite the four millennia that has defined his existence. His cold voice echoes disappointment. "You haven't finally met your match, have you?"

"Never," I growl.

"Don't get mad. You're allowed an off day." I feel his eyes on me, waiting. "Occasionally."

His threat hangs in the air. Each passing second awakens the Beast inside, igniting my rage. Rage for letting the girl leave, rage for needing her soul at all.

Rage for remembering things I shouldn't.

A satisfied smile curls on my master's lips. "Nice. Very nice."

I cannot watch him take pleasure in my torment, feed from my anger. Cannot let him know the thoughts that refuse to release me.

Her eyes. Her lips.

Her.

I weave through the club, watching my brethren, dark creatures of every assortment, consume the sins of the naïve teen crowd. The creatures snap their beaks and claw the air as they drink in the lust, greed, and envy of the crowd. The teens have no idea that many of them may not survive the night. They are all lambs to the slaughter.

For the first time in centuries, their actions bring disgust. I have to get away, get a hold of myself before my master notices there's a problem.

I leave the club, inhaling the stale cold air of the rotting city. I reach the train and descend the steep stairs that lead to the subway platform. My thoughts are heavy, laden with emotions I shouldn't be feeling. Not anymore.

I stare down the dark tunnels, trying to clear my mind. But the harder I try not to think of her, the more her blue eyes haunt me.

Images spring to life in the empty shaft. Abandoned feelings crest over me. Anguish, rage, shame.

And love.

Profound, burning love.

My world spins apart as the train station melts away, replaced by a life I don't want to remember. The time before my fall.

My life as human…

I'm so innocent in my memories. A blond boy, no older than seventeen. Tormented. In love.

"Run away with me. It's the only way we can stay together," I whisper.

"I can't leave my sister. There has to be another way."

The sight of her melts me as always. Chestnut hair that reflects the sun and hangs in waves around her face. Her slim build underneath her simple dress. Deep blue eyes that see straight through me.

"Your father will never allow us to be together." I pull her closer to me.

"We have to try. I can't leave Lorelei. I won't." Tears flood her eyes.

Even then, I knew it was just a fantasy. We could never be together. Why did I let myself fall in love with her?

A sharp pain resonates through me as the memory speeds forward and I remember the day I've tried an eternity to forget. The day I'm destined to remember forever…

"Why are you crying?" I watch the tears spill over her cheeks.

"You were right. Papa…he won't listen. He's forbidden me to see you. Promised me to another."

The sadness in her eyes overwhelms me. I take her hands in mine, breathing her in.

The scent of her hair, warm sugar and vanilla, fills every inch of me.

The feel of her skin against mine, so smooth, warms me.

I want to etch her into my soul, to never forget the way she makes me feel, how she fills the very depths of me.

"I know." I say as I lead her into the forest surrounding her farm. Our forest.

"I won't marry someone else. I can't. You were right; the only way we can be together is if we run away. Tonight." Her words bounce off the trees and echo through my thoughts.

She melts into my arms, shivering. I tighten my grip and pull her into a hungry kiss. "What about Lorelei? Or your mother?"

"My sister will understand. I can't be with someone else. I won't."

"They'll never forgive you."

"I don't care. We have to leave. Now."

I hesitate. Torn. I have waited for these words, prayed to hear them. But now that she's mine, I know I can't condemn her to a life on the run. I won't.

Her eyes widen as the moments click by.

One.

Two.

Three.

"Why are you hesitating?" She asks. She steps away from me, her face contorted. "You don't want me now, do you?" Her voice turns cold. Distant. "You said this was the only way."

A gasp escapes my lips as I relive every moment.

"We can't be together. You'll grow to hate me. I vowed—"

"I can't believe what you're saying. You lied to me. This was your idea." Her voice cracks. Tears stream down her face and she turns away. And runs.

"Elle! No!"

"Go," I yell to the apparition of myself. "You idiot. Go after her!" I watch myself plunge into the thicket after her, hearing myself beg for help, pleading with the angels to give me this one thing, to let me have a life with her.

Water fills my eyes as I remember how this ends. The angels won't listen.

They never listen.

LACRIMOSA

I pace the subway platform as my heart slams against my chest and sweat consumes my brow. Rage bubbles through me, feeding the monster I've become. Suffocating anything good that still exists.

The train screeches into the empty station. I board, my mind filled with the familiar taste of vengeance.

For Elle. For the fate I chose. For feelings I never wanted to feel.

For everything.

I walk from car to car, searching for someone that will make me forget. Someone to relieve my pain.

An older couple

—*too easy.*

A mother and her young child

—*no excitement.*

A priest

—*Just...no.*

The train stops, allowing more souls to enter.

A group of would-be Goths followed by fear-eating dark creatures

—*if only they knew what hunts them.*

A couple of gang-bangers

—No thrill.

Still, no one to appease the Beast inside.

I reach the last car, my last chance. Two young men eye an attractive girl clearly on her way home from work. I listen to their thoughts, see their plans to rape and torture her.

My attention shifts to their prey. So naïve, so innocent.

Perfect.

I walk past the would-be assailants and stand next to the girl. She nervously glances at me and smiles, tilting her head a bit.

"Hi." I push into her thoughts and open her mind.

"Hi," she says. A demure look colors her face. A moment of fear passes over her eyes. Fear and excitement.

Oh, yes. She's just what I need.

"A beautiful woman like you really shouldn't ride the train so late. It isn't safe." I move closer and her body tenses. I look over her shoulder to the two men staring at us. Ramming my thoughts into them, I flood their minds with torturous images. Their anguish stems my hunger, allows me to control my frenzy and take my time with the girl.

"Those men mean to hurt you." I nod to the boys trapped in a maze of their own torture. "Let me escort you home, keep you safe. Okay?" My voice casts a spell as my thoughts become hers.

Faint pink hues paint her cheeks. "Um, okay. That's very nice of you."

"Oh, it's no problem. No problem at all." I allow her mind to see a taste of my plans. A not-so-innocent kiss. A brief caress. She smiles at me, flushing with the thoughts I plant.

"This is my stop," she says as the train slows. "Thanks again for riding with me."

"The pleasure is mine," I whisper in her ear. "But please, let me walk you home. Just to be safe."

A flash of panic and then a smile. "Sure, okay."

I lead her from the train, through the deserted streets of the city. My need explodes across my tongue and I can barely control myself. *Slow down*, I remind myself. *Enjoy her.*

I pull her into a dark alley, lean her against the cold brick building. A soft breeze flutters past and I smell the sulfuric scent of the dark creatures waiting to feed.

Almost time.

I press into her. "You really should be more careful with strangers."

Her body stiffens against mine. I feel her heart pound against her ribs as her breathing grows erratic. A seductive mix of fear and desire colors her features.

Close your eyes. Give into me.

Her eyes roll back as I lean in and tease her neck with my lips. Her jaw, her mouth. A barely-there moan escapes her lips.

I've won.

Demonic shapes form from the shadows around me. Tall and short, beaked and clawed, they move invisibly toward their next meal. *Wait. Soon you can feed.* They stop and allow me to finish, their need nearly eclipsing my own.

"Are you sure about this?" I ask my victim, already knowing her answer.

She grabs my waist and pulls me to her until the space between us is gone. "Yes," she says through trembling lips.

I draw her into a soft kiss. The mix of chaotic emotions—fear, lust, need—send me into a frenzy. I pull her into a hungrier kiss, moving my hands to the small of her back. She wraps her leg around me, her desire matching mine.

I retreat, teasing her. She moans and pulls me back.

I take what I need, gripping her body and ripping apart her soul. The sweet nectar unleashes the monster within. Her eyes spring open, wide and filled with unmitigated fear. The color drains from her skin as every crevice, every line in her face hardens with terror. She tries to close her mouth as her fists pound against my chest. I tighten my hold on her body and force her lips open.

I take her breath.

Her life.

Her soul.

And wait for my release, for the pain to ebb.

Nothing. Only more fury.

I drop the girl's lifeless body. Demonic sounds pierce the night as the creatures move in, their beaks snapping around me.

LACRIMOSA

They rip at her body, feasting from the discarded torment and flesh.

My anger, my torment, grows with each heartbeat.

CHAPTER 5 – TRANSCENDING PAIN

NESY

There are few things I hate more than feeling weak. Needing help or failing top the list. The worst, however, is knowing that all three just happened.

My soulless human form sleeps without me. I had to get away from her body, her chaotic feelings, if only for a moment. I never wanted to be locked in flesh again. But glamour, illusion, will never fool an UnHoly like Aydan. No, I had no choice but to become human again.

I stare at the human girl, wondering what her life was like. Did she always feel so off balance? So confused? Did she ever feel love and hatred as I do in her body? Or has she always been nothing more than a shell created to serve the Council? I know the answer even before the question is fully formed. She is flesh and bone, memory and emotions. Nothing more. No soul, no higher purpose. A tool to serve the Council when we must interact with the humans we are sworn to protect. A vehicle that allows us to get closer to the UnHoly and the Dark One.

Shards of golden light reflect from my skin and dance around the room as I contemplate the night. My wings, an intricate web of spun gold and translucent feathers, unfurl behind me. Finally released from the confines of humanity I can relax. Think.

My emotions, human emotions, got the better of me tonight. No doubt the Council will want an explanation. And soon.

A true warrior should've been able to block those feelings and focus only on the mission.

A true warrior never would've lost control.

A true warrior wouldn't have failed.

I think of my training, think of what Mikayel, the head of my order, would say if he knew of my weakness.

Of course he knows.

"Where's your control, Sentinal?" I can almost hear his voice booming in my ear. "Focus. Practice."

But I have practiced. For centuries.

I joined the Sentinals so I could forget. Adam. My human life. Everything.

Trained in combat and dedicated to control, the path of the Sentinal was my best hope for survival. My time on Earth had scarred me. Secrets and feelings no angel should possess were permanently tattooed to my soul.

Images of my training stream through my thoughts. Decades learning to handle a sword. Even more time spent learning the ways of the UnHoly and the Dark One.

I trained my mind, closed off my heart, transcended all emotions. I forgot.

Until tonight.

Tonight's events rewind and I relive each heart beat, looking for the moment I lost control. Aydan fills my thoughts.

Amber eyes…*so like his*.

The feel of his body against mine…*inviting, familiar*.

The taste of his lips…

Adam.

I broke every rule. Lost control. Endangered my order. It's a miracle Zane and Cass found me. A miracle Aydan didn't walk outside and discover the truth. A miracle the Dark One wasn't there.

I have to fix this: find the UnHoly, finish my task. Before the Council comes and Mikayel asks questions that have no answers.

I draw in a deep breath and stow away my thoughts. *Control, Sentinal. Stay in control. That time is gone. It has no meaning to you now.*

Yeah, right.

"I see you're awake." Zane, my best friend and confidant, stands in the doorway. We could be twins, our angelic statures identical except for his jet black hair and the dark emerald green glow to his skin and robes. It's the color of the Mediators, angels whose job it is to protect humanity from the evil seduction of the dark creatures and relay messages from the Council. It's that last part that worries me.

Do they know?

Zane helped me transition from my life on Earth. After sixteen years in human form, you forget a few things about being an angel. He filled in the holes, healed my mind, reminded me of my duty. It was Zane who introduced me to the Sentinal order, Zane who encouraged me to trust Mikayel. I owe him my life a thousand times over.

A thousand-and-one if you count tonight's fiasco.

"Hey, I was just coming to find you. Where's Cass?"

"She's confirming your orders." Zane clenches his jaw, something he only does when he's angry. Really angry.

This can't be good.

"Orders? What orders?" My voice screams the unspoken question—how much does the Council know?

"You had to know they'd see everything. What happened? Why isn't that UnHoly gone?"

"Being human happened." I turn away, unable to handle his interrogating glare. "There's something wrong with my host—her mind isn't clean. She still has memories, feelings."

"Impossible. I took care of it myself."

"Well I don't fail, whether I'm trapped in a human body or not. My host has to be the problem. It's the only explanation."

"Are you certain?" Zane's accusing tone fills me with anger, doubt.

"Of course I'm certain. What else can it be?"

The question lingers as my mind crafts the answer. My past. My memories. My feelings.

No! I refuse accept that. I purged everything centuries ago.

"You were only in form for a few hours, too fast for your host to change you." Zane pins me with his stare.

"What are you saying? That this has to do with last time?"

He furrows his brow and reaches into my mind. "Does it?"

Images and feelings race past my vision. Aydan singing to me, the feel of his skin on mine, the taste of his lips.

Blazes. What's wrong with me?

"Your form isn't the problem, Nes. Is it?" Zane takes a deep breath and retreats from my thoughts. "You're going to have to manage the emotions—yours, the girl's, whatever. You said you could handle this. The Council expects this taken care of quickly." I open my mouth to speak and Zane raises a quieting hand. "And I expect you to do your duty."

The disappointment in his voice stings more than my failure. "What do you want me to do? I didn't expect any of this to happen."

"I expect—"

Before he can finish his thought, Cass appears next to him. She's shorter than either of us, with long black hair that reflects the indigo color glistening from her skin and wings, the color of her order, the Anointed. Where Zane healed my mind so many centuries ago, Cass healed my heart.

"So, did you tell her?" Cass smiles, a stark contrast to the scowl still etched on Zane's face.

"Yes. She understands her duty."

"My *duty* was never a question, Zanethios." This is how it always is with Zane. I do something a tad reckless, and he lectures me about duty. Most days the routine is comforting.

Today it only illuminates my shame. My failure.

Cass ignores the frustration in my voice. She's used to the constant bantering between Zane and I. "So," she says. "Tomorrow you'll enroll in Aydan's high school, find him, and finish your task. No problem."

"Whoa, what? High school? No one said anything about high school."

"You should've thought about that at the club."

"Zane, stop. She'll get it done." Cass smiles at me. "We've been ordered to stay with you until you've completed the assignment."

"Why? I've never needed a team. Or a babysitter."

"You've never missed an opportunity to vanquish either." Zane's voice is flat. I've never seen him so disappointed, so angry, with me.

I want to argue, justify every action. But the words won't form. Zane is right. I messed things up. Just me. I let the stupid emotions of a teenage girl confuse me. Let myself feel broken. Let myself remember.

That will never happen again.

East Side Prep looks more like a large brownstone than one of the best prep schools in the city. I climb the steps, unfamiliar doubt surfacing in my all-too-human thoughts. But not just doubt. Fear. Something feels wrong. Evil. Maybe the UnHoly isn't the only dark creature walking the halls of this school. Maybe there is something worse, much worse.

I get my schedule from an office clerk and walk into the European History class, late. The loud bang of the door announces my presence to everyone. Not that I care. I'll be gone by tomorrow and the UnHoly along with me.

I hand the registration slip to the teacher and search. Ayden's easy enough to spot: back row, dressed in black, whispering to his tablemate, a black-haired, Goth boy I recognize from last night. Neither of them have a care in the world.

Let's see how long that lasts.

I stare too long into his amber eyes, feeling an ache of yearning that twists in my abdomen. *Inhale…1…2… 3…Release…1…2…3…Control your thoughts, Sentinal.* The mantra repeats as I ignore the urge to jump into his arms and lose myself in his touch.

"Pick whatever seat you want," the teacher says, pausing. "Nesy, is it? Nesy Walker?"

I nod and move towards the cluster of desks closest to Aydan.

Aydan's conversation seeps through my thoughts along with something that makes my skin crawl. The same evil I noticed before. I steal a glance at Aydan, trying to locate the source of my newfound anxiety.

"So, I think I know what you're doing after school," the Goth boy whispers to Aydan. "Just save some for the rest of us."

"No promises," Aydan says as he looks my direction. His eyes find mine and for a moment I forget my purpose.

Again.

"That's why I like you, Aydan," Goth boy laughs. "You always take care of yourself first."

Sit by me, Nesy. Aydan's voice rings in my ears. I glance away, pretending not to hear him. Goth boy watches. Waits. And I have to wonder, is he the source of evil?

I feel Aydan pull me toward him. Catching his gaze, I smile and deliberately slide into the vacant seat two desks in front of him.

His frustration fills the air between us. It's all I can do to keep from laughing. Being in this body, being undetectable to him, has some perks after all, even if I have to endure these stupid emotions.

"Looks like she's going to make you work for it. Interesting." Goth boy chuckles, a chilling sound that makes me again question *what* he is.

Another surge of quiet fury rolls from Aydan into me.

"Don't worry," Goth boy continues. "Her fight will make it all the sweeter in the end."

His words explode a sense of dread through me. Whatever he is, he's not human. No doubt about it.

I turn and look straight at Aydan, daring him to make a move. His lips turn up in a seductive smile. Hunger filters through his eyes. Followed by...

Anguish.

The teacher's voice pulls my attention back to class. "The werewolf legend originated in Bedburg," he says. "Peeter Stubbe...murders...a demon."

I know that legend all too well, know the details they don't print in the history books. I lived that legend.

All at once I remember the forest near my home, the wolf that stalked the edges, the warnings.

And the attack.

My emotions attempt to spin away from me as pieces of that time spring to life. *Not again.* I start the breathing mantra, determined to wrangle my emotions. Within a single heart beat, my mind is my own. I swallow back my feelings and focus on my task.

Aydan.

His thoughts float through me as I see his need to rip me from my soul. I understand his weakness, my way in.

Abruptly, the connection breaks. Something has changed. I look to Goth boy. He glances around the room almost like he's felt it too. I follow his gaze to a quiet girl sitting in the corner. She looks out of place, her clothes—a black dress that looks more like a tunic and lace-up boots. So different from the other students. Her auburn hair and ghostly green eyes stir more memories. The room begins to shrink.

Green-eyed girl pins me with her stare and the walls close in around me. It's all too much to absorb: the teacher's voice talking of legends I've lived, vacant eyes that are too old, too familiar, an evil I've sensed only one other time.

And a voice, sweet and clear.

Help me. Please. Someone help me.

The events combine and form a tempest in my soul, one I can't contain. My breathing falters as the words continue their pleading in my head. I quiet my thoughts, force some control. But it's no use. The voice won't stop. A voice that can't exist anymore. A voice that died centuries ago.

The voice of my human sister.

CHAPTER 6 – PREY

AYDAN

She's here, in front of me. Just my luck. I obsessed about her all night, working out a plan to find her and take her soul. After the disappointment in my kill last night, I knew nothing would satisfy me until I had *her*.

Only her.

She stares at the strange girl hiding in the back of class, one I don't remember seeing before today. She is a plain girl with out-of-date clothes, notable only for her flaming auburn hair and green eyes, features that are eerily familiar.

I feel like I should know her, like I *need* to know her.

My master watches Flame with an intense interest that seems odd for such an ordinary girl. What does he see that I don't?

I look back toward Nesy. A pained expression blankets her face, an expression that makes me want to do something I've never done.

Protect her.

The feeling is strange. Distasteful. And a problem.

My master would never understand the need to protect a human. Honestly, neither do I.

The teacher assigns a meaningless task and sits. Flame doesn't hesitate; she walks over and stands next to Nesy. My body tightens. Adrenaline courses through my veins, preparing me to strike. But why? Flame is no threat. No human is.

Flame pulls out a chair and sits. She warns Nesy about me, tells her to avoid me at all costs. My master watches them. And me. *Hold back,* he warns. *Wait.* I don't understand his sudden concern. I can handle two human girls.

The girls continue to whisper, their voices drawing everyone's attention, including the teacher.

"Anything you want to share with the class, Miss Eisner?" His words are laced with frustration.

"No sir," Flame chokes. "Just making sure the new girl has everything she needs for your class."

I stifle a laugh. *That's my job.*

Flame glares at me. Nesy does as well. Did they hear me? Feel my thoughts?

Interesting, my master and I think simultaneously.

Very interesting.

I need to get closer to Nesy and see what she knows. I stand, my chair scraping against the hard floor. I feel her body stiffen as I come up behind her. She trembles and my need for her grows to a feverish pitch.

Be careful, my master cautions.

I shake off his warnings and press into her thoughts. *Look at me.* I repeat the phrase until Nesy turns. *Look at me.* Our eyes lock and the room spins away, fading to something else. Someplace else.

CHAPTER 7 - DEATHLY BETRAYAL

NESY

"Elle!"

I hear his voice surround me as I run away. I can't bear to look at him. Not now. Not after his betrayal.

He promised we could be together. Promised he loved me. Promised...

I crash through the thicket, my body tense. Something else is in this forest with me. Something...wrong.

My head screams danger and I look around. Searching.

Through the trees I notice two yellow eyes, staring.

I freeze, my feet glued to the spot. My heart pounds so loudly I'm sure the wolf can hear it. *What do I do? What do I do?* My mind begins to spin away from me.

"Take her. She's the one I've prepared for you." The voice seems to come from the forest itself. Cold, steady, unearthly. A low, guttural, growl rips through the trees.

My body springs forward and I run. Three steps, that's as far as I get before the wolf is on me, dragging me to the ground.

I open my lips, the sound gone before I can scream. Blinding pain rips through my body. Along with the wolf's teeth.

I struggle against the memories, my eyes still locked with Aydan's. Can he see what I see? Does he know what I am?

His face blanches and anguish flashes through his expression. He's gone before I can figure out what's happening. But I already know one truth—

He saw it all.

A hand brushes against my shoulder, bringing me out of my vision. I shove it away, barely holding on to enough control to keep my identity secure. I have to get out of here, get away before everything is lost.

I try to stand. Another hand grabs me, stronger this time. "Are you okay?" The voice of the green-eyed girl. She looks at me. *Sees* me.

This is so not good.

The bell rings as I grab my books and run from the room.

"Wait. Let me help you," she yells over the din of the other students.

Pieces of memories continue as I run across the quad. I forget to breathe, forget my training. Forget everything.

Everything except the memories that never end.

I reach the back fence, unable to escape myself. I slide down the wall of the old portable classroom, fragments of my life surfacing in my thoughts.

My sister...*Why did you tell? Why?*

Adam...*Why did you let me leave?*

I remember their actions. Remember my love for them both.

My chest clenches, nausea coats my throat.

It took too long to forget that life. Too long to lock away those feelings.

And now, seeing things through human eyes again, it's all back. Every last memory. Every last feeling.

Incessant thoughts throw my world off balance as the nausea continues to buffet against my body. Too many questions. Too many doubts.

Nesayiel. Stop it! I scream inside. *Find your control!* My thoughts begin to slow.

Inhale. 1...2...3.

Release. 1...2...3.

I shove aside the images, ignoring the endless questions.

Inhale.

My focus sharpens.

Release.

And I remember who I really am.

A Sentinal.

Mikayel's Sentinal.

I will not dishonor him. I will not dishonor myself. One by one I release each thought, transcend each feeling. I think only of my assignment. And walk to my next class, ignoring the chaos raging beneath my hard façade.

I use my morning classes to devise a new plan. Take Aydan at lunch. Simple enough, especially since I'm certain he's now hunting me. I stretch my neck, back, shoulders, feeling my true form pressing against my host. I hate the confinement of my fleshy prison.

The bell rings, indicating the lunch period. I stand, ready to find my target and finish my task. I've had enough of being human. Pushing through the crowd, I pour out of the door into the sea of students.

"So, we meet again," Aydan whispers, his breath warm against my neck. He leans against the hall outside my classroom. Waiting. Just like I knew he would be.

"Looks like it." Everything melts away except for him. I feel his pull at my soul, feel him lure me in.

I resist his urgings and lock my thoughts away. Stash my feelings. Remain in control.

He leans into me, trying again. "I'm Aydan."

"I know. I'm—"

"Nesy."

Looks like I'm not the only one doing a little profiling. I just hope he hasn't figured *everything* out.

Kids bump into us as we remain locked in each other's presence. His fingers graze my hand as his eyes meet mine. *So much like Adam.* I dismiss the thought with a single breath. Aydan is far from human. And I could never love an UnHoly.

Get back to work, Sentinal. I focus my mind, lightly fingering the hilt of my dagger stowed under my hoodie. "So, what do you guys do around here for fun?" I tilt my head, lick my lips.

Aydan twitches.

Perfect.

Someone else crashes into me, breaking the momentary bond Aydan and I share. "Hey, I was hoping to find you. Let's go get some lunch." The green-eyed girl grabs my arm.

Who *is* this girl?

"Oh, I'm sorry. I'm Lori. Come on, you don't want to hang out with this loser."

Actually, that's exactly what I want to do.

Again she tugs at my arm, pulling me away from him.

"Ah, Lori. You should at least get to know me before you call me a loser." Aydan blocks our path. "Who knows, maybe you'll like me." He winks at her.

Oh yeah, he's good. Very good.

"I know enough to keep her away from you." With that Lori pulls me past Aydan and his laughter.

So much for vanquishing over lunch.

I let Lori push me through the throng of students filling the quad, studying her. She has a familiarity to her that melts away my exterior. An innocence that compels me to protect her. From Aydan, from me.

In all the centuries I've served humanity, I've never felt such an urge. That's more Zane's style.

The feeling is unnerving, surreal. And yet, I can't imagine anything more natural, almost like I'm supposed to care about her.

Lori and I find a low wall in the back of the school. Far away from the other students. Far away from Aydan. She sits, her eyes never leaving mine. I mentally feel for my wings, look at my human skin. Everything angelic remains hidden. She can't see me.

And yet…

"You really need to stay away from Aydan." Her voice trembles as she reaches for the angel-wing charm around her neck. It's the most normal thing about her. Everything else—her blazing hair, her too-old eyes, her antique dress—screams of another time altogether.

"So what's the story between you two?" I watch her carefully as she answers. Something about her is definitely not human.

"He's just bad news. A lot of girls fall for him. And, well, they tend to disappear."

"What do you mean, disappear?"

Lori's eyes glaze over and she looks like she's lost in some memory. "Disappear. As in never come back."

She knows too much to be mortal. "What happened to you?" I ask.

A veil of sadness settles over her face, a sadness too familiar to ignore. Again, I feel compelled to protect her. Heal hear. I think of my friends. Cass could heal her heart. Zane could fix her mind. "You can tell me," I say.

Lori fumbles with the charm and sucks in a sharp breath. I watch as her expression hardens, the cloak of sadness replaced by determination. "Aydan's into risky things. You know, bad-boy stuff. Sex, drugs, that sort of thing. Some girls like it. My friend liked it. She went to a party with him and his band. No one heard from her for a week." Lori pauses and bites her lip. "The police found her in some hell-hole on the west side, totally messed up. The cops said she ran away. But I know Aydan was behind it. He's evil. And if he decides he wants you, Nesy, he won't stop until he gets you."

There was something she wasn't saying. Something important. I shake my head, removing the concern from my mind. She's not my task. "Don't worry. I can take care of myself."

The bell rings and students move around us, rustling their papers, talking too loud, laughing. I stare at the strange girl—so mysterious. So familiar.

"I really can take care of myself," I say again.

"Not against him you can't. I've never met anyone who can."

Good thing I'm not just *anyone*.

Lori stands and turns away, wiping the lone tear sliding down her face. Words float through my thoughts, words I've heard somewhere else.

Don't go. Please don't go. He'll take you back with him. I'll never see you again.

As quickly as the voice enters my head, it's gone. I replay every syllable, trying to lock on to the elusive memory.

It's no use. The memory is gone, leaving only the voice of my dead sister.

Again.

CHAPTER 8 – BETRAYED HAPPINESS

NESY

My emotions swirl inside as the day continues. This job is so much more difficult than I had expected. I want to blame my humanity for my problems. Blame the imaginary memories my host *must* still have. Blame Zane for not cleaning her thoroughly.

But my human body isn't the problem. I am. Just like Zane said. I think of my long-dead sister and all that she has meant to me. I cried when I decided to leave her. I wonder, did she cry for me when I died?

I walk into my last class, Study Hall, discouraged. Confused. I have to finish this assignment. Prove to myself that I'm the warrior I think I am and not some love-struck girl caught in her own memories—memories of a boy long since dead. Memories of a sister that no longer exists. Memories of a time that can't ever be.

Adam.

I shouldn't be thinking about you again. About that life.

I sit at an empty table in the large expanse of the library. The room is quiet except for the questions screaming through my head, their incessant loop, mesmerizing. It lulls my body into a stupor. My eyelids flutter and I yawn. I can't fight my fatigue, can't resist my body's need to sleep. I slump over my books as dreams form around me. Large grassy fields, the scent of pine and soap, the sound of laughter as I die over and over again.

The visions pulse in and out, changing into something new.

A hand in mine...*hot*.

Breath on my neck...*sweet*.

The feel of lips on my own...*forbidden*.

I pull back from the boy in my dreams.

Black spiky hair. Tall, lean silhouette. Penetrating amber eyes.

Aydan.

I rip myself from the dream, my heart pounding wildly in my chest.

"Dreaming of me already?"

I feel the color rise in my cheeks. *Azryel's Wings*. I pull the fragmented pieces of my mind together. Consume my feelings. Orient myself: last period, Study Hall, library.

"You know, Mr. Presley hates it when people fall asleep in class. You're lucky he didn't catch you." Aydan pulls out the chair across from me and sits.

"Yeah, well, it happens." I can't hide the anger in my voice. What the heck is wrong with me? Sentinals don't sleep—especially when they're on the job. "So, where's your friend? The way you guys talk, I assumed you went everywhere together."

"He had someplace to be."

Good. Time to finish this before anything else can go wrong.

"I guess it's just you and me then."

The corners of Aydan's mouth twitch. I stare too long, remembering the taste of his lips. *Focus, Nesy. Focus.* "So, what are you doing after school?" I ask.

"Hanging out with you."

"Interesting. And what exactly are we doing?"

"You asked me to walk you home."

"Funny, I don't remember asking."

"Yeah, but you want to."

Yeah, something like that.

I smile and take his hand in mine.

We leave campus as the bell rings. Cars and people fill the streets around the school. Goth boy is nowhere. Neither is Lori. Finally, a chance to vanquish in peace.

The bustle of the city makes it impossible to hear, so I step closer to Aydan.

"So?" Aydan asks. "Where do you live?"

I lean into him, painting a confused look on my face. I seem open, vulnerable. The perfect victim.

"I said, where do you live?"

"Oh! Chelsea. I usually take the train," the lie flows easily from my mouth.

He smiles, his eyes radiating hunger. "Sounds good. But, let's not go there. Maybe the park. I know some out of the way places I think you'd like."

Out of the way places? Just what I had in mind.

Aydan places his arm around my waist and steers me up the crowded streets. My body reacts too strongly to his touch. *Inhale…Release…Inhale…Release…*I continue the breathing mantra with every step. I refuse to mess up this time.

The walk uptown is long, punctuated by the everpresent pulse of the city at the end of a day. Aydan's hands never leave my body, as though he's afraid to lose me. On the way to the park, we talk about school, music, his band. He's easy to be around. And nothing like I expect. Not that I'd actually spent any time with the UnHoly. The thing is, I could like Aydan. A lot. If it wasn't for the whole soul-sucking thing.

I find myself wanting to hear about his life, the things that make him happy, the things that annoy him. Each moment draws me closer. He's nothing like the monsters I'm trained to kill.

Not even close.

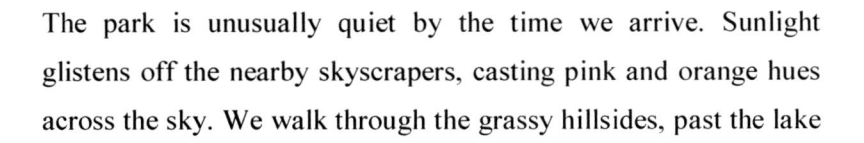

The park is unusually quiet by the time we arrive. Sunlight glistens off the nearby skyscrapers, casting pink and orange hues across the sky. We walk through the grassy hillsides, past the lake and reservoir. Parents play with young children, couples lock in tight embraces. I need to get Aydan alone.

"I want to show you something." He tightens his hold on my hand.

The groups of people thin with each step. As does my commitment to my duty.

"Here." Aydan points to the bridge in front of us. "My favorite bridge in the city."

I look at the smooth architecture of the cast iron bridge, carved to look like Gothic windows in a cathedral. There is a delicate beauty and strength to the bridge, and I find myself again surprised by this UnHoly. "It's beautiful," I say. "Why is it your favorite?"

"I don't know. I've just always liked the way the iron curves at the base. It's strong and delicate at the same time. I like the irony it represents."

Definitely not what I would expect from the UnHoly.

The sun drops, casting shadows around us. Aydan slips his arm around my waist and leans into me. His lips brush mine.

I know I should resist him, but I can't.

I don't want to.

The kiss deepens and I lose myself to him. My energy begins to drain as I feel my soul—my angelic soul—slip away. It feels strange, almost as though something, someone, is trying to…

Kill me.

The world stops and I push him away, remembering *what* he really is. Remembering my task.

I turn away and finger my dagger.

"My turn," I say. "I want to show you my favorite place in the park." I take his hand and lead him back towards the lake.

"Which is?" he asks.

"A surprise."

"Oh, I like a mystery." He slips his arm around my waist and I struggle to keep my body from trembling.

Long shadows change the landscape while dark creatures make their way toward us, cloaked in darkness. Their odd insect-like shapes bend the shadows further, while the putrid scent of their flesh wafts past me. I close my eyes to avoid registering their presence. No doubt the creatures expect me to be their next meal.

I don't think so.

Pulling my emotions in tightly around me, I focus only on my job. I won't get more than one chance to finish this. I'd better make it count.

"What are you thinking about?" Aydan's breath sends a chill across my skin.

"Nothing." Ignoring my body, I focus on the task at hand.

I guide him to a large courtyard near the lake. Dusk settles around us, casting an inky hue over everything. In the distance, fluorescent lights flicker on the upper terrace of the courtyard. We sit on the bench overlooking a large fountain.

"Here. My favorite place in the park." I nod towards the sculpture sitting in the middle of the fountain—a peaceful angel that looks down upon cascading streams of water. She reminds me of Cass.

"Hmm? The Angel of the Waters?" Aydan furrows his brow. "I'm surprised. I would've thought that angel too passive for you. You seem more the aggressive type. A warrior. Not something as…well, weak."

Does he know? It's a reasonable question. I replay every encounter from the club to the kiss. I may have been a little reckless—okay the kiss was *really* reckless—but there's no way he could've figured out the truth.

"Can I ask you something?" He turns my head towards his.

"Sure." My lips tremble. Darn human body.

"Why did you run off at the club?"

"I didn't run off," I lie. "I had to leave."

"No, you ran off. I'm just curious why."

"It was nothing. I just had to go."

"Because it almost seemed like you were—"

"I was what?"

"Scared." A seductive smile forms on his mouth.

"Of what? You?" I reach behind my back for the dagger. I need to time this just right.

"Yeah."

I collapse any space between us, and catch him off guard. Our lips are barely apart, my fingers wrapped firmly around my knife. "And what do you think now?" I can feel him shudder. Feel his heart pound against mine. "Am I still afraid?"

"Terrified." He draws a deep breath, parts his lips and kisses me.

It deepens, again pulling on my soul. I don't resist. Not yet.

I raise my dagger level with his heart, mentally speaking the words I need to cast him out. He tastes my soul as I cling to my humanity and—

"Hey, Aydan."

The unexpected voice pulls me back. I stow the dagger in my jeans, fear tightening every muscle. Taking a labored step backwards, I feel my face flush.

Aydan stares at me, a pained expression in his eyes. "Hey," he says, his breath coming in ragged spurts. "What's up?"

Two familiar figures walk through the shadows. Aydan's band mates. "Just hanging out," the weak, not-so-human guitarist says.

"We didn't mean to interrupt anything." Aydan's friend from school looks curiously at me, a smile spreading across his face.

I study him closely as a sense of dread laces through my senses. Just like earlier. Goth boy's black hair hangs in a ponytail down his back. He has a strong jaw and chiseled features most girls would find attractive. He wears a t-shirt that reveals something I hadn't noticed before, a series of Celtic tattoos covering his neck and jaw, eventually disappearing under the confines of his shirt.

The marks of the Beast.

He takes a step toward me, extending his hand. "I don't believe we've had the pleasure." His voice is as cool as ice. And just as unyielding. "I'm Azza."

My heart pounds against my ribs as the adrenaline rushes through me. Our gaze meets and I understand everything. Black with no hint of pupils. The eyes of unspeakable evil.

The Dark One himself.

Azzaziel.

How did I not notice him before now? What's wrong with me?

I step out of his reach. I can't let him touch me, *see* me. Not here, alone, with a mob of dark creatures ready to feast on me.

Azryel's Wings, how did I ever let this happen?

"Nice to meet you," I say, taking another step away from him. I look at Aydan and stow every emotion. His eyes dart from Azza to me and back. His expression is hard, angry.

And desperate.

"I should go," I say to Aydan as I back away, eying both Azza and his friends.

"Don't leave on our account." Azza slithers closer. "I'm sure we could get some others to join us and make a party of it."

The air stands still around me, stopping time. One...two...three seconds pass before the words will form. "No, really, it's okay," I finally say, stepping into the shadows. "I'm already late. My mother will be worrying about me." I continue to back away, keenly aware of Azza's stare. His thoughts reach out to mine. I shield my identity, making sure he senses nothing more than the scared musings of a normal human girl.

Leave her alone, I hear Aydan say to his master. *She's mine.* His words chill me to the bone.

Azza's laughter fills the air as I finally reach the stone stairwell that leads to the upper terrace and duck into the darkness, cursing my mistakes.

Again.

Why couldn't I just vanquish that UnHoly already? If I had just finished my task, Aydan would be in the Abyss.

And Azza's whereabouts would be…

A mystery.

My mind slows. Azzaziel. The Dark One himself. Hanging out in high school. Why? It doesn't make any sense.

My heart continues to pound too fast in my chest. I've never let myself get this close to blowing it this big. I should have felt Azzaziel's presence, should have sensed him coming. Mikayel will never accept these mistakes. Unless…

Maybe if I can figure out why Azzaziel is here, what he's up to, maybe then Mikayel will ignore my little failings.

Who am I kidding? Mikayel won't let any of this pass. None of the Council will.

Nor should they.

CHAPTER 9 - SUCCUMB

AYDAN

I never intended to serve Azza. No one ever does. But it sure beats burning in the eternal flames of the Abyss.

At least, that's what I keep telling myself.

Truthfully, most days I obsess about killing my master. I used to think being his apprentice, binding myself to him and learning the secrets of the Dark Ones, would give me the strength I needed to end his reign.

Not any more.

Now I know the truth, becoming the Beast will only tie me to him for an eternity. None will be able to kill me. Any honor will be forever gone. And I will be nothing more than a slave to my master...

Forever.

"Why are you here, Azza? I almost had her." My voice bounces off the stone walls surrounding the courtyard.

"No, young apprentice, she almost had you." The disdain in his voice is palpable.

I've disappointed him. Again.

An unintended growl escapes my throat. "You don't think I can handle her?"

"I don't trust her. She's more than she appears. Much more."

"Since when is a human too difficult for me to handle?"

"Since you wanted one for more than just a meal." Azza's words slice into my heart. "Am I wrong?" he asks.

I stiffen with anger as I consider his words. My shoulders slump with the weight of my truth; I do want her for more than a meal.

So much more.

I bite back the feelings I've never wanted, clinging to my familiar anger. Balling my hands into fists, I drink in my anguish, letting it calm the Beast. "You are not."

"Then you must stay away from her for now." Azza glares at me, a primordial show of force.

"No," I say before I can think. So much for control. "I *will* have her." I've always been too impulsive. Especially when I'm angry. "All of her."

And I'm more than angry tonight.

My rage engulfs the space, exploding into an inferno I can't contain. I don't want to contain.

Centuries of doing *his* bidding.

Meeting *his* needs.

Fighting *his* battles.

It's time I took care of me. And right now, Nesy would fill my needs.

Memories I can't shake spin me into a fury. Pictures of Elle, of her death. I feel it like it just happened. Centuries of purging these feelings gone. And all because of this girl.

Nesy.

My world slips away and I again taste vengeance on my tongue. I do want Nesy for more than a meal. I need her soul to erase these feelings—I need her to pay for waking them in the first place.

I clench my jaw, stifling the rage I feel for her. For the life I regret. For everything Azza has turned me into. Releasing a low growl, I storm off, walking toward the stone staircase that leads to the upper terrace overlooking the fountain—her fountain. Nesy's face follows me, burned into each stone. She whispers to me. Taunts me. Each step brings me closer to my undoing. But still I push on, desperate to outrun the she-devil.

I feel a light brush against my skin as I start up the stairs. I spin around and stare into the face of my master. A primal scream, my scream, splits the silence.

I can't be contained. My human forms drops to the ground in a heap. Black bat-like wings unfurl to their full span. My body, nothing more than muscle and flesh stretched too-thin over bone, rises to its full stature. My eyes are the only part of my humanity to remain.

The Beast is awake.

Another howl pierces the night air. "Yield to me!" Azza bellows.

He towers over me, black wings and claws that match my own extended, gnashing the space between us with his sharp fangs. He expects submission. Demands it.

My fury blinds me—anger, shame and memories too difficult to forget. I ram my shoulder into my master, ripping my claws through his skin.

"Yield, Disciple. Now!" Azza growls. He wraps his spindly talons around my throat and squeezes.

My strength fails as I gasp for air. Too much grief. Too much shame. I'm weaker than I should be. Weaker than I've ever been. *Why?*

I tighten my neck against his grip. My muscles tremble, and still I refuse to submit.

A feral snarl escapes his lips. A reminder.

I cannot win.

"You must feed." Azza releases his hold, sending me to the ground. "After which, I expect you to make amends to me."

Never a good thing.

I remember the last time I was forced to make a deal with Azza. That choice cost me my life. What will he expect from me this time?

My soul?

Worse?

"Now, go. Feed. Tomorrow we will deal with your feelings for this girl. *If* that is what she truly is."

LACRIMOSA

I watch as Azza and the dark creatures fade into shadow. Slipping back into my discarded body I walk home, defeated.

And hungry.

CHAPTER 10 - REMEMBRANCE

AYDAN

I jam the key into the lock of my apartment, unable to think of anything but Elle. My home, nothing more than a studio, feels even smaller tonight. The walls close in as my mind continues to spin. Every feeling I'd abandoned, every moment I'd locked deep inside has been released by Nesy. But why? How?

If she's even human at all…don't trust her…she almost had you…

Azza's voice bellows through me, silencing my own tortured musings. *Not human.* I never considered that possibility. Nesy's image fills my thoughts. The smell of her hair, so like Elle's. The curve of her waist. The life in her eyes. Nothing about her is off. She is human. Completely human.

Which means she can't be Elle.

Elle's dead.

I cast aside my thoughts and focus on my anger. Nesy has awakened more than just my memories of Elle. She's rekindled my hatred for Azza. I've committed too many heinous acts at his bidding. Paid too high a price for one choice made so long ago.

LACRIMOSA

Each thought stirs the Beast inside, a reminder that I will never escape my fate. Never escape my choices.

I plop on my couch-bed, weak from hunger and guilt. My entire body aches for the one thing it can never feel again—the feel of Elle's touch on my skin.

The Beast screams for food. I know I won't be able to stave off the hunger much longer. But I can't continue this charade either. I hate everything I am, everything I'll soon become.

I close my eyes, my head in my hands. I need to get it together. Need to find a way through this hell. I look up, staring at the only piece of art I've ever owned. Michelangelo's *Fall from Grace*. Not an original, of course. But something I've kept with me for decades.

The picture screams of my life: Adam and Eve, their fall from Eden, the human-faced serpent.

The Beast again stirs inside, begging to be fed. I ignore my urgings, feel my own rage and disgust surge. The picture begins to change as my torment increases, swirling to life. It morphs into a replica of me, Nesy, Azza. I watch as the figures dance across the paper, highlighting the end of everything I was.

Mesmerized, my eyes begin to close. And I fall...

Into my past.

I'm running towards the screams that rip through the dark forest. My humanity slips away with every step, Mikayel, Sariel. Keep her safe. Please.

"You're too late." Azzaziel steps through the trees, standing in shadow. His laugh fuels my rage.

"What do you want from me, Dark One?"

"You know who I am. I'm flattered. Most humans don't recognize me, even when I'm standing right next to them." Azzaziel steps into the filtered sunlight, his black hair, solid black eyes and tangles of Celtic markings burned into his neck giving away his true identity. "But then, you aren't like most humans, are you?"

My eyes widen. Chills explode down my spine. "Azzaziel." I choke on his name.

"And you must be the Council's newest addition. Aydan, is it?"

My human body goes stiff.

"Don't worry, I'd recognize you anywhere, even if you'd been more careful. But, you really should practice better control; prevent your angelic skin from glowing through your human form. Otherwise these people may think that you're possessed. And you know what these pagans do to the ones they think are possessed, don't you?"

I ignore him and push through the thicket. Elle's body is sprawled out on the forest floor, bending at odd angles. Her flesh is torn and shredded around her legs and torso.

"No!" I scream, collapsing next to her. I pull her tattered body into my arms. "No." My voice falters. "I'm so sorry, my love. This is my fault. I never should have let you go."

We rock back and forth, my body trembling.

My dream changes in front of me, as Elle impossibly turns into Nesy. I try to fight against the nightmare now playing out in front of me, the hell I've survived all this time. But it's no use. I can never escape.

I carry the broken body of Elle-turned-Nesy into town.

Azzaziel watches, an amused look on his face. "Are you sure you want to get involved? I doubt your bosses would approve."

Like I'm listening to him at all.

The dream's images come faster and faster. The farmers and hunters running after a wolf. Dogs attacking. My dagger flying through the air...

The wolf howls in pain, my knife sticking from its thigh. I watch as it stands on its back legs, slowly contorting, changing. In moments the wolf is no longer there. Only a man. Peeter Stubbe. My human boss for more than two years. And a dark creature serving Azzaziel.

How did I not know?

Azzaziel's sadistic laugh fills the space in my thoughts. "What kind of angel are you, Aydan? You can't even manage to recognize one of my own."

My mind folds in on itself as I toss and turn. I need to end the nightmare, end these memories. But they refuse to yield.

The villagers take Peeter to the town magistrate and beg for justice. I force my will into the humans. Force cruel, vile thoughts into their weak minds. Not an ordinary execution for the murderer, but days of torture and a brutal death the world will never forget. Peeter Stubbe will pay for Elle's death. Forever.

"You really think that I would allow you to hurt my pet?" Azzaziel stands too close to me.

"Do you really think I care?"

"I know you do." His truth hangs in the air. "But I think I have a solution to this. And the many other problems you face."

"What other problems?" My voice sticks on the words as fear wraps around my throat.

"The Council will not let you live in Celestium now. You must know that."

In truth, I'd never thought about the Council or Celestium; only retribution for the death of my love. "And?"

"I will not allow an angel to kill my servant."

The threat coats my skin, erupting a fresh set of shivers down my spine.

"Fortunately, I think you have talents I can use."

The town's magistrate stretches Peeter on a rack. His bones crack as his executioners pull his arms from their sockets. The pressure in my chest releases with each horrific act.

"You need vengeance for Elle. Almost as much as your human body needs air. But the Council will cast you to the Abyss. You have broken your vows." Azza circles me, whispering every taunt. "You've experienced human love. You've tortured and hurt those you were supposed to protect. You'll never be allowed to remain in Celestium."

"And when they cast you out, I want you to come and work for me." Azzaziel smiles. Waits.

"What do I get out of it?"

"Retribution. Justice. A chance for a life outside of the control of the Council." Azza leans closer. "And my loyalty."

I can't believe I'm considering his offer. Can't believe what I'm about to do. "You'll let me do anything I want to Peeter? Exact any form of revenge I wish?"

Peeter's voice fills the night air as his limbs continue to release from their sockets.

"Oh yes." A smile dances on the Dark One's face.

"And if the Council does not cast me—"

"They will."

"But if they don't, our deal is off. You won't look for me."

"Agreed."

Don't do this. He can't be trusted. I shake the voice from my head, my need for revenge greater than any loyalty I feel to Celestium; or to myself.

A moment passes.

And another.

"Do we have a deal, young angel?" Azzaziel's stench crinkles my nose, causing my stomach to clench.

I square my shoulders, swallowing my concern. My disgust. "Yes."

Even in my dream state I feel the tears sting my eyes. Peeter's trial, his torture and execution, replay; a dirge of evil I, alone, orchestrated. One I've forever regretted.

"Have you had your vengeance? Are you prepared to join me?" The smile on Azzaziel's lips sends chills down my spine.

But I ignore them. Ignore him. And walk to Peeter's farmhouse. One thing left to do.

I break into the house and light every candle. One by one I set the fabrics covering the windows and tables ablaze. The fire dances around me.

"You don't need to die like a heretic." Azzaziel walks through the burning wall and faces me. "What you did, what you feel, it's only natural. The Council really should understand that. After all, you couldn't help but fall in love with the girl. Just ask Mikayel. I'm sure he'd understand."

I turn away. "I've decided not to join you."

Azzaziel's laughter weaves through the crackling fire. "Your oath cannot be undone. And the Council will banish you."

"They may."

The flames continue to flicker around me, catching the hem of my trousers on fire. I feel my flesh begin to burn. I flinch, clench my jaw, ball my hands into fists. The pain is excruciating. It blinds my vision, fades my thoughts. Don't move. Don't move. Don't move. The words barely form, the agony eclipsing everything.

"So you plan to die then? As a human?"

I can't speak as the flames climb up my trembling body. I swallow each scream, desperate to stay in command of my humanity.

"I admire your control."

A feral sound pushes up from my abdomen, exploding from my mouth. I don't recognize the sound; can't tell its source. All I know is the agony bursting through my enflamed skin.

The scene spins, too many things happening simultaneously. Azzaziel laughs and disappears from my sight. The room explodes in light and my body continues to burn.

It's almost over. My physical body is nearly gone. Soon, my angelic heart will stop.

A hand grips what's left of my body. His touch sends wave after wave of pain rippling through me.

"No Aydan. You won't die. Not now. Not in this way."

I know the voice and what it means. The Council is here.

"Release yourself. Or I'll do it for you." Mikayel's voice is unyielding.

"Please. Just let me die." I can barely speak. Just a few more seconds and it'll be too late.

"No. That would be too easy."

I feel my angelic soul rip from my body, stealing my breath. The pain fades within seconds.

"You *will* face the Council and atone for what you've done. You will not die a coward. Or become a servant to Azzaziel."

I want to scream "No, you don't understand. Let me do this!" But the words refuse to come. My human shell—what's left of it—falls to the floor. I look at Mikayel and tilt my neck. "Just finish me. Here. Now."

Mikayel tightens his grip on his sword. He wants to, I feel it. "It's not my decision to make," he says through gritted teeth.

I bolt upright, startled. Sweat pours from my brow as I struggle to gain control over my pounding heart. An icy breeze brushes my skin, followed by the distinctive scent of rotting flesh and sulfur.

My master is here.

"Reminiscing about the past were you? Sometimes it's better to just leave it alone." Azza's tones wash over me, sending fear into every crevice.

"What do you want, Azza?"

"Still angry, I see. Why not put that to good use instead of wallowing in your misplaced sense of shame? You haven't fed, have you?"

"No, but—"

"That's twice you've overlooked my commands. If I didn't know better, I would say you're making a habit of ignoring me." Azza's taunt lingers.

Time slows as he waits for my answer. I feel my heart beating against my chest, hear the blood pumping through my veins. Swallowing hard, I focus. I can't do anything stupid, not now. Not when Azza is this poised to strike. "I am only what I've pledged myself to be. Your servant."

"Not servant. Apprentice. You will be as powerful as any Dark One once you complete your oath and we find our Seer to feed you."

I flinch as the Beast inside awakens. Confusion paints my thoughts as I war with myself—my soul versus the monster I'm destined to become. The monster I am already. Am I ready to release myself entirely? Succumb to Azza and the Beast?

I was.

I'm not so certain now.

Azza pins me with his cold glare. "I've come to ensure your loyalty and make certain you feed. To do this, I've decided to pick the victim this time."

My eyes widen. *Not Nesy. Please, not Nesy.* My mind reels as I wait for Azza to continue.

"Come, she waits for you at the club. We'll go together. This time, I'll watch you carry out your task."

I open my mouth to speak, the words drying to dust. Inside, the Beast stirs, anxious to be fed.

And my soul dies a little more.

He will find the Seer one day and force me to drink her soul. He will find her.

Maybe he already has.

CHAPTER 11 – CONCEALED TRUTH

NESY

I blew it. I blew it. I blew it.

How did I ever get myself into this mess? I know better than to let my emotions get in the way. Know how to avoid the likes of Azza and the other dark creatures that loom these shadows. And yet, I've managed to do everything…

Wrong

I think again about my human host. I've never lost control like this before, never felt so chaotic. It has to be this host, doesn't it? Some strange residue from her last assignment. Something Zane missed when she was cleaned. It can't be me—my memories, my erratic emotions. It just can't.

I sigh as the truth screams through me. There is no one to blame for any of this but me. Only me.

Aydan skulks away from his master, as the dark creatures retreat into shadow. I let myself slide down the cold stone stairwell, my body no longer able to shoulder the weight of my failures. The Council isn't going to like this. Not at all.

Moments slip into seconds, which slip into minutes. I wish I could stay here and pretend that none of this ever happened.

Not warrior-like I know, but sometimes it feels better to pretend.

The wind rustles around me. So much for fantasies.

"What happened? Why are you sitting on the ground in the cold?"

Zane. Leave it to him to find me in the midst of one of my less-than-Sentinal moments.

Perfect.

"Well? What happened?"

I stand, trying to make the words form. It's risky telling him everything, but he's always been a friend. No reason to assume he'd go all tyrannical on me now.

"Aydan's not alone." They're the only words I manage to force past my throat.

"Not alone? What do you mean?"

"Azzaziel. He's here."

"Here? That's not good." Zane, the master of understatement.

"Yeah, I know it's not good."

Zane begins to pace. "How did you find him?"

"He sort of found me?"

He stops midstep. "What does that mean, Nes? Does he know who you really are? Because if he does, you're in great danger and we need to talk with the Council. Now."

So much for not being a tyrant.

"Relax. I was careful. He interrupted Aydan and me. While we were...well, while I was about to vanquish him. I'm sure he doesn't know who I am. But, he doesn't trust me. I need a new plan."

"Stop worrying about Azzaziel. You know the rules. Focus on Aydan; let Mikayel deal—"

"No! No Mikayel. He asked me to do this and I said I could. I'll get it done. Without Azzaziel suspecting a thing."

"I don't know, Nes. It seems like an awfully big risk to take just to prove your worth as a Sentinal."

"This isn't about vanity. It's about doing my job, like always."

Okay, so maybe it isn't only the job. Maybe I do need to prove myself a little. After two botched attempts, I need this.

"Fine," Zane says, his voice stiff. "But get it done."

"I will."

"Soon."

I've had enough of Zane, enough of his expectations. Why is he so angry? So concerned? "I said I'd get it done. Now drop it."

Zane's focus narrows. "I think Cass and I should come along. Just to help."

I open my mouth to argue. I want to tell him that the last thing I need, the last thing I want, is for *him* to help me. Sentinals don't need help from the *lesser* angels. But I can't. And he's right. After more failures than I've ever committed on a job, maybe I do need his help. Maybe I need him.

"Fine," I say, my jaw clenched. Unfamiliar fear trickles through my hardened shell. What if I can't finish this? I wrestle back the feelings aside.

Failure isn't an option.

Not now. Not ever.

CHAPTER 12 - FEED

AYDAN

The club is quiet, typical for a Monday night. No one crowds the entrance as Azza walks in, nodding at the dark creatures guarding the robes. I follow a step behind, my mind torn. The dark creatures smile, baring their fangs, anticipating the meal they expect me to provide.

But I can't. I won't. Not now.

Maybe not ever again.

My mind tosses over my life with Azza. Frustrated. Angry. I've never enjoyed serving him; but I've never had this kind of a problem either. What's wrong with me? Why can't I stop thinking about Elle? About Nesy?

Azza motions me to join him at the back of the club. We slip into a booth overlooking the stage and dance floor. Music echoes off the walls as the scant patrons dance or talk in tangled huddles near the bar. I search, praying she isn't here. Frustration riddles my muscles as I stretch my neck, back, shoulders.

"You have something to say to me," Azza says. I feel his cold stare penetrate my defenses.

I know what I should say, what he wants to hear. But I can't lie. The Beast stirs, reminding me of my need to feed. Guilt and shame coat my tongue.

Enough of this.

"I can't do this anymore. I won't."

"Can't do what, exactly? Can't live as a 17-year old boy, forever young? Can't skate by with no rules? Dominate anyone you choose? Feed off the fear of these humans?" Azza's words drip with disdain. "What is it that you think you *can't* do?"

I clench my jaw as a wave of fury begins to make its way up my throat. "This. Kill for you." I force the words out through my gritted teeth.

"You don't do it for me. You never have. You kill for you and you alone. You kill to meet your own needs. I simply allow my demons to take your leftovers."

He's right.

And I hate him for it.

"Don't sulk, Aydan. You chose this life. All of it."

No! I want to scream. *You did this to me.* I turn to my master, my cold expression mirrored in his eyes.

"You chose to ignore the Council," Azza says. "They would have offered you a chance. But you decided to leave Celestium. No one else. You picked this fate."

"That isn't what happened," I spit. "You forced—"

"The Council wanted you to stay. Only Mikayel objected. But he would've yielded to the others. You had a chance at another life. A life without me. That was our bargain. You decided to leave. You decided to follow me. I am not to blame for your choices."

My silence screams the truth of his words.

"I know you've enjoyed this life," Azza says as a smile forms in his eyes. "Found pleasure in killing the way you do."

"At one time. Maybe."

"Absolutely."

I turn away and try to pretend that I was never his apprentice, never wanted the life he offered. But I did at one time.

I did choose this.

"What's changed, Aydan? The girl?"

Nesy. A picture of her blond hair and haunting eyes flits across my thoughts. It awakens the Beast. And my heart. I want to consume her power. Protect her soul. The opposing feelings battle inside, stealing my breath.

Azza watches, a cold fury seething in his expression. "You would sacrifice everything with me for her? A worthless human girl?"

"I thought you said she was more than human."

"She is. But *that* is not the point."

"Then what is?"

"You. Are you willing to risk everything for her? Would you give yourself over to my demons, be consumed by them as you scream for their mercy? Would you do that for her? Because I promise you, she won't do the same for you. She'll kill you if she gets the chance. I hear it in her thoughts. See it in her eyes."

I turn away, unwilling to accept the truth I know.

"If she is what you crave, take her. Enjoy every inch of her. And when her lust and fear has fed your soul, kill her. Consume her body. Her power."

I contemplate my master's words. He's never been wrong about our enemies. Not once. But is she really my enemy?

The Beast screams the answer, leaving only one solution.

An image of myself drinking her soul fills my vision. I feel her power flowing into me. Feel her death. Bile coats my throat. My eyes begin to water. And my heart feels as though it's being carved from my body.

I can't do this. I don't know why, but I know I will never be able to do *this*.

Not to her.

Uninvited feelings permeate my mind. Loyalty. Fealty. Devotion.

To someone other than my master. To a stupid human girl.

Azza's thoughts become my own. He demands my allegiance, regardless of my feelings on the matter. Or perhaps, because of them.

I stretch my neck, willing the visions to stop. Azza is right; my allegiance belongs to him and him alone. I made that choice centuries ago.

I face my master, asking the question I fear. "You've picked *her*, haven't you?"

Azza's laugh brings no relief. "Oh no, you're not strong enough. Whatever she is, there's a power you can't yet face. She will be yours after you have fed."

Not Nesy.

"But, you will kill her. Soon."

A boiling rage surges with his threat.

His eyes narrow. "Tonight I have a smaller prize in mind. One that will not resist you. Her death will prove your loyalty for now."

No! forms in my thoughts. But the Beast pulls on me, stifling my voice and urging me to fulfill my oath to my master, regardless of the cost.

"Nesy's death guarantees your fealty later."

"Who?" It sounds more like a growl than an actual word.

Azza nods forward. I follow his gaze to the bar adjacent to the booth.

A familiar girl. Alone and unaware.

Not Nesy.

I can't control the Beast. I must feed before a frenzy starts and I lose all control. I walk to my prey and sit next to her.

Don't do this, part of me says. But my need for sustenance is overwhelming and will not abate. Whispering in her ear, I prepare my meal. "You attend East Side, don't you? Mandy is it?"

A smile glints in the girl's large brown eyes as she tosses her chestnut brown strands over her shoulder. "Yeah."

"Here on a Monday? I'm surprised. I thought girls like you avoided this place during the week. What would your parents say?"

"My mother couldn't care less. She probably doesn't even realize I'm gone." Mandy leans in. "Besides, being here is a lot more fun than staying home. Especially with you around."

I feel my hunger cover the contours of my face, feel the Beast growl. "Well Mandy, you're just full of surprises tonight, aren't you?"

"I guess I am."

Every word she speaks, each toss of her hair and pout of her lips explodes my appetite. I can't resist the Beast's pull. Not with such an easy kill.

There are no strange memories to confuse me this time. No longings for a girl long dead. No feelings of my heart being ripped to shreds.

Just the familiar satisfaction as her soul feeds the Beast.

Why resist what I am?

"So, want to get out of here?" I ask.

"I would, but I'm here with a friend. I think you know her. Lori. She's warned me all about you."

That's the second time that girl has interfered with my plans.

"And what do you think?" I ask as I brush my finger across her throat. "Are her warnings justified?"

Mandy takes a deep breath. I see her pulse throb in her neck, feel the erratic beat of her heart against her chest. "Definitely." She moves closer to me.

I smile and push into her thoughts, showing her everything she wants. "Leave with me."

A sexy pout covers her lips as she stands. "Let's go."

Very easy prey.

I place my hand on the small of her back and guide her out the door. Azza follows, unseen to all but me. Dark shadows dance along the edges of the alley behind the club. Azza's creatures wait, watching the hunt. Their beaks and claws clack in anticipation.

I push my body against the girl, rubbing my hands across her arms. She shudders in response.

For a moment Nesy floods my vision. *Stop this. Stop.* Her voice taunts me and I pull back, hesitate.

But the Beast won't stop.

It never has.

Do this! The pull of all that I am is too strong. I push against my urgings, clinging to my feelings of guilt and shame. The Beast consumes them, leaving me no way to resist.

I focus on the girl who offers her soul to me. Leaning in, I taste her lips.

"I shouldn't do this," she whispers.

"I know you want to." My voice weaves around her, casting my spell. She melts into my arms, her breath nothing more than short, shallow wisps.

I feel her quiver as I again taste her neck, her jaw. "I came for you."

Her aroma, a mixture of sweet peas and the life coursing through her veins, sends me into a frenzy. My body shakes. There's no turning back now.

She arches her back, giving herself to me.

"Do you want me?" I ask, already knowing the answer.

"Yes," she whispers.

I pull her into a hungry kiss. She releases herself to me and I take her air.

Her life.

Her eyes spring open as I drink her soul, extracting it from every cell. She screams into me, pounds my chest, writhes against my hold.

I tighten my grip and deepen the kiss that will end her life.

The girl continues to beat on my chest, her strength growing weaker. And weaker. Her soul flows freely into me as her color begins to pale and her movements slow.

I drain every last drop of her soul from her.

Her body drops from my grasp as her life force coats every crevice, filling a need too deep to ignore. Satisfaction and disgust buffet against me.

"Feel better now?" Azza emerges from the shadows, pride glinting in his eyes. Pride and satisfaction.

He owns me.

Azza leans into me, whispering into my ear. "The next time you displease me, I will choose a closer victim. One I know will bring you great pain to kill."

I clench my jaw, fighting back the rage born from his words.

Nesy.

Screeches and howls fill the night as Azza's creatures pour forth from the shadows and feed on the dead girl. I watch them shred her body, eat her flesh. My knees wobble as I spit out the bile filling my mouth. Lightheaded and dizzy, I am forced to face the truth. This *is* who I am now—nothing more than the Beast. Destined to serve Azza and rule the dark creatures. Destined to kill.

I don't know which feeling to experience first. Anguish. Guilt. Shame. They meld together and crest over me. I face my master, one thought on my mind—

Better to die, than to be his servant.

In a single heartbeat, I prepare to attack. Azza will pay for the centuries I've served, for every act I've committed at *his* bidding.

A sudden blast of wind streaks through the dark alley, stopping me cold. Bursts of emerald, indigo and golden light fill the space as three angels emerge from the center of the brilliance, swords drawn.

I hear Azza's howl as he steps back from me and disappears into shadow. The angels run to the half-eaten carcass strewn across the concrete, their wings unfurled behind them. They toss aside the demons, slamming them into the stone wall of the buildings that line the narrow corridor.

"Cass, Zane, trap them," the golden angel orders as she turns to face me, poised to strike.

Two angels chant and bursts of light erupt from their hands. A cage forms around Azza's creatures. They howl and gnaw at their prison.

The Beast surges through me, releasing a feral growl. "You have no purpose here, angel." I push out of my host body, sending it crashing to the ground. My wings extend to their full expanse, as I steady myself for the attack.

"*You* are my purpose, UnHoly." The golden angel's voice echoes through my skin, resonating in my soul. "It is time for you to meet your end. Feel the eternal flames of the Abyss."

She lunges towards me. But I anticipate her move and duck. I grab for my weapon, the short sword of the UnHoly. Forged of black metal it bears the creed of the Beast, of Azzaziel's realm. *Meus tripudium est prognatus ex tuae tormentum et poena.* From your torment, my joy is forged.

I may not want to serve Azza, but I will not be taken out by some angel with a sword. The Beast won't allow it. "I will never submit to you, Sentinal." I slash at her, coming up empty.

She moves too fast and each blow catches only air.

Not good.

"You cannot beat me, UnHoly," she taunts. "The Abyss waits for you."

Each word infuriates me, baiting the monster inside. I hack the space around her, fueled by my newly found power—a power supplied through Mandy's death.

The angel parries each blow, countering with force. "Your time here is finished," she yells as her blade pierces my side.

The blade sends a wave of pain across my vision. The Beast screams and rage floods my senses. Black blood leaks from the wound, splattering on the pavement. I suck in a breath, ignoring the searing anguish.

Lunging forward, I rake my sword across her arm. The cut slices through her armored skin. She sucks in a breath, her eyes wide with shock. She counters my attack, slicing the air around us. Metal screeches against metal as our fury collides.

A soft white light empties into the alley. The strange girl, Lori, spills out of the club, screaming "No!"

Impossible. She shouldn't be able to see any of this. The golden angel is as surprised as I. Finally, my chance.

I barrel into the angel, pinning her against the wall. Wrapping my clawed hands around her throat, I squeeze, ready to end this once and for all.

"Let go of her," Lori yells.

Azza, emerges from the shadows, cloaked in his humanity. "Ah, our Seer." He says as he grabs the not-so-human girl. "At last."

A scant "no" escapes her lips before Azza cups his hand over her mouth. "Now, Aydan. It's time."

I watch Lori and Azza disappear into the shadows, my claws still around the angel's throat.

"Unhand me," she snarls, her voice hoarse. She thrashes against my hold, unable to move out of my grasp.

Blurs of indigo and emerald light run towards me.

"No, stay back. Guard the others," the golden angel commands, still pushing against my hands.

My claws dig into her neck and a trickle of silver liquid snakes down her skin. I stare into her fierce eyes, admiring her determination and strength.

My breath catches in my throat as I see her. Really *see* her. Deep blue eyes that seem to reach into my soul. Chaos simmering under a surface of calm. I furrow my brow, unable to free myself from her glare.

"Nesy?" My claws open and I stumble backwards. "It can't be," I whisper.

Released from my grasp, the angel pushes past me. "Lori! Lori!"

"Elle!" Lori's voice floats through the shadows. "Help me."

"Lorelei?" The angel says, choking on the word. She opens a portal into the shadow, ripping a hole between the worlds. Her gaze meets mine and for a moment time is suspended.

"Elle?" I whisper, watching the three angels disappear into the void.

Elle.

CHAPTER 13 – CONFESSED EMOTIONS

NESY

I squeeze into the pitch darkness with Cass and Zane, our glowing skin the only thing illuminating the darkness. A breeze drifts through the surrounding mist. The scent of the Dark One, ripe with putrid flesh and death, flows with the wind.

"It sure smells like Azzaziel here. He must have come this way." I say, wrinkling my nose. Moss covered stones poke up through the ground, looking more like decaying ruins than anything else. Mist floats between the stones and the ground. This place is like nowhere I've ever seen, no where I've ever been. The space in between the worlds.

Azzaziel's realm.

Muffled screams fill the air around me. I run towards the sound, desperate. Lori saw me. As an angel. She called me by my human name from so long ago.

Not possible.

"You're too late," a voice says, seeming to come from the stones that surround me.

I draw my sword in a single motion and spin in the direction of the sound. "Show yourself," I command.

Tendrils of black smoke emerge from the stones, forming a face.

Demonic smoke. Great!

"The girl you seek is not here." The smoke-voice says.

"Where is she?" I growl, frustrated. "Show me."

"I cannot show what I do not know." The smoke thins until it disappears entirely, replaced by a suffocating silence.

I really hate demonic smoke. Nothing more than a trickster, you can never really trust it.

"She's not here," Cass whispers "I can't feel her."

"That's not possible," I snap. "Azzaziel was only a second ahead of us. Lori has to be here somewhere. It's a trick." I pound the cold stone wall next to me.

Elle...Elle...

Lori's voice repeats my human name over and over, looping endlessly. For a moment I begin to think she could be my sister.

I shake the wish away, angry. "Blazes!" I yell into the darkness. "We should've been faster. We can't let him hurt her."

"She is *not* your assignment." Zane's frustration is palpable. "We shouldn't even be here. Your duty is to—"

"Don't lecture me about my duty, Zanethios. There is no way I am letting Azzaziel hurt that girl."

"Then take care of Aydan, as Mikayel ordered you to. The Council will send others to take care of the Dark One." Zane clenches his jaw.

I'm sick of his anger. His judgments. "And Lori?" I yell. "Who protects her?"

Cass stares at me, a look of shock on her face. Yelling is not exactly Sentinal behavior.

She moves closer and I feel her heart reaching for mine. "Why is she so important to you? What aren't you telling us?"

I ignore her question, still hoping against hope that Lori and Lorelei are the same person, that my sister lives.

Definitely not Sentinal behavior.

"She called you Elle." Again Cass pulls forward my emotions.

No. I won't let her into my heart; not now, not until I can figure this out.

"She *saw* you. She saw all of us." Zane's voice frays my already frazzled nerves. "How is that possible?"

I pace, unable to think clearly. "Zane, what do you know of the Seers?"

Zane looks surprised at the question. "Seers? Azzaziel killed them off centuries ago. Why? What does this have to do with that girl?" Zane shakes his head, trying to find the answers in my thoughts.

I lock eyes with him, feeling every ounce of pain, every moment of frustration as I shove him from my mind.

"Why did Azzaziel go after them?" I ask, still staring at Zane. "The Seers?"

"He needed their souls. According to the rumors, he was trying to make an army of UnHoly, one that could defeat the Sentinals. An army as strong as Azza, but subservient to him. The Seers were the key to his play. Or at least, that is what the rumors said. Drinking the soul of a Seer could give the UnHoly unmatched strength. The Seer's soul would awaken the Beast in a way that would make the UnHoly immune to the swords of the Sentinals. They would not be able to kill them. Only Mikayel's sword could prove fatal. Just like with Azzaziel." Zane's expression softens as he speaks. "But that was before."

"What do you mean *before*?"

"The Seers are gone, Nes. And Azza has no army."

"What if he didn't fail? What if the Seers are still alive and in hiding?" My mind whirls around tonight's events. The mist swirls at my feet, matching emotions swirling through me.

"Impossible," Zane says. "The Council would know if he had raised an army. And the Seers *are* dead. We've had no reports of their presence for more than a century."

I turn away. I don't care what the Council thinks, the Seers are not dead. Not all of them.

Azza just took one.

"Nes, what aren't you telling us?" Zane's tone is laced with impatience, frustration. And worry. "Nes?

"Lori saw us. In angelic form. You know what that means. She must be a Seer. It's the only explanation." I inhale the rest of my thoughts, not willing to tell them—tell him—everything. "That's why we have to find her; before Azzaziel can kill her."

"If she is a Seer, Nes, she's already dead."

Anger coils around my body.

"There's more, isn't there?" Cass asks. "Lori called you by your name, your past human name. Nesy, is she—?"

I can't answer the question; can't force myself to say the words. I'm not ready to accept that truth, no matter how much I may want it. I'm not ready to accept the emotional torrent it would bring.

"Is she what?" Zane looks from Cass to me. "Nes?"

Nothing. Only silence.

"Lori is Nesy's human sister, Lorelei." Cass looks at me. "Isn't she?"

I can't speak, can't think, can't breathe. I walk away, anger and pain filtering through my thoughts.

The breeze, the unholy stench, wraps around me, reminding me of where I am. I have to find Lori before Azza ends her life.

Something warm drips down my neck and arms, a thick silver liquid that sizzles as it hits the ground. My blood.

Perfect.

My head is woozy and I grab one of the moss-covered stones, trying to steady myself.

"Let me look at your wound," Zane says, reaching for my arm. There is no anger now, no frustration. Only concern. "Please."

I flinch and pull my arm close. "It's fine. A scratch."

"That isn't a scratch. It's deep. You need a healer to look at it."

"No!" I snarl. "I'm fine."

Zane sighs. "You aren't fine." He walks away, his wings rippling as his shoulders tighten. "In fact," he says as he faces me again. "You haven't been *fine* since we took this assignment." Zane's eyes narrow and he clenches his jaw.

So much for his concern.

"What are you talking about?"

"You. The way you've been acting over the last two days." His venom-filled tone matches mine.

I turn away, a storm of emotions smoldering through me. "I said, I'm fine," I hiss. "Now drop it. We need to find Lori."

"Azryel's Wings, Nes. Wake up." Zane grabs my arm and spins me towards him. I wince, my skin still burning from Aydan's sword.

"Zane, stop." Cass stands between us. "This isn't the time. Besides, Nesy isn't herself tonight. Think of what she must be feeling."

Cassiel. Always trying to calm every situation.

"That's exactly my point. She shouldn't be *feeling* anything. She is a Sentinal."

"Zane, come on," Cass pleads.

"No, she needs to hear this." He looks past Cass to me. "Something's wrong with you. Ever since you met Aydan, you've been sloppy. You've had three chances to vanquish him and what have you done? Run away. Hesitate. *Feel* something for him. You're acting like a confused little girl. Where's the five-hundred-year-old warrior, huh? Where the blazes did she go?"

"I am not acting like some little girl." My anger burns through my cells.

"Yes you are! And you're risking all of our lives in the process."

"When have I ever taken unnecessary chances with my life? Or yours?" My voice pounds against the stones.

"Since the moment you looked at that UnHoly."

Here it comes. Another infamous Zane lecture.

"You've allowed yourself to wallow in some memory from your past—a memory you were supposed to have released," Zane continues, anger pouring from his words. "You refuse to attack him when he's alone, but you confront him when Azzaziel waits in the shadows. You run off to chase some girl you think might be your human sister, even though your orders are clear. You're letting your childish human emotions rule your well-trained mind. And you expect us to play along like everything is okay.

"Well Nesayiel, guess what—everything is *not* okay." His voice booms around me.

He's voiced every one of my fears, every concern. And right now, I hate him for it.

"Zane, stop." Cass's soothing voice floats through the air, providing a fragile veil of serenity.

"Don't try to use your power on me, Cass." Zane steps away from her, still glaring at me. "Look, I know you're used to being in control. Always right, no mistakes. And I can deal with that holier-than-thou attitude. But you're acting like a first-year Sentinal, and you're going to get yourself killed."

I'm sick of his accusations, his interrogation. It's time to remind him who's in charge. I draw my sword, aiming it at his neck.

Zane remains where he stands, his shoulders square and his jaw clenched. "You'd strike me down? Risk Mikayel's wrath, your life, just to avoid hearing the truth? Really?"

Blazes.

I growl, slamming my sword against the stones next to us. Sparks shoot in every direction. It isn't enough. I need to release this rage, need to hit something. Vanquish something. Again I slam my sword against the stones and walk away; before I do something really stupid.

"We're both worried about you Nesy," Cass says, the soft, timbre of her voice filling my thoughts. She's using the powers of the Anointed again. "We know something's going on between you and Aydan, something beyond your human emotions.

Something...wrong." She approaches me, putting her hand on my shoulder and lifting my chin.

Our eyes meet and I feel the comfort of the Anointed pass between us. She enters my heart, my feelings. My pain and confusion fade almost immediately. But I know it won't last. It never does.

"You're confused. Hurt. So many unanswered questions." Cass smiles. The burdens of the past few days continue to lift from my shoulders. "Questions about Aydan and Lori. Your life before."

The relief isn't real. Or deserved. I shove her out of my heart and walk away. Her words are too much for me right now. I want my pain and torment. Need them to remind me of my oath, my duty.

"Your feelings scare you, Nesy. And more than anything, you hate being scared."

I can't look at her, can't let her see the truth reflected in my face. I am scared. Too scared.

"It's okay. This is just part of the human experience."

Enough lectures for one night.

"Stop patronizing me, Cass." My fear and pain turn to anger in a single heart beat. "I'm not scared," I say through gritted teeth.

Not much.

Before Cass can respond the corridor explodes in a blaze of indigo light, stopping time. A winged being, larger than the rest of us, emerges from the light. He wears long purple robes that flutter in the breeze. His auburn hair hangs down his back in waves. His piercing green eyes look as though they could reach into the depths of your soul.

They can.

"Nesayiel!" His voice booms causing the stones to vibrate.

Raphael. A member of the Council.

Awesome.

I'm in some serious trouble.

"Let me see your arm," Raphael says.

I face the angel, my heart beating too fast against my ribs. "Raphael. Why—?"

"I came at Mikayel's request to tend to your injuries." His indigo tinged wings tuck in as he reaches for me.

"There must have been others who could have done this."

"Yes. Many. But I also bear a message from the Council."

I stare at the Healer, anxiety permeating every cell. This is *so* bad.

Raphael takes my arm and examines the still bleeding wound. "It has been a long time since you allowed an UnHoly to pierce your armor."

"Yes." I choke and I remind myself to breathe.

Raphael smiles, quiet as usual.

Sometimes the Council really annoys me.

"And you have had an encounter with Azzaziel that you have not reported?"

I can't seem to figure out how to form the word "yes", so I say nothing.

"You are to report to the Council." Raphael says. He turns to Cass and Zane. "All of you."

"But, the girl," I say too fast. "We must find—"

"She is safe. Her memories, purged." Raphael wraps his large hand around my laceration. "And she is not your assignment."

Why do people keep saying that?

Raphael squeezes my arm, whispering "*Apage.*" He blows on the wound and I watch it fade into nothing. "Now, the Council is waiting," he says, his voice firm.

I flex my healed arm. "Thank you."

"Thank Mikayel. You should have come to me yourself. The Council will want to know why you did not. And why your duty has not been done."

Just what I need, another guilt trip.

Raphael walks to my friends. "You both would be wise to remember your duty as well." As the last word fades, Raphael vanishes in a burst of blinding light.

"What the blazes did he mean by that?" Zane asks, stretching his wings behind him.

"What do any of the Council ever mean?" Cass replies. Her body shudders slightly. "But I think we'd better listen."

Zane smiles and nods. "Like it or not Nes, we're going to Celestium."

"No. Not yet. First I need to find Lori. Talk with her."

"There's no way I'm letting you violate a direct order. Raphael said she was fine. Whatever it is you *think* you need to say to her will have to wait. We need to go. We're in enough trouble already." Zane glares at me. Again.

"You mean *I'm* in enough trouble."

"Yeah, well, you are the one with the most to answer for." A smile plays on his lips as his voice relaxes. I don't know what he finds so amusing in this. "You know we'll protect you as best we can with the Council."

"I thought you were angry."

"Oh, I am. I'm pretty certain you've lost your mind actually." Zane puts his arm around my shoulder, avoiding the gash that remains on my neck." But, that doesn't mean I won't stand up for you."

"Thanks," I say. I like the feel of his arm around me, like the safety he always represents. "I don't know what's wrong with me. Something about this case, about my stupid human form, it's just so dang—"

"I know. Hard." Zane squeezes my shoulder and for a moment I can believe things will be okay.

"Yeah."

"You need to figure out why it's hard, Nes." Zane pins me with his stare, reaching my soul. "Before you see the Council. Before they ask questions that could land you in the Abyss too."

Time stops for a brief moment before Cass sidles next to us.

"It'll be fine." Cass's eyes hold the concern her words hide.

"Yeah, sure. Fine." I push away the smoldering feelings that burn through me. The Council will never understand any of this. Heck, I don't understand it.

Mikayel expects more from me than this. So much more.

And so do I.

"I'd better go. You guys find Lori, okay?"

"No. You heard Raphael. We're coming with you. Lori will have to wait." Cass says.

"But—"

"But nothing. We're all going to the Council. Now." Zane and his sense of duty.

I force my thoughts into the shadows behind us, filling it with a piercing golden light. The ground shakes as the scene fades and a void forms—our portal home. I think of the questions the Council will ask, the kinds of answers they'll expect to hear. Explanations about Lori and Aydan. My emotional connections to them. The memories of a human life long gone. Without the right answers, my fate with the Council will be grim.

We step into the portal.

And I pray for a miracle.

CHAPTER 14 - COMPLICATIONS

AYDAN

The angels disappear into the darkness, along with the shattered pieces of my world.

Elle.

It can't be her. It just can't. I watched her die. Held her lifeless body in my arms. All the intimate moments, the tight embraces, the shared kisses. I would have known if she were anything other than human. There's just no way.

It's not possible.

My mind caves in on itself as I think about every moment Elle and I shared. Every moment I need to forget.

If I can...

She stands in the fields, herding the goats. I am in awe. Her soft hair and pale skin. Surely nothing in Celestium is as beautiful as the girl standing before me.

My skin prickles in the cool breeze that wafts past. I have to meet her. Talk with her. The Council has warned against interfering with humans. But they couldn't have meant her. This apparition.

This angel.

"Hello," I say as I approach.

She looks down, shy.

And even more irresistible.

"I'm new here," I say, tripping over my words. "I work on the Stubbe farm, keeping things in order when Mr. Stubbe is away."

She stays silent.

"My name is Adam."

Her face flushes as she steals a glance.

"What is your name?"

"Elle," she says, her voice barely audible.

"I'm sorry, I didn't quite get that." I have to hear her voice again.

"Oh," she whispers. She lifts her head and looks at me. "My name is Elle." Our gaze meets and I'm locked in a sacred moment, just the two of us. Her eyes search mine and I wonder if she knows what I am. But it isn't my wings or my glowing skin she seems to see. It's my soul—the part of me I show no one.

In that second I know. . .

I will never forget her.

I scroll through the times Elle and I shared, still unsure if Nesy could really be her. But even as I try to find a way to convince myself it isn't true, I know the truth.

Nesy and Elle are the same person.

And things just got complicated.

Too complicated.

CHAPTER 15 – MORAL OBLIGATION

NESY

My life as a Watcher was nothing like it should have been. Taking human form was so different from what I'd expected, what I was prepared for. To begin with, I'd never imagined I could forget being an angel. I never thought I'd fall in love. And I certainly never expected to be murdered.

Mikayel saved me from that life. Just as he'd saved me during my training as a Sentinal. He seemed to understand the permanent stain the human emotions had left on my soul. Understood the nightmares that plagued me during those first centuries—the time before I learned to master my weaknesses. Before I learned control.

His teachings had helped me in ways I could never quite express. Ways that forever defined…

Me.

And now, as my weaknesses, my flaws, resurface and my emotions unravel, I realize the truth.

I never mastered anything. I *am* damaged. Broken.

And I always will be.

I shake my head and shove aside my self-pity. This is not the time to wallow. Broken or not, I'm still a warrior.

I just need to remember everything that means.

I abandon my shame and push through the vortex into Celestium. The entire landscape glows like a prism in the sun. Streaks of emerald, indigo, ruby and gold dance around the sky. Inhaling deeply, I reach for the calm that always flows into me at home.

But I find no solace this time. Neither the love of my realm, nor the peace that surrounds me can dislodge the rock of fear growing in my stomach.

"Come on," Zane urges. "They'll be waiting for us."

"You mean me," I correct, my voice as shaky as I feel.

"Don't worry. You'll be fine. Just answer their questions and keep the whole 'I can't control my emotions' thing to yourself," Zane says.

If only it were that easy.

I walk into the massive Council chamber with my friends. Large bronze doors carved with intricate reliefs of angels and demons greet us. The doors open and we pause.

Cass squeezes my hand, Zane nods, and we begin to walk into the enormous room.

"Just Nesayiel." Mikayel says, his voice echoing off the gilded walls. "We will speak with you two in a minute."

I inhale my fear and step forward. I have no answers to the questions they'll no doubt ask. No way of explaining my mistakes, my feelings for the UnHoly.

I tuck my concern behind my warrior's façade and hide every emotion.

Time to face my fate.

The chamber itself is large, adorned with pictures of angels—Mediators, Anointed, Guardians, Sentinals. Every painting is depicted in amazing detail. They shimmer, giving the illusion of movement.

A lone golden chair sits in the center of the room. It faces a large alter with four majestic thrones. And in the thrones, the four I am most terrified to see. Gabriel, Raphael, Sariel, and Mikayel. The Council Elders. They rise as I enter the chamber, cold and detached. All except for Mikayel, whose anger is almost palpable. He glares at me, slicing through my mask and into my soul. There is little I will be able to hide from him.

Blazes.

"Good, you're here," Gabriel says, directing me to sit.

"I came as soon as Raphael requested."

"But the question is why didn't you come earlier? Why did I have to send someone for you?" Mikayel frowns, his voice hard.

"I don't think I understand."

"Then I'll clarify." Mikayel looms in front of me. "Why haven't you reported? Why does your assignment remain unfinished? And why didn't you report your encounter with the Dark One?"

I clench my jaw and force myself to focus. "You know about Azzaziel?"

"Of course I know," Mikayel bellows "The point is *you* should have been the one to tell me."

Guilt covers me. I hate seeing my master so enraged, hate knowing I'm the reason for it. "I just thought—" The words die on my tongue. How could I possibly explain this away?

Gabriel stands, placing a hand on Mikayel. "I think what concerns us, Nesayiel, is that you have never once broken protocol."

I feel Gabriel push into my thoughts. Feel them all enter my mind. I can't resist. I must grant them access or face their wrath.

"When you failed to report Azzaziel's presence, failed to secure the UnHoly on two separate occasions, we became...concerned." Gabriel waits for me to respond. His gentle, relentless eyes lock with mine.

The Council examines my thoughts, searches my feelings.

My heart beats once, twice, three times before my mind becomes my own. I wait, breath held, for someone to say something. Anything. Some hint that my weakness, my shame, remains undiscovered.

"Perhaps it is best to send another team back with you." Sariel looks to Mikayel.

They know.

"What do you think, brother?" Gabriel stares through me. "Shall we send another team? Just to make sure she can handle this."

"That won't be necessary." I choke on my own words. Of course it's necessary. I'm broken. "I can handle the UnHoly. I will finish this. I just need another chance." I've never failed. And I refuse to start now. I won't admit defeat. Not to the likes of *that* UnHoly.

Mikayel examines me with his gaze, questioning my abilities. "Two humans have died since you arrived. Not exactly confidence-inspiring."

Raphael stands and joins Mikayel, both of them glowering at me. Nothing like being scrutinized.

"You're ability to vanquish Aydan is not in question, Nesayiel. But with Azzaziel now part of the equation, additional help would be most prudent, would it not?" Raphael looks at my now-healed scar. "Especially given Aydan's ability to find your weakness."

"What weakness?" I don't have any weaknesses. That is, if you ignore the whole I-can't-control-my-feelings-around-Aydan thing.

"With your armor. Did he not burn your skin with his sword?" Raphael already knows the answer.

"He did."

"Then he has somehow figured out how to evade your defenses. Perhaps a second team would—"

"Would not understand him as I do." The words pour out of my mouth too fast. "I know how he fights. I know how to beat him, armor-penetrating sword or not."

"And Azzaziel? What will you do if he discovers your presence? Engage him? Prove yourself by trying to defeat him?" Gabriel's questions sear me with their truth.

I hate it when he does that.

I stare at the floor, my silence screaming every word I can not bear to say.

"You have three days. No more." Mikayel stands next to me. "If Zanethios has not reported that you have completed your task, I will come myself. Regardless of the reasons for your failure. Do you understand?"

Mikayel's threat steals the air from my lungs. He never comes unless an *angel* has committed a crime.

"Yes, Sir," I manage to say.

"As for Azzaziel, you cannot defeat him. He is not your target. You are to track his movements only. Keep your true identity hidden from him. Once he knows what you are, he will try to persuade you to join him. Azza has been known to be very persuasive in the past. You can not risk falling to his words." Mikayel's expression relaxes and his voice lowers.

"Report in often. Let me deal with the Dark One. Not you. Am I clear?" His voice cracks.

"Yes, Sir." I ignore my swirling emotions—fear, anguish, and shame—and leave the chamber, suffocating under the weight of Mikayel's words.

And his expectations.

"So, do they know?" Cass whispers.

"They suspect."

"Are you sure?" she asks.

"Yes. Mikayel said if I didn't finish this in three days, he would come himself."

"That's not good." Zane's voice is barely audible.

"I know."

"So, what are you going to do?" Zane asks

"My job." I ball my hands into fists, desperate to leave the shrinking chamber.

"But can you?" Cass asks. Her words sound more like an accusation than a question.

"I'm not willing to risk everything because of my stupid emotions, human or angelic. I learned to control these feelings once, I just have to do it again. A Sentinal never gives in to feelings. Not ever."

"Cassiel and Zanethios, please come in now." Gabriel's request holds none of the malice of Mikayel's demand. *They* are obviously not in trouble.

"But you are no ordinary angel." Cass whispers as she starts through the doors.

"I am what I've trained to be—a Sentinal."

CHAPTER 16 – ANSWERS REVEALED

NESY

I walk to the libraries of Celestium, my mind full of Mikayel's threat and my failures. I have to find a way to finish this. I won't disappoint my master, not after everything he's done for me.

The archives are housed in a remote chamber, far away from the Council. I walk to the center of the small space flanked with private nooks. It looks empty. Perfect. I doubt my brethren would understand my need to know what happened so many centuries ago.

"Harahel, I know you're here. You're *always* here." I wait for a response, wondering where the archivist could have gone. Harahel is the master of the libraries of Celestium. If there is anything to discover about Aydan, this is the place to find it. I pace across the floor, begging the documents to materialize in front of me. A pointless act. Only Harahel has the key. There is no way to gain access without his approval.

I just hope he'll grant it.

I call for Harahel again, my confidence waning as the moments continue to click by. Mikayel's words trickle through my thoughts again.

Three more days. Finish this or I will come and do it myself...

Mikayel never makes idle threats. If I fail again, I'll be the one going to the Abyss.

Not going to happen.

I picture Aydan; see myself vanquish him as he burns in the eternal flames. The images tear through my heart and cripple me. Waves of nausea buffet against my body and my legs tremble. I grab the corner of the lone counter in front of me. *Relax. Breathe.* I attempt to start my breathing mantra, but it's no use. Something about Aydan prevents me from doing what I must. Even thinking about hurting him fills me with an uninvited pain, as if I will die too.

I have to understand why. Now.

"Harahel," I call again. "I need you." My voice echoes through the empty chamber. The ground begins to shake, rattling the few adornments on the walls. Navy blue light floods the dark room.

Finally.

The azure light coalesces in front of me. Harahel steps forward and tips his head slightly. He's tall, like most of the angels in Celestium. His deep set eyes match the navy color of his robes. His hair hangs in a wavy mass of dark brown around his shoulders. He looks far younger than he should, considering his existence predates that of the Council.

I nod, ready to make my request. "I've come—"

"I know why you are here. You seek answers about the UnHoly. My question is why, Sentinal? Mikayel has not sent you. He does not know of your presence here."

"No, he doesn't. But there is something I need to see about Aydan's fall."

"Is it not enough to know that he fell? Why must you know how?"

"It isn't *how* I am searching for. It's *why*."

I watch as the archivist considers my request and nods again. "Knowledge is something to be pursued by all, not hidden away in some dark recess. I am proud that a Sentinal has figured out the need for examination of the past, when deciding how to proceed in the future. I will get the information you want."

He leaves and returns in the time it takes one human heart beat to pass, carrying nothing but a single piece of parchment. "Take this," he says as he hands it to me. "It will tell you everything."

"It's blank." I turn the paper over in my hands. "How do I read it?"

"The path to knowledge begins with a question. I suggest you start there. You may use the alcoves for your contemplation." Harahel waves a hand and a blue light directs me to the corner of the room. "Return the parchment when you have discovered what you need."

"I will," I say.

I go to the alcove and sit, staring at the blank scroll. My hand trembles. Can I do this? Do I really want to know everything? I think about Aydan. About Lori. My instincts tell me who they are. What if I'm right? What if everything I've worked so hard to forget is the key to finishing this? Am I really ready to confront my past?

The questions bounce in and out of my thoughts as my wings flutter nervously behind me. I draw a deep breath and pull on my strength as a Sentinal—what's left of it.

I have to do this. There is no other way.

Harahel's words ring through me. *The path to knowledge begins with a question.* I consider the myriad of queries continuing to bombard my thoughts and settle on one.

Why did you fall?

The question caresses my thoughts. I whisper the words, wondering why it really matters, what I'm hoping to discover.

My heart beats too fast as the parchment comes to life. Images blend into the fibers and move like a projection on a screen. Pictures of Aydan. The Council.

His fall.

LACRIMOSA

Aydan tumbles onto the floor of the chamber as Mikayel releases him. "Stay," Mikayel barks, his sword pointed at Aydan's chest. "I will deal with you later." He sheaths his sword and fades into the air. Aydan stands facing the empty Council table. His body glows with an almost translucent light that fills the room. His wings unfurl behind him.

I can't trust what I'm seeing. Aydan. So beautiful. So different from the Beast I saw tonight. The Beast I almost killed.

My body begins to tremble as the images swirl and change.

"Aydan, do you know why you are here?" Gabriel's voice holds no malice.

"Yes, Sir. I have broken my vows and I must atone."

"That is correct. Let us start with the demon. The werewolf you hunted." Gabriel studies Aydan carefully.

"Peeter Stubbe. He was working at the Dark One's bidding." Aydan's voice quivers when he speaks.

"Azzaziel?" asks Sariel. "Are you sure?"

"He is," Mikayel responds. "Azzaziel was present when I retrieved the angel." Disgust fills every syllable.

"And yet, you did not report his presence to this Council. Why?" Raphael's eyes fixate on Aydan.

"I was...overcome, Sirs."

The Council pauses, considering his words.

Several moments pass in desperate silence. Finally, Sariel speaks, his tone controlled. Dangerous. "So, you loved a mortal? A young farm girl? Despite the vows you took?" Aydan says nothing. "And you love her still?" Sariel asks.

The words bounce around the great hall.

"And you sought vengeance for her death. Killed those you were meant to protect." Mikayel spits every word. "These are your actions, yes?"

Aydan looks down, stoic.

"You understand what you have done, do you not?" Gabriel's voice still holds no malice.

Aydan's continued silence echoes the confession the Council demands.

"Speak!" Mikayel's voice booms.

Aydan says nothing.

Nothing of his feelings for the mortal.

Nothing of the shame carved on his face.

Nothing of the rage still blazing through his eyes.

"So that is it then? You will say nothing on your behalf? No explanations for your deeds?" Raphael stares at the young angel.

"Aydan. Since you have chosen silence, you give us little choice. You will go to the antechamber and await our decision." Gabriel motions to the Sentinals guarding the large doors of the chamber. They take their positions next to Aydan.

Mikayel stands, his expression hard. "Why are we waiting?" he asks, his voice unyielding. "The rules are clear. He should be cast out."

"Everything is very precise with you now, Mikayel. So different from before. Life is seldom that simple. It never has been, especially when we intertwine ourselves with humanity." Gabriel looks at his brother angel, his face wearing the same peace that fills his voice.

"But the rules—"

"Are not as absolute as you wish them to be. Something you know better than most." Gabriel's voice matches Mikayel's intensity. "Aydan, leave us. We will have our decision soon."

The images fade as the parchment goes blank.

"No, there has to be more." I whisper. I still don't understand. I quiet my mind and form a new question. The real question. The one that's haunted me for the past two days.

Are you Adam?

The empty canvas in my hand responds immediately as colors wash over the beige vellum.

Images of my sister, so much like Lori. My time with Adam. Intimate moments that still leave me breathless.

A life I vowed to forget. Forever.

"Don't go with him. Please. Just forget you ever met him." My sister grabs my dress, her ghostly green eyes begging me to listen. Auburn hair drapes over her shoulders.

"I thought you liked Adam. He likes you." I pry her fingers away.

"But, he'll take you away. He will. He'll take you someplace I can't follow. He isn't like me…like us."

"Lorelei, you're just being silly. I'm not going anywhere. Adam and I will get married one day. And we won't move away. You'll see." I take her trembling hands into mine. "Now, you have to let me go and see him. I promised."

"I'll tell Papa everything. I will. He won't let you marry a farm hand."

I drop her hands and walk away, ignoring the pleas of my sister.

The images speed forward.

Lorelei's betrayal as she tells Papa everything…How could you?

My screams as the wolf attacks…Thank you for saving me, Mikayel.

And Adam.

His body encased in flames.

I stand, desperate to escape the truth in my hands. Trembling, I stifle the scream rising up my throat. The sound of my pounding heart floods my ears.

I watch the fire consume Adam's body, hear his screams as he dies.

The pictures stream faster and faster.

Azzaziel. The Sentinals. A battle.

And Mikayel, ripping an angel from my beloved Adam before he dies. An angel with amber eyes and translucent skin that shimmers.

Aydan.

"No!" I cry, my voice nothing more than a whisper. Tears flood my eyes and spill over my cheeks, dampening the still streaming movie in my hands.

Aydan paces across the Council floor, waiting. "I'm sorry, Elle. I should've have prevented this. All of it." His voice cracks.

"You should not feel shame for your actions," a voice calls out.

"Azzaziel?"

"You were only avenging the death of your beloved. A noble cause. Why should you be punished for an act of justice?"

"You can't be here," Aydan hisses.

"And yet, I am."

"I would rather die at Mikayel's hands than join you."

"After what they are doing to you? This sham of a trial? And for what? Because you dared to love another? Seems quite hypocritical to me. Why don't you ask Mikayel to tell you about his true feelings on angelic love?"

"Go away, Azzaziel. I'll never join you."

"You cannot undo your vow to me. I am looking forward to training you, young Aydan."

The Council chamber grows silent save the sound of Aydan's footsteps as he continues to pace like a caged animal with no escape.

Moments click by. Aydan's expression hardens with each step.

I can feel his rage through the pictures. Taste the bitter acid of his emotions as they coat my tongue. Torment digs into his features and I fear what comes next.

Aydan bursts through the heavy chamber doors. "I will not stay here while you wrestle with my fate. Release me to the Abyss—it is my wish. I do not regret what I've done. Not any of it. And I would do it again. So, let the flames burn me for an eternity. It makes no difference to me."

Mikayel appears next to him, sword drawn. "As you wish," he says, his lips twitching.

Booming thunder rattles the Council chamber as the ground beneath Aydan's feet splits open. His wings unfurl, ripping themselves from his back. He falls backwards into oblivion, a shower of feathers all that remains in the chamber.

"And now you are mine." Azza's voice rings through the hall.

And Aydan continues to fall.

"No!" I scream. My legs won't hold me a moment longer. I crumble into a heap on the cold floor of the library. Bits of memory stream past my eyes, emerging from the depths of my soul. Every intimate embrace, every stolen moment. I'm lost in the depth of a love I feel for the man that still holds my heart.

But he isn't a man anymore.

He is the UnHoly. A Beast. The one I must kill.

If I can.

CHAPTER 17 – GRIM DILEMMA

NESY

Morning arrives encased in the memories of my life as Elle. I loved Adam then. Adam who is Aydan. Craved him. It's a life I need to again forget.

The peace I found only when I was safely nestled in Adam's arms...*forget it all.*

The security no one but he offered...*release that life.*

The need I had for his touch...*bury it away.*

I'd learned to lock away the memories once, transcend the feelings that lingered in my angelic heart.

But that was before.

Now that my memories of that life are unleashed, now that my feelings are awakened, I have to face the bitter truth.

I will always love Aydan.

I stare out of the window of my small bedroom, my human body asleep. The sun rises above the nearby buildings, casting beams of pink and yellow light bouncing off the glass encased skyscrapers. The scene is breathtaking. Calm.

And completely lost on me.

Nothing will make me feel calm. Not until Aydan is gone and my emotions purged.

"Hey," Zane says as he walks into the room. "You okay?"

"I guess." I turn from the beautiful view and look at my dearest friend, wondering. How much does he know? "What happened with the Council?"

"We got the 'your-loyalty-is-to-Celestium' speech. No big deal."

"They think I'm going to fail."

"They think you can't separate from your emotions. And they're worried that we'll cover for you."

"And would you? Cover for me?"

"Would I have a reason to?" Zane stares through me, pushing into my thoughts.

I block the uninvited intrusion, not ready for him to know everything yet.

"This looks serious," Cass says. "What am I missing?"

"Nesy's going to ask us to choose between her and the Council."

"I didn't say that. I just asked what you would do if my plans differed from theirs."

"Do they?" Cass asks.

"No. Not really." I turn back to the window. I want to tell them I can't do this. Want them to tell me there's a way out that I won't have to kill the one I still love.

I feel Cass's hand on my shoulder. "You know we'd do anything for you, Nesy. But Aydan is evil. You have to finish this."

"He wasn't always this way." The words pour out before I can stop them. All I can think about is the way he was as Adam—his kindness, his love.

"None of them were."

I turn to my friends, lost in a fantasy I want to be real. "What if he could find his way back to us?" I ask. "Stop being evil?"

"Impossible," Zane says. "It's too late for him."

"Why?" There has to be a way. Some path of redemption. I'm not ready to lose him again, no matter what he's done.

"Because he likes killing too much," Zane answers. "He's Azzaziel's right-hand man. There's no redemption for that kind of evil."

My silence betrays my thoughts, confessing everything I won't admit.

"It's him, isn't it?" Cass asks "Adam."

I nod.

"I'm so sorry." Her embrace showers me in pity.

I step away from her. "Don't. I won't have you feeling sorry for me. I'll figure a way out of this and fulfill my duty." I look from Cass to Zane, disgusted by the pained expressions on their faces—reminders of all of the ways I've failed.

"Are you sure you can?" Zane asks, his body tight with anxiety.

"I'm a Sentinal. Trained by Mikayel himself. Of course I can."

Cass furrows her brow. "And you're in love with your target."

"That was a long time ago. I'm not that person anymore. Neither is he. We both left that life—and our love."

"Still, asking you to kill the one you love is more than any one should have to bear, even a Sentinal. Perhaps they should—"

"No, I will not ask for a new team. I don't love that UnHoly. Not anymore. And I don't fail. Not ever."

"Why are you being so stubborn?" Zane's forehead wrinkles. His mouth twitches. "If you're wrong, if you can't handle this, Aydan *will* kill you. Or worse, Azzaziel will figure out who you are. He'll torture you until you join his ranks. We've all seen it happen before."

"Not with me, you haven't." I clench my jaw, refusing to acknowledge the truth of his words. "Look, I know I can handle this. It's just another assignment like all the others. I'll do my duty, regardless of anything else. I owe Mikayel that much." I feel my emotions subside. Feel my warrior's mask harden. Centuries of training take over and slowly I become everything I've been trained to be. . .

A cold, heartless, warrior.

"I am not broken. I will do this." I say the words more for myself than my friends.

"This isn't about your being broken, Nes. It's about being smart. A Sentinel would know that, would see when they're outmatched." Zane's voice is barely audible.

"I'm not outmatched," I say through gritted teeth. "Not even close." I look at my physical body still sleeping. "Now, if you two will excuse me, I need to slip into form. I have a *demon* to vanquish." The lie sticks in my throat.

"Nesy—"

"I'm fine, Cass. But seriously, get out of here and let me get dressed. There's a chance he hasn't figured out who I am. I need to get this finished before he does. Then I can forget all about Aydan. About everything."

Yeah, right. No chance of that.

CHAPTER 18 - CONFLICTED

AYDAN

Azza expects my allegiance. Demands it. But things are different for me now. The mere thought of taking his vows fills me with disgust.

I can't go through with this. Not anymore.

I think of the Seer, Lori. There is something familiar about her too. Something that pulls on the fringes of my memories. I reach for the fragmented pieces of that former life, desperate to unlock the riddle of who the Seer really is, but I can't.

I only know her presence binds me to Azza forever. He won't stop now. Not until I've been branded. Not until I've fully become the Beast.

This was always the price for my vengeance so long ago. But now that it's time, now that the Seer has been found, I'm torn.

I don't want this life anymore.

I want Nesy.

She reminds me of everything I've lost. Everything I still have to lose. If only I could find a way out of this fate.

My mind swims in the possibilities, a drop of hope blooming in my chest. Maybe I can find my way back to Celestium.

The Beast claws through me, shredding any possibility for a different life. My eyes water as every death I've caused streams past.

It's too late.

There have been so many lives ruined. So many atrocities committed.

Hope withers and dies and I'm resigned to the disgust of who I am and the only option left to me—

A life spent as Azza's slave.

A life filled with killing.

A life as…

the Beast.

CHAPTER 19 – FINDING LORELEI

NESY

I arrive at East Side moments before class. Aydan is bound to be at school, if for no other reason than to feed off the students' torment and pain as they learn about their classmate's death.

Was that only yesterday? It seems like a lifetime ago.

The campus is quiet. Solemn. Grief counselors meet with small groups of students helping them process the loss. They huddle together. Some cry. Many seem curious, whispering questions. "Was it a drug overdose?" "Was she attacked by some psychopath?" "Did she kill herself?" The questions are endless.

And all wrong.

Aydan is to blame. Only Aydan.

Two innocent deaths on my watch. Two more reasons why I have to finish this now. Today.

Before I change my mind.

My morning classes creep by with no sign of Aydan. No sign of Azzaziel. Strange. They should be here. I reach out my thoughts, searching. Every feeling leads me back to school. They're here.

Somewhere.

The bell for lunch rings and I head out amongst the throng. The students are not as sad, not as shocked. They walk with their friends as death fades from their conversations.

I walk too, still looking for any sign of Aydan. Tendrils of emotion seep through my façade as seconds turn into minutes. My body tenses and I imagine the feel of his hand in mine.

No. I won't do this. I won't pine for him.

Focus, Sentinal. I ignore the waxing tide of feelings threatening to overcome me. Desire, guilt, rage. *Sentinals do not give in to emotions.* I repeat the words, desperate to embrace my training. None of it works as the tempest continues to rise, swirling through me. Confusing me.

I make one last attempt to find Aydan amongst the crowd at lunch. My mind splinters as pictures of my sister filter into my thoughts. Images of a suicide. Her suicide.

Help me Nesy. Please. Make me strong. This is the only way...

I try to dismiss the voice, the images, and focus only on my job. It's no use. Lorelei's pleas are too compelling.

"Nesy."

Not in my head.

"Nesy."

That voice is real.

"Are you okay?"

I spin around and face my past. "Lori?" Her name scrapes across my throat. I stare into her eyes. She's alive, just as Raphael promised. Alive with no memory.

I hope.

"Hey! I was looking for you." I say.

"That's funny, I was looking for you too."

"Me? Why?"

"I wanted to make sure you were okay. You know, after last night and all." Lori stares relentlessly into my eyes and I see the truth. She *is* my sister. My human sister. Impossible or not, Lori and Lorelei are one. "I needed to see that Aydan didn't really hurt you." She looks from my neck to my arm, scrutinizing my skin.

So much for no memory.

My body stiffens and I fumble for the right words. "Um, what do you mean? Hurt me how?"

"You don't need to play dumb with me. I know what happened, same as you."

I remain silent, unsure of exactly what to do or say.

Lori takes my hand and leads me to the same low wall where we talked two days ago. She sits, motioning for me to come next to her.

"I know who you are," she whispers. "I know *what* you are."

I say nothing, praying this isn't actually happening.

"You're an angel." Lori smiles at me, looking more like the six-year-old girl I left behind so long ago. "You came to protect me. Just like in Germany."

Guess I can't pretend this isn't happening anymore. "Lorelei?"

She nods. My world fractures as both lives collide. I wrap her into a tight embrace, unwilling—unable—to stop the flood of happiness I feel. "I can't believe it's really you. How much do you remember? From last night? How much?"

"Everything. You and Aydan were fighting. Azza took me away. I thought he was going to kill me."

I did too.

"An angel rescued me. He frightened Azza away and brought me home." Tears glistened in her eyes. "The angel tried to make me forget you, tried to change my memories. But he couldn't. I hid them away, just like Momma taught me." Lori fumbles with the winged charm around her neck, biting her lip. "I've waited too long for you to come back to me to forget everything now."

"I don't understand. You shouldn't be alive. You can't be."

"But I am."

"Then you must be a…" I couldn't bring myself to finish the sentence. To admit the truth.

"A Seer."

I nod.

"I am."

"I thought the Seers were a dead race."

"We almost are. In fact, Momma said I was the last one. I'm not sure I believe that though." She releases a labored breath and closes her eyes. After a moment she shakes her head, opens her eyes, a sad smile forming on her face. "Most of my kind were killed by a powerful monster with large black wings, empty eyes."

"Azzaziel."

"Yes. Aydan's friend, I think. He's much worse than Aydan."

"You said 'most were killed' by him. What happened to the rest?"

"Suicide. It's the only way to keep him from stealing our souls. Momma killed herself to protect me. She was a Seer too."

Lori's eyes cloud over as her tears spill over cheeks—just like they did the day I left her for Aydan, the day I died. "I'm sorry, Lori. I didn't know."

"She died to save me. I never understood that choice before last night. But now…now I think it's the only way."

"No. I don't believe that."

"Azza knows who I am, *what* I am. He's relentless. He'll hunt me and he won't stop until I'm dead, until he's claimed my soul."

The thought of Azzaziel or anyone hurting Lori sickens me, strengthening my resolve. I have to end this.

First Aydan. Then Azzaziel. Mikayel's warnings or not. I will not let him hurt my human sister.

"Why does he need *your* soul?" I ask, knowing there's more to this story.

"I don't know. When Azza took me, he called me the one he'd been searching for to fulfill his plans. He said he'll follow me to the ends of the Earth, that I'd never be safe now that he can recognize me." More tears fill Lori's eyes. "Nesy, I'm tired of running. I've been hiding for centuries. I can't do it anymore. I'll die before I let him touch me again."

"What if I could find a way to protect you? Make it so he could never hurt you again?" I don't care that she isn't my assignment. I don't care about Mikayel's warnings or the Council's wishes.

This is personal.

"You can't protect me all the time."

"I'll find a way. I swear it." I hug my sister again, determined to keep my promise. "I'm here for Aydan. But that doesn't mean I'm willing to let Azzaziel take you. I have to figure this out. In the meantime, I need you to hide. Keep yourself safe. It'll only be for a day or so."

"Momma's choice makes more sense." Lori lowers her head, mouthing one word. "Suicide."

"No! That's not an option. There are horrible consequences for that—things far worse than losing your soul." Lori will not pay for my failures.

"Before I agree to hide again," Lori says, wiping the tears from her eyes. "I need to ask you something." Her hands again fumble with the winged charm around her neck.

"What is it?"

She takes a deep breath. "Do you know who Aydan really is?"

An involuntary shutter ripples through me at the mention of his name. "Yes," I whisper.

"You know that he was Adam? Before?"

Hearing the words from her lips somehow makes everything worse. More real. "Yes. I know."

"And you're sure you can still do this? Protect me from him, from Azza?"

I fight back the rush of emotions and ignore the crushing weight of despair threatening to rip me in two. Aydan is not Adam. Not anymore. He is an UnHoly, one I'm ordered to kill. I have to say the words. Force myself to admit the truth. "Aydan isn't the person I fell in love with in Germany." The words scrape across my lips. I swallow, desperate to quench my suddenly dry mouth. "He's nothing more than a monster. And I always chase away the monsters."

"But he had you pinned last night. Maybe he's too strong for you."

Why does everyone keep thinking that? He is *not* too strong for me.

"He caught me off-guard, nothing more. That won't happen again."

A slight wind ruffles my hair, carrying the putrid scent of the Dark One. Azzaziel. My senses go to full alert as I begin to scan the crowd for him. "Lori, I need you to tell me exactly what Azza said when he took you last night." My angelic form pushes against my body, poised to fight. "Every word." I turn back to my sister.

"He—" The words fade on her tongue. Her eyes roll back into her skull and she begins to convulse.

Spasm after spasm rolls through her body as she slips off the wall.

Azryel's Wings, not now. "Someone help!" I shout. "Please!" Panic breaks through my hardened façade as I struggle to reign in my true self.

A few teachers run toward me. Cass and Zane materialize, visible only to me.

"Help her," I cry again.

A teacher bends over and tips Lori's head back as her mouth foams. "It looks like a seizure. Get help."

A student runs off towards the office. I remain, unable to move.

"I've got it, Nes," Zane says. I feel his hand on my shoulder, feel him calming my thoughts. "I'll protect her. Go and find the source." Zane opens his palms. A burst of bright emerald light emanates from his hands, bathing Lori. Her convulsions quiet.

Thanks, I say through my mind. *Don't let anything else happen to her. Please.* My desperation seethes, turning to rage.

"Just go. Hurry." Cass holds Lori's hand.

Fueled by anger, I search the throng of onlookers. *He has to be here.* Our eyes meet immediately—black pits that hold no life. I see his face, the Celtic tattoo glistening on his neck, his black hair tied back. A smile curls his lips as I push through the crowd, anxious to ring his neck.

I plow through the students to the spot where he stood.

Too late. He vanishes into smoke seconds before I reach him.

"Looking for me?" His voice snakes around me.

"Leave her alone, Azzaziel," I say to the crowd. "This isn't about her."

"I'm sorry, but you're wrong. It is exactly about her. I've been looking for her for a long time."

I turn towards the voice. Azza reappears in human form across the quad. His face is painted with a sadistic smile. I want to run to him. Engage him. Kill him.

But I won't. Because that is what he wants. Mustering all of my resolve, I square my shoulders, speaking to the air. "Soon, Azzaziel. You'll pay for everything soon." I turn and walk back to Lori.

"I'm looking forward to it, little angel. More than you know."

I ignore his taunt, thinking only of Lori. "How is she?" I ask when I reach her.

"Weak, but alive," the teacher answers. "The ambulance should be here soon. I'm sure she'll be okay."

I look to Cass and Zane.

"She's fine. Who's the source? Aydan or Azzaziel?" Zane asks.

Azzaziel. Lori's the Seer he's been hunting, I think. *He wants her soul and we need to figure out what he's up to. Determine if he really is forming an army.*

The paramedics make their way across the quad.

There's more. I promised I'd keep her safe. I won't let Azzaziel hurt my sister.

"She's your sister? From Germany?" Cass asks.

So it seems. I can't take my eyes off Lori. She looks so peaceful, just like when she was young.

"He's not your target, Nes." Zane's voice draws my attention to him. "And neither is the Seer."

I know. But things are different. She will not pay for my mistakes. We have to protect her. At least until we figure out why Azzaziel is so bent on killing her.

"You just worry about Aydan." Zane grabs my arm.

Blazes! I wish he'd give the whole do-your-duty thing a break.

I pull away from him. *Will you help me protect her?*

Zane is stoic.

"Will you?" The onlookers spin and stare at me. I turn away.

"I'll talk to Sariel. He'll send the Guardians to keep watch over her," Cass says.

Okay. But quietly. I'm in enough trouble with Mikayel.

"He'll want to know." Zane isn't going to let this go.

And I'll tell him later. Right now, I just really need you to keep my sister safe. Please. Even in my thoughts I sound desperate.

Zane nods. The paramedics place Lori on a stretcher.

Go with her. I'll meet you there. I watch my friends vanish as the ambulance takes Lori away.

Things have completely spun out of control. Aydan's my lover. Lori's my sister. And Azzaziel knows exactly who I am.

Great.

How am I supposed to finish this now?

CHAPTER 20 - FURY

AYDAN

The quad bustles with activity. Lori, looking more dead than alive, is wheeled off campus. The angels, Nesy's friends, follow, guarding over the young girl. Do they know who she is? *What* she is?

Anger ripples through me, rustling my wings. He did it; he really did it. *No!* I scream through the silence in my thoughts. *No!*

Azza's laugh fills me as he taunts Nesy. "You'd better keep a close watch on her, little angel. I have big plans for her. And Aydan."

Nesy screams in frustration, leaving campus. She disappears into the endless throng of onlookers. She'll never believe that I had nothing to do with this. Never see me as anything other than her target. Azza's apprentice. The UnHoly.

And she shouldn't. Not now.

I try to picture a life without Azza and his crazy obsessions. One without the Beast urging me to feed.

Only me and Nesy

—nothing more than a fantasy.

Our love forever strong

—and a lie.

No violence, no Azza

—there will never be "no Azza", not for you.

I need to pretend it can happen. Pretend I'm not a killer.

Lies, lies, lies.

My stomach clenches as hunger again fills my body—never-ending hunger. And a reminder. There is…

No.

Way.

Out.

CHAPTER 21 - BROKEN TEARS

NESY

I sleep in the chair next to Lori's hospital bed, reliving the fragments of my former life. Memories of Lorelei. The times we spent collecting eggs, making butter, milking cows. Mundane tasks I enjoyed with my sister. Until Adam.

After he came, my world changed, becoming promises and secrets. Dreams and desire.

In my mind, I feel his kisses, his embrace. I needed him then. Craved him. Every moment we spent apart felt like an eternity, every moment together—heaven.

But that was another life.

My thoughts change as images of Aydan's killing sprees alternate with the pictures of my life with Adam, tormenting my sleep.

More than once, I startle awake only to see the concerned faces of my friends and the Guardians. Their expressions remind me of how messed up I am. No Sentinal gets involved. No Sentinal *feels* these feelings.

No Sentinal falls in love.

Focus, Nesy. Do your duty. Zane's voice, a constant reminder, replays over and over in my thoughts.

I look at Lori, alive because of the machines pushing oxygen through her body. Each pulse of the machine rips a piece of Aydan-Adam away. No matter what he was once, he's nothing more than a monster now. The UnHoly.

My target.

I wipe away the tears filling my eyes and say goodbye to the life I once lived. *Time to end this.* For good.

"You should rest. You've barely slept." Cass hovers near me, her skin bathing the room in an indigo glow.

"I feel fine, Cassiel. Focused. Ready." I glance at my friend.

"Are you sure?"

"Yes." I swallow the doubt rising through me. "Zane's right. Aydan is a monster. He'll never be anything more, he can't."

"We'll make sure Lori stays safe. Do what you must." Cass embraces me. "Be careful," she whispers.

"I will." I walk from the room to the elevator at the end of the hall, oblivious to everything but the job in front of me. I've let this go on too long, let myself remember things best forgotten, let myself feel.

No more.

The elevator slowly descends and I again picture Aydan's death.

The weapon, my dagger…*a close kill, personal.*

The words, whispered…*into his ear.*

The time, during an embrace…*so he never forgets*.

This ends tonight.

The elevator bell sounds as the door opens on the ground floor. I walk forward, bumping into the person in front of me.

"Sorry," I mumble, scarcely aware of where I am or who I've just run in to.

"Nesy?" Aydan's voice sharpens my mind into focus. "Is Lori okay?"

I stare into his eyes, the only things that remind me of Adam. My body goes stiff. "What are you doing here?" I spit through gritted teeth.

"I wanted to check on Lori."

"Why? Did Azza ask you to come and finish her off? Feed your little friends?" Venom fills every word.

He steps closer.

"Don't touch me," I snap as he reaches out for me.

The nurses look up from their work station. Like I care. Maybe a scene is just what I need.

"It's okay. She's just upset." The nurses calm immediately, no doubt influenced by Aydan's hypnotic voice.

That's not going to work on me.

"Come on," he whispers, again grabbing for my hand. "We need to talk."

I pull away. "Fine. Outside."

He raises his eyebrows and inhales deeply. "Sure."

"And don't try to contact your master. This is between you and me."

"Agreed."

The wind bites into my skin as we walk outside. I pull my leather jacket close around me and lead Aydan to the courtyard situated between the two hospital buildings. The tall structures cast long shadows throughout the empty garden. I focus my thoughts and finger the small dagger hidden in my jacket.

Aydan follows me to the far end of the courtyard, facing a small prayer garden. In the center of the garden sits a small sword-wielding angel. Another reminder.

Inhale...1...2...3...Exhale. I feel my control falter as I prepare for the inevitable. Aydan stands behind me, his breath thick on my neck. Inside, my emotions begin to unravel as my body reacts to his closeness. "Why did you come?" I ask, my voice scarcely more than a whisper.

Aydan places his hands on my hips, causing me to drag a ragged breath. I step out of his touch and face him. "Answer me."

"I came to check on Lori. And you."

My fragile hold on my feelings begins to crack. "Why?"

"I didn't cause her injury and I didn't want it to happen. I needed you to know that."

Do your job, I remind myself. I picture the plan, preparing myself. But my focus is fractured. My mind wrestles, torn between fulfilling my oath and asking the questions that were burned into my soul centuries ago.

Do your job…*Why did you leave me?*

Cast him out…*Why didn't you tell me?*

I refuse to give into my emotions. Refuse to play this game with myself anymore. I'm better than this. I know I am.

Am I?

"Why would I care what you need, UnHoly?"

Aydan says nothing as he steps closer.

I don't move. My wings flutter through my disguise and Aydan smiles. "You know who I am?" I ask.

"Yes."

"Then I assume you know why I'm here?"

"Yes."

"Good." I reach into my jacket, slipping my fingers around the small dagger. "But, before you meet your end, I want you to tell me who you are."

Aydan collapses the space between us. "You already know who I am."

I raise my weapon and point it at his chest. "I want you to say it."

"Why? If you plan on carrying this out, why does it matter who I am?"

"Say it," I order. Tears sting my eyes and spill over my cheeks.

Aydan leans into the dagger, allowing it to dig into his human flesh. "I am Adam," he whispers.

Electric currents flow between us, engulfing me. For a moment, I'm lost in him.

Focus, Sentinal, I scream, desperate to ignore my emotions. I push against the familiar scent of soap and pine that fills my senses and ignore the urgings of my physical body.

Keeping the dagger level against his heart, I look into his eyes—Adam's eyes. "Why didn't you tell me *what* you were?"

"I could ask you the same thing."

I grind my teeth. Silent.

"I couldn't say anything. I thought you were human. I wasn't supposed to love you at all." Aydan's breath caresses my skin as he speaks.

"And when I died? Why did you join Azzaziel?" I push the dagger into his skin.

"To avenge you," he says.

My hands tremble. "Don't blame me for your choices. My Adam never would have joined my murderer." My voice shakes on every word as I fight against everything I want.

My former life.

Love.

Adam. Aydan.

He raises his hands. "You're right. Everything was my own doing." He leans his body into mine, allowing the blade to puncture his skin. "Do it, Nesy. Say the words. Pierce my heart. Send me to the Abyss and end my suffering. Please. I won't stop you."

I inhale a sharp breath and shove the blade deeper.

His eyes widen and his body goes rigid. "I never meant to hurt you," he forces through gritted teeth.

"You didn't," I lie. Tears burn my eyes. "You hold no power over me. Not anymore." I pull the blade slowly out of his wound. I want him to feel every moment.

"Yes I do," he says as he slips his hands around my waist and pulls me to him.

Our combined electricity explodes across my skin. The dagger falls from my hands. His breath caresses my neck. "You still smell like vanilla," he whispers.

I open my mouth, desperate to say the words that will cast him aside and end this. But every word dies on my tongue.

He covers my mouth with his in a kiss that melts my bones. Steels my breath.

My eyes widened with rage. Fear. I pound against his chest, pushing against his skin.

He tightens his hold on me.

I frantically hammer against his chest. Scream into his mouth.

He deepens the kiss. My mind goes blank, my eyes roll back.

And I'm his.

I arch into him, threading my fingers through his black hair. A slight moan escapes my lips as he breaks through my walls and fills every part of me.

All I see is Adam.

All I feel is our love.

Nothing else matters.

He pulls away as the kiss ends, my world in ruins. "I've never forgotten you," he says. He places his hands on my face and brushes his mouth along my jaw. Every touch burns into my skin, my soul. "I love you, Elle. Still."

I try to speak. Tell him I've never forgotten him. Tell him we can be together.

Tell him I love him.

But my mouth won't work. And I know how this must end.

"I…can't," I choke as I push him away.

He reaches for me.

I step away, into the darkness. Tears still falling down my cheeks.

Aydan falls to the pavement, a mixture of human and demon blood pooling around his pierced heart.

CHAPTER 22 - FALLEN

AYDAN

I wasn't supposed to fall in love. Angels never do. But something about Elle changed everything. I don't know if it was her gentle manner or the fiery spirit that lived just beneath the surface. Either way, she was intoxicating. She understood me from the moment we met, almost as though she could touch my soul.

I met her a few months after I arrived in Bedburg. I wanted to marry her, give up my angelic life and live out my days with her. Something the Council would never allow.

Her father betrothed her to another and I went mad. There was no way I could share my Elle.

I thought of running away with her. But can you ever really run away from yourself?

My eyes flutter open as the image of Elle and our life together fades away. I look around, wondering how I made it back to my apartment.

Was everything just a dream?

The pain radiating in my chest gives me an answer.

Azza stares out of the window, stiff. Angry, no doubt. I haven't been acting like the UnHoly he trained me to be. Not by a long shot.

"How did I get here?" I ask.

"I found you outside the hospital, bleeding and unconscious."

I sit up on one elbow and clutch my chest, groaning.

"The wound to your human flesh will hurt for a while. But, overall you're intact. Looks like the Sentinal returned to finish her work."

I thought about Nesy. The taste of her lips on mine. The vanilla scent of her skin. She kissed me back. She wanted me as much as I wanted her.

I try to hide the smile I feel on my face, hide the love I still feel for her.

Azza glares at me. "Strange."

Does he know?

"What's strange?" I ask, pretending to feel nothing.

"Sentinals never miss. Let alone twice."

I hide my feelings away and try to act like the Beast I am. "Maybe I'm just stronger than she is."

"Mikayel would not have sent her if she couldn't complete the task. My guess is that something else got in the way." His gaze intensifies. "Something you may know about." He tilts his head and waits for me to answer.

"I have no idea why she missed," I lie.

Azza pounds into my thoughts, rifling through my mind. Good thing I know how to block intrusions—just the way he taught me.

I stow my memories, my feelings, deep inside; somewhere Azza can't invade. A moment passes. And another. Every moment of my life with Azza streams in front of me before I feel him leave my thoughts.

"We must figure out why the Sentinal is so hesitant to vanquish you. It could help us learn how to defeat her."

I stare at my master. "What—?"

"I will not let these attacks go unpunished. You will bring her to me. And then you will kill her."

No. Not her. I will not let him hurt her.

The Beast stirs, ready to carry out my master's bidding. I want to rebel, find a way to defy his orders. But I can't. I'm tethered to him.

And I hate myself for it.

"Kill her and Mikayel will think twice about sending any more Sentinals after you." Azza watches me, waiting for my reaction.

"But, if we hurt her, Mikayel will come himself. Why would we want that? We've avoided a direct confrontation with him for centuries." I try to stay calm and ignore the Beast smoldering inside.

"You sound scared. I expected more from you than fear. If you don't think you can handle her, I'll be happy to take care of this myself, while you watch, of course." His threat unleashes my fury.

Visions of his plans for Nesy spread across my mind. Images of fire and ash, the Sword of Death slicing into her tender flesh, the smell of her burning skin. My stomach churns into convulsions. I can't prevent my physical body from reacting to the movie playing in my head. I run to the bathroom and empty myself.

Nausea grips my body, sending wave after wave whirling through me as I release my fear, my pain, into the basin. After several moments, I return to Azza. Empty. Spent.

A sadistic smile spreads across his face. "So, shall I be the one to end her life?"

I have to protect her.

"No," I whisper. "I'll take care of her. You need not be involved."

"I knew you'd see things my way." Azza turns to leave. "Oh," he says over his shoulder. "One more thing. You *will* tell me if you discover why she hasn't hurt you, right?" The threat lurks between the spaces of the words.

I grit my teeth again. There's no way I'll be able to keep him from her. Not now. "I will tell you everything," I lie. "As always."

"Good," he says as he slips from the room.

I sink onto the couch, my head in my hands and my mind racing. There has to be a way out, a way to keep her safe. I won't allow my love to tear her apart again.

I drift into a restless sleep, the pain from my wound ever-present. Hellish pictures wrap around me.

Visions of my lips on Nesy turning her blood to poison

—I won't allow this.

Intimate embraces that turn her body into flames

—I'll never hurt you.

The sound of her screams as I end her life

—I'll protect you. Somehow.

I toss and turn, trying to shove aside the nightmare. But it's no use. There is only one way this can end.

In death. Hers or mine.

I wake, drenched in sweat, calling her name.

I can't let this happen.

I breathe in my emotions, allowing them to focus my thoughts. Pacing, I think of everything I've become since Elle's death. The hundreds of lives I've taken without a second thought. The misery I inflicted for fun. Thousands of human bodies emptied of their souls. Hundreds more used to satisfy my lust. Guilt and shame squeeze the air from my lungs.

I don't deserve you, Nesy.

I picture every detail of her. The exact color of her wings. The glow of her skin. The endless blue of her eyes. I need her as much as my body requires air. As much as the Beast needs the souls it feasts upon.

I need her forgiveness for everything I've become.

The lives I've destroyed

LACRIMOSA

—*I never meant to become this.*
The choices that define me
—*I never wanted this.*
The Beast I am
—*save me from myself.*

The walls of my apartment close in on me. Along with my guilt. I walk into the city, determined to find the only one who can help appease my shame. The moonless night engulfs the city while the nearby cathedral bells sound the time. One, two...twelve tolls echo through the concrete valley. I walk past the club and its hordes of dark creatures eager to be fed, ignoring their howls.

Ignoring my own hunger.

Azza's threat lingers in my thoughts.

If you can't handle her...take care of this myself...you will tell me what you know...

The words echo through my mind, consuming everything else. I have to find her. Protect her.

Love her.

"It's time to feed." Azza's uninvited voice rips through me, awakening the Beast. "I can feel your hunger. I think it's time I chose another meal for you."

"I don't need—"

"If you are to defeat the Sentinal, you need your strength. I want you to take Lori. Finish what I started."

"What?" I ask, scrambling to find a solution. "What about Sariel? Aren't his Guardians protecting her?"

The ground trembles beneath my feet as Azza materializes, towering over me. His demonic wings stretch to their full height as he reaches his taloned hand for my neck. "Are you refusing?"

I step out of my master's grasp. "No. I just thought the Sentinal was my priority."

Azza closes the distance, grabbing me by the throat and bringing me closer. "It is. And you require more strength for that. You will feast on Lori." His putrid breath stabs my skin. "You will drink her soul to prepare you for the marks."

I close my eyes as fear explodes across my human skin. There is no escape.

Azza tightens his grasp. His wings begin to flutter as he lifts me from the ground. "Are. You. Refusing. Me?"

I release the feral growl that races up my throat and send my host to the ground. My wings unfurl as I scream "No."

I'm unable to refuse the direct order from my master, no matter how hard I try. My vows won't allow it.

Azza opens his hands and I fall forward. Vengeance fills every cell. "I will go," I say, desperate for a way out of everything I've become.

Everything still to come.

CHAPTER 23 – BETRAYAL

AYDAN

The hospital ward is quiet, patients sleeping and nurses attending to paperwork or talking amongst themselves. A lone Guardian blocks Lori's door.

"I'll take care of him," Azza says. "You take care of Lori. But be quick. I doubt he's the only Guardian here."

Azza flicks his wrist as a loud crash emanates from the walls, catching the Guardian by surprise. He looks at Azza and nods before spinning toward the sound. He follows the sound as I slip into Lori's room. My body tenses and the Beast wars with my mind.

I don't want to do this. I can't. But there is no choice now, not since Bedburg. Not since I bargained with the devil.

"Hurry," Azza again says as the door between us closes.

Lori's eyes dart back and forth underneath her closed eyelids. Dreaming.

Does she dream of Nesy as I do?

I part my lips and kiss my prey. Shame coats my throat as hunger fills my senses. *Just do it*, I tell myself. Unable to hold back the Beast any longer, I press against her and sip her soul.

Lori's eyes fly open and startle me. She shoves against my chest. I pull back for a moment and she screams.

My hand slams against her mouth, an act of instinct more than intent. "Shh," I warn. "Don't make this any worse than it already is."

Terror glints in her eyes. Her scream stops, her mouth closes.

"I don't want to do this, Lori," I say as I move my hand away from her mouth. The Beast urges me to finish.

Lori again pushes me. "Then don't," she blurts out. Another scream escapes her lips.

Not good. Not good at all.

"If you do that again, I'll have no choice but to kill you."

Lori resigns and falls back, silent.

"Good, you understand me now."

She nods. "The angels will be back. *She'll* come back. You can't win this."

Every word wraps around me. She's right. I lost this fight centuries ago.

I stare at Lori, see the little girl now grown. Same flaming hair. Same haunting eyes. Same fierce expression.

How did I not see this before?

Lori's blood pulses fast through her neck. Her fear seeps into me.

"Please don't kill me. I know you don't want to."

Every moment I wait brings agony as the Beast urges me forward. I need to take her, rip her soul and let it nourish me. Fulfill Azza's dark purpose.

A week ago, I would have without hesitation.

But now...

Now I remember who I was once

—an angel who broke his vows.

Now Nesy has returned

—to kill me.

Now I just can't.

I push away from Lori, fighting against everything I am. I feel my true self bleed through my human form. "I don't want—"

The room floods with a golden light. *Her* light.

Nesy materializes in front of me, nothing more than an apparition. She hovers between Lori and me—here but not here. Her stare reaches into the horrors of everything I've become. For a moment, I forget how to breathe.

"She knows what you've come to do," Lori says in answer to my unspoken questions. "She knows who you are."

My legs wobble as the room begins to spin, the image of Nesy slowly fading away.

"What else do you know?" I ask.

"She still loves you. And you...you love her too."

The words carve into my skin as I repeat them over and over in my thoughts. *She loves you. You love her.* Is it even possible after all this time? After everything we've become?

Does it even matter anymore?

Lori's words continue to play through my mind, reminding me of all that I've lost. Forcing me to face what I still have to lose.

Nesy.

My soul, what's left of it.

Everything gone, as soon as I fulfill my vows to Azza.

"Ah. So this is why the Sentinal has not killed you." My master's voice booms through the small room as he walks towards me.

Lori slides under the covers, her hospital monitors beeping frantically.

"And why you refuse me," Azza whispers into my ear. His foul stench turns my skin into gooseflesh. "I do not tolerate disloyalty."

Something in me snaps. "And I will not let you hurt Nesy," I say. "Or Lori."

I release my human host and reach a clawed hand for Azza's throat.

Time to end this.

The hospital doors fly open and three Guardians pour through the doorway. The ruby radiance of their skin bathes the room in an eerie crimson glow. Behind the Guardians, two small angels follow. The same angels from the alley.

Nesy's friends.

"You are not welcome here," the lead angel says.

"And neither are you," Azza replies as he pushes past me, his sword drawn.

The room erupts in a flash of chaos as swords clash. The sound of metal on metal mixes with screeches and howls.

Guardian versus Azza.

Guardian versus me.

I don't want this. Any of it. But the Beast in me will not abate. I draw my sword and fight the angels, determined to exact my death.

I hear the leader fall before I see it, his scream echoing in the room.

"One down," Azza yells as my stomach turns.

I need a way out of this.

Nesy's friends stay clear of the skirmish, running to Lori's side. They whisper to each other and a cage of light explodes from the emerald angel, the Mediator.

"Thanks, Zane," the other angel calls, one of the Anointed judging by her indigo robes.

Azza laughs, walking away from the battle still waging between me and the two Guardians. "Your silly cage will do nothing to save the human," Azza taunts.

His words distract me. And the Guardians I fight.

They leave me, forcing Azza into the hall.

Azza laughs as he again strikes at the angels, landing blow after blow against them, carving into their skin.

The nurses tend to their charts, oblivious to the battle waged around them. They talk and laugh, carefree. If only they knew how close they are to death.

"Azza, let's go," I plead. My mind wars against itself, the need to protect Nesy's brethren—my brethren once—with the Beast's need to kill.

I am distracted. Unfocused. A Guardian turns to me and drags his sword against my chest. My wound opens, as does my heart.

"No!" I scream, unable to contain who I've become any longer. I round on the angel. Jab and thrust, slicing through his armor. His skin.

The angel retaliates, landing blow after blow across my battered body. The battle rages in the hall. Cries and growls. Metal and metal. The cacophony of war sounds is deafening.

Nesy's friends watch, still protecting Lori.

I try to ignore them. Try to focus on the battle.

The Anointed's voice fills my head. "*Succurre,*" she says. "Help us, Nesayiel."

I turn my head and our eyes meet. Everything stops. "No" I mouth. Not now.

A sharp pain interrupts the moment as the ground moves underneath my feet. I wobble, bile coating my mouth. Cold steel digs into my back. And I stumble.

A whoosh of air rushes past me. The sound of a sword—Azza's sword—circling overhead. The burnt smell of the angel's skin fills my nostrils as Azza pierces his heart.

"That's two."

The last Guardian counters, pointing his weapon at Azza's neck. "Time to end this, Dark One. *Divina virtute in infernum detrude daemones.*"

Azza's cackle splits the air. He wedges his sword between his skin and the Guardian's sword. Pushing hard against the blade, he sends the Guardian's weapon clattering to the ground. "That one only works on the weak. I am not weak."

Azza rams the tip of his sword into the angel's chest.

The scene spins out of control as I stagger to my feet.

The Mediator pulls out a dagger and runs for Azza, lodging a blade deep into his flesh. Azza's scream sends chills down my spine. He rounds on the angel, fury in his eyes.

I step between them, ignoring my fealty to Azza. Ignoring my pledge to kill angels on sight and claim them for Azza. Black blood oozes from my wounds. It soaks my skin. My mind folds in on itself.

"Azza, let's go!" I urge, forcing my mouth to work. "They've called the Sentinals."

"Oh good," he replies. "Maybe your lover will come and we can end all of this."

His words slice open the unseen wound in my heart. Cold steel presses into my chest. "I think we're done here," the

Guardian hisses. He pierces my skin and I pray for an end to my misery.

    I drop my sword and succumb to the angel.

        Relieved.

    But the Beast will not give in, and I cannot ignore my vows.

    I watch the Guardian turn away for a brief moment. Picking up a discarded dagger, I lodge it deeply into his heart.

    "No!" Her voice fills the narrow corridor.

    The voice I crave.

        The voice I need.

            Nesy.

CHAPTER 24 - DANGEROUS TRUTH

NESY

My mind whirls, taking in the scene. Two Guardians dead on the floor. Another lays at Aydan's feet. Aydan's hands hold a dagger, still wet with my brethren's blood. Nurses and doctors walk the corridors, unaware. Patients sleep in their rooms. Except for Lori.

This can't be happening.

I cast my human form to the ground, not thinking. Brandishing my sword, I enter the fray.

No one else dies because of my failures.

Anguish streaks across Aydan's face as I run towards him. Pain rolls off him in waves. "Nesy, I—"

Too late for my sympathy.

I run past him and lunge into the real cause of this horrific scene. Azza. He falls back into Lori's room.

"Get up, Azzaziel," I snarl. "Time to finish this."

"Aydan, your lover has spunk!" he yells into the hall. "I like that," he whispers at me.

I ignore his words and hold my blade steady against him.

"You can't beat me. Didn't Mikayel teach you that?" Azza steps forward, pushing his sword against mine.

"Care to bet your life on that?" I counter his attack, matching each blow. My blade pierces his shoulder.

Azza groans. "You'll pay for that, little warrior," he spits. He unleashes a torrent of blows, each one powerful enough to knock me from the room.

I strengthen my stance. Block and counter, slowly regaining my ground. Until something hits me from behind.

"You?" I ask as Aydan hits my back a second time.

Him, I can beat.

"Aw, how sweet. The lovers are reunited," Azza taunts as I round on Aydan, careful to keep them both in my sight.

Zane approaches Aydan from behind, dagger drawn.

"You don't want to do that, Mediator."

"Oh, I do. I *really* do." Zane strikes as Aydan spins out of the way.

Fast. Despite his injuries.

Impressive.

Azza takes a step back and I confront him, my sword level with his heart. "Time for you to leave."

"As you wish, Sentinal." Azza's body fades into smoke.

I jab at the fading image, slicing nothing but air. "No!" I scream as the last of Azza's image disappears.

I spin to face Aydan, my heart full of rage. A growl escapes my mouth as words dance through my thoughts. Accusations of murder. Confessions of love. Everything I cannot bring myself to say out loud.

His eyes reflect the torment I feel. It consumes me as I again feel like we are sharing a similar thought.

A similar wish.

Everything whirls to a halt as the scene moves forward in slow-motion, one frame at a time.

Aydan releases his dagger and drops to his knees…"I'm so sorry."

Zane tries to attack as Cass pulls him away…"Kill him, Nesy. Now."

Lori stares into my eyes, shaking her head slightly…"He loves you. Still"

The scene is too much. It overloads my senses, my resolve. I close my eyes and breathe.

1…

2…

3…

My mind clears.

"End this, Nesayiel. Now." Zane's angry voice booms in my ears.

I grip the hilt of my sword with both hands. Standing over Aydan, I prepare myself to finish this at last.

My gaze locks with his. He was everything to me once.

Aydan's tear-filled eyes mirror my torment. Every second that passes cracks the foundation of my world, shattering me to pieces.

"It's okay, Nesy. Do it," he whispers. I watch him close his eyes and dig his nails into his palm.

I tighten my grip and raise my sword. "I'm sorry," I mouth, ignoring the tears that fill my eyes. In one bold stroke, I thrust the blade forward.

It sails from my hands, landing with a crash on the floor.

Aydan opens his eyes, confused.

"Go," I whisper. "Get out of here."

He reaches for my hands.

"Go now!" I yell as I collapse to the ground. Aydan falls into his host and runs from the room.

"Nesayiel, what are you doing?" Zane yells.

Cass holds him back. "No, Zane. Stay out of it."

"The heck I will," he says as he wrenches himself free, retrieves my sword and runs after the UnHoly.

What have I done?

My mind implodes under the weight of my choices. My failures. The Council will cast me out for this.

"He wasn't to blame, Nesy," Lori says. She edges herself onto her elbows.

"What?" I ask, still surprised that she can see me.

"Aydan. He wasn't to blame for the angels' deaths. He tried to resist. Tried to refuse. But no one can resist Azza for too long."

My lungs stop working as piece after piece of my world shatters with the mention of Aydan's name.

"He loves you," Lori says. "Just like in Germany. He would do anything for you."

I stare at my sister, unable to process her words.

Love? Was it even possible between us anymore?

Zane storms back into the room, yanking me from my thoughts. "He got away," he snarls. "And it's your fault."

He's right. It is my fault.

"Zane, stop. You don't understand." Cass lays a hand on his shoulder, exuding a calm that only the Anointed can muster.

"I understand that he almost killed Lori," Zane says, casting aside Cass's attempts to console him. "He killed a Guardian, Nesayiel. Your brethren. How can you let that pass?"

The room grows thick with my silence.

"You are sworn to protect humanity and serve Mikayel. Do your duty. Go after him and end this. Now."

"Zane!" Cassiel barks.

So much for calm.

"No, Cassiel. You're too easy on everyone. Compromised or not, she has to do this. Now!"

"Zanethios! No!" Cassiel pushes into the room, trying to force a calm that won't come.

Zane exhales a deep sigh. "Nesy, if you can't do this, Mikayel will have no choice. You will die, Nesy. Is that what you want?" Concern and anger press through his words.

There's nothing I can say to answer him. Part of me *does* want to die.

"Do this now, or I will get the Council to send people who can. Last chance." Zane's disgust fills the empty spaces in my heart, shredding it further.

"Enough!" I yell. My voice feels as though it's coming from someone else. Someplace else.

I struggle against the tide surging inside. *Sentinals don't feel. Sentinals don't show emotion. Not ever.* I repeat the words over and over, letting them caress me. Calm my thoughts. Remind me of my duty.

I can do this. I have to.

For Mikayel and all he's sacrificed for me.

For my sister and her faith.

For my friends.

For me.

Within moments, my pulse slows and I can think again. I inhale my pain. Drink the love I still harbor for the UnHoly. And shove it all aside, becoming the Sentinal again.

No room for emotions.

No place for love.

Yeah, who am I kidding?

"I have two more days to finish this," I say through gritted teeth. "I'll get it done." I sheath my sword and fight to hold myself together.

"You should have done it already."

"Zane, she can't." Cass looks from Zane to me.

Don't say it. Don't.

"She's still in love with him."

Blazes!

"What?" Zane asks as he glares at me.

I turn away, unable to speak.

"Is it true? Do you love that…that…UnHoly?" His voice cracks on the words.

I want to say yes, tell him everything.

My confusion…

The poisoned love…

All of it.

"I'll take care of it. Of him," is all I manage to say.

"Do it now, or I'll be the one to tell Mikayel everything."

"Zane, don't you see what this is doing to her?"

"And don't you see that our first duty is to humanity and the Council?"

"Look, I know what I'm doing," I say, clinging to my role as a Sentinal and all that it means. "I'm not about to die for a love that doesn't exist anymore. I'll take care of this. I will. Before Mikayel's deadline."

"You'd better."

I push past Zane, retrieve my host and go in search of Aydan.

The only being I'll ever love.

The one I must kill.

CHAPTER 25 – TORTURED SHAME

NESY

I head for the subway station, desperate to outrun the feelings threatening to overturn everything I've struggled to become.

Guilt.

Shame.

Anger.

Longing for the Beast that holds my heart. Still.

The station is empty with the exception of three guys tagging the tunnel. They stare at me with hunger in their eyes.

Bad idea.

"Hey baby, whatcha doing out so late?" The leader of the group walks over.

Really, really bad idea.

Rage sears through me, burning my skin. I want an outlet for my anger and shame. And this guy fits that need perfectly.

Not within the rules.

But I haven't exactly been into following rules of late.

The leader stands next to me, too close. He wears a serpent tattoo on his arm that peeks out from his torn t-shirt. "I said, what are you doing out so late?"

"None of your business," I say as I face him. I tap my heeled boots in annoyance, begging him to mess with me.

"We'd like to make it our business." A second guy walks over. The scent of his foul odor invades my senses.

Now I really want to fight.

I feel the corners of my mouth pull into a smile as I glance at the boy behind me. His dark eyes match his dark skin. Trouble.

"I'm only going to say this once," I say to tattoo guy. "Leave me alone."

"Or what?" he asks.

Thought you'd never ask.

"This," I reply, swinging my arm back and grabbing the guy behind me. I pull him over my head and drop him to the concrete with a loud thud. His eyes roll to the back of his skull and he groans.

That felt good. Too good.

Tattoo guy steps back, afraid.

Not so fast. Thought you wanted to play.

I swing out my leg, tripping him as he continues to step back. He lands close to his friend and I stick the spiked heel of my boot into the fleshy part of his neck. Someone steps behind me. In a flash, I pull my dagger and aim it at the guy approaching. He stops moments before colliding with my knife.

"Like I said, leave me alone." I dig my heel into tattoo guy's neck just enough to break the skin. A small trickle of blood leaks from the cut. "Understand me?"

Tattoo guy nods feebly.

"Good." I release him, straighten out my clothes and board the newly arrived train. The disgruntled crew remains on the platform as the train lurches forward.

I grab the railings and slip into a seat, drunk on adrenaline.

I shouldn't have enjoyed that so much. Shouldn't have enjoyed it at all. Guilt adds to the mix of emotions as the train rocks forward. The motion lulls me into a stupor, blurring my thoughts.

Each moment that passes loosens my defenses, tearing pieces of my warrior's façade away. Until the mask falls away completely. And my world crashes in on itself.

Pictures stream around me. Through me.

Mikayel's sword slicing into Aydan...*pain radiates through me.*

Aydan's body exploding into flame...*my skin sears.*

The look in his eyes as he screams my name...*my heart shatters into a million pieces.*

My human body trembles. My lungs refuse to work. The train continues uptown, the wheels screeching on the tracks. My nerves grating.

Death and love twine together, binding permanently to my soul. My stomach seizes violently and for a moment I know I must be dying as well.

"Get a grip, Nesayiel. You're better than this." I repeat the words over and over, battling against my feelings for Aydan.

Nothing works. My emotions rage out of control. My thoughts loop. And I remain lost in a labyrinth of torment.

The train grinds to a stop and I rise, forever trapped in my own hell. My body moves of its own will, dragging me out of the train and up the stairs. A blast of cold air bites into my skin as I walk.

Something pulls me forward, forcing every step my legs take. I have nothing left to fight against it, no way to resist.

Dark creatures nudge out of the alleys I pass. I feel them pour into step behind me. Some take the form of large insects, snapping the spaces around me. Others are more like snakes, hissing taunts in my ears. And still others resemble birds, their sharp beaks and taloned claws brushing against my skin.

Like vultures, they've all come to feed off the dead.

I push forward, ignoring Azza's creatures careening around me. Ignoring their foul stench.

Ignoring...

Everything.

A demon steps in front of me – tall, human-looking save its sallow skin that's stretched too tight over the bone. A Jinn. It claws my arm and shreds my skin.

I keep walking.

The Jinn clicks its beak and raises another taloned hand. It gashes open a fresh wound as more dark creatures spill into the street. They crowd around me, halting my movement.

My skin sizzles as they lick my wounds and feed off my anguish.

Fight back, Nesy! Fight back. I yell through the ruins of my mind, desperate to regain myself.

It's too late.

The creatures continue to press in, absorbing my agony. Drinking each dark emotion, leaving me empty.

Sentinal! Wake up! Remember who you are! Aydan's voice floods my senses.

My lungs remember how to breathe as his words continue. My focus begins to sharpen and I wake from my nightmare.

Please, Nesy. For me. Fight back!

The voice seems to come from outside of my head. I turn to face it as razor-sharp pain tears through me and the taloned demon carves into my chest.

CHAPTER 26 – DARK PASSIONS

NESY

Aydan's words continue, filling the empty spaces in my heart, my mind, my soul. Instinct replaces torment as centuries of training take over. I whip out my sword, swinging it in a large arc over my head. The blow lands on the Jinn, severing its clawed hand.

"No more!" I scream as the mob scatters, confused by my sudden strength.

Hacking and slashing the space around me, I clear a large circle. "*Divina virtute in infernum detrude daemones,*" I yell, condemning the dark creatures to oblivion.

With each word, the ground beneath me rattles. A massive hole opens, claiming the demons. Those that escape my sword retreat to the safety of darkness. Until, finally, I am alone.

I focus my thoughts and look around. For the first time since leaving the hospital, I'm aware of my surroundings. A large cathedral stands before me, built from massive stone bricks. Several gothic spires cut into the fog that descends in the early morning hours. The facade of the church is adorned with stone carvings. Images of the angels—Mediators, Anointed, Guardians and Sentinals.

My brethren.

I've come home, more or less.

For a second time, I'm compelled to walk, clueless about my destination. I cross the left side of the cathedral until I come to a courtyard sitting between the cross sections of the building. I open the small iron fence protecting the cloister, straining to see in the navy darkness. A large bronze sculpture adorns the center of the garden, an image of Mikayel as he triumphs over the Dark One.

Over Azzaziel.

I stare at the statue, so perfect in its details—the Sword of Truth grasped firmly in Mikayel's hands, the strong muscles of his shoulders as he battles, and the broad expanse of his wings. Carved images of the planets, scientists and animals wrap themselves around the base of the angel. A perfect union of Celestium and humanity.

And a reminder.

My oath to the Council pounds through my thoughts. My obligation to protect. My role in the forever battle against evil. My duty to resist temptation. Resist the Dark One.

And my job to vanquish Aydan.

A pang of deep longing ripples through me. I'm torn between my promise to send Aydan to the Abyss and my need to keep him safe. The opposing forces fragment what remains of my mind, breaking me down once again.

I close my eyes and center my thoughts. *Let go of him. Let go of that life.* I picture my life as a Sentinal—the training, the commitment to live a life detached, the oath to serve. It's everything I am. Everything I've wanted.

Until now.

Now there's Aydan.

Black, spiked hair. Smooth, pale skin. His image floods my thoughts, looking exactly the way he did that first night. Same black jeans, same leather jacket.

I draw a ragged breath and let the fantasy unfold. The musky pine scent of his skin. The feel of him next to me. The sound of his voice as it resonates through me.

In the recesses of my thoughts, Aydan wraps an arm around my waist and pulls me close. His other arm drapes across my chest and in my dream, I am forever safe.

His heart beats too fast against my back, mirroring my own. His hot breath caresses my neck, igniting waves of desire I shouldn't have. I give myself to the dream, melting into him as he presses his lips against my neck.

My body trembles. "Stop it, Nes," I whisper to myself. "This isn't real."

But I want it to be, more than anything.

"You're a warrior," I say. "Purge your emotions. All of them. You can't give in to this. You can't be weak." I know I should push the dream aside. Detach from the longing in my heart.

"I don't find you weak at all." Aydan, the real Aydan, moves his hands to my hips and turns me to him. "Not in the least. I love your human form." He presses his body to mine.

His touch sears me. I pull away, barely able to speak. "Aydan? You're here?"

"Be with me," he says, kissing my jaw, my neck, my shoulder. Every spot his mouth touches closes the empty spaces inside.

A storm of desire gathers in my soul. Not just desire—need. "I shouldn't…can't—"

Aydan stops and looks at me, his amber eyes as beautiful now as the day we met in Germany. "Tell me you don't love me."

I try to form the words. Try to lie. But every cell, human and angelic, reaches out for him. Every thought, only him. I fall back into him, giving in to everything I desire.

He wraps me in a hungry kiss, erasing the pain, the torment, the anguish. All that remains is my need. My love.

"Let me have you. Love you," he says, his voice trembling.

I open my mouth to respond, the words nothing but dust. A single moan escapes as he draws me into another kiss.

Somehow he reaches every dark corner of my soul, healing the betrayal and pain from so long ago. I want for nothing but him. This moment.

For an eternity.

My duty flits through my thoughts. My promise to vanquish him. My oath to remain detached. To purge all emotions.

Not going to happen. Not with Aydan.

This is what I want now. What I need.

This moment with Aydan, right now, this fulfills me in a way I never thought possible.

I part my lips and succumb fully to the moment. My body feels as though it will implode as heat fuses my cells from my belly to my head. Our tongues greedily explore each other. I thread my hands through his hair as he slides his mouth along my jaw, my neck, my arms, leaving a burning trail crisscrossing my body.

My senses overwhelm, sending stars shooting across my vision. My body quivers and the last of my defenses dissolve. Nothing matters anymore.

Not Mikayel's wrath.

Not Azzaziel's rage.

Only Aydan's love.

And my burning need for him.

CHAPTER 27 - SACRIFICE

AYDAN

Morning arrives in a blast of color that ignites the courtyard, setting the sculpture of Mikayel ablaze. I sit on the bench, Nesy wrapped in my arms. For the first time in centuries, I don't feel like a demon, can't hear the Beast inside.

It's a moment I want to hold onto forever.

But wanting it won't make it so.

I have but one future. And it doesn't involve anything I want. Anything good.

I stare at the image of Nesy's sovereign, remembering the last time I faced him. There is no way he will ever understand Nesy's choice in me.

I don't understand it myself.

There is so little left of the angel I once was. But with Nesy I feel alive. Pure. With her, the mistakes of my life are forgiven.

Mikayel will know of last night. He always knows. I've put Nesy in danger again. Just like I did in Germany.

I really am nothing more than the Beast.

I think of the consequences of our actions. My death. Her fall. An eternity encased in the flames of the Abyss.

For both of us.

How could I do this? My body shudders as the pictures replay across my vision.

"Are you cold?" Nesy asks, pulling me closer to her.

Her touch orients me. So perfect.

"What are you thinking?" she asks.

"Mikayel. He knows doesn't he?"

Nesy releases me and sits. "Yes. Probably. He usually knows everything."

"There's only one answer for us, Nesy. One future." I swallow hard. I have to do this, do what I should have done already. I have to let her go. "He'll never allow this. Us." I say.

"I know." She pushes further away, her face pained. "I took a vow. I have to—"

I slide next to her and place my hand to her chin, tipping her head towards mine. "Vanquish me by tomorrow."

She buries her head in my chest. "I can't do it," she says. "Not now. Not ever."

"Yes you can. You must."

She will not die again because of me.

"But—" she starts to say.

I place a finger on her mouth. "I love you, Nesayiel. I have since the day I saw you on the farm. I know who you are now, who I am.

"We can have one more day to be together. One day. I want us to spend it in each other's arms. Then, when our time is over, you will do your duty. You *will* send me to the Abyss and end this. You will restore Mikayel's faith in you."

I watch as tears fill Nesy's eyes, spilling onto her cheeks. Her pain matches mine. "I...I can't," she says.

"You must. Otherwise, Mikayel will just send another team. Or worse, he'll do it himself."

She stares at me, her breath coming in hard, shallow gasps.

I don't know how to comfort her, how to make her see that this is the only way. "I want you to do it. Only you. Sever my ties to Azza. Send me to the Abyss tomorrow. Promise me."

Her eyes begin to dry as determination passes through her expression. She places her hands on my face, sending a chill down my spine. "I love you, Aydan."

"I know. And I want you to do this for me. I don't want to be Azza's monster anymore. I don't want the Beast to be all that I am."

"One more day?"

"One more day."

I pull her into a tight embrace, determined to soak in every ounce of her, let her heal the dark corners of my soul. I tip her face to mine, sealing our promise with my lips. She presses into me, stealing my air. Her lips tremble as they speak of everything she cannot say.

Her love.

Her need.

Her fear.

"Aydan," she says as the kiss ends. "I need something from you." Her voice cracks on the last word.

"Anything."

"You can't kill again. Not while I'm with you. You—"

"I know. And I won't." I softly kiss her lips again. "I'm done feeding. For good."

The Beast protests.

"You'll grow weak?" she asks.

"Yes."

"You'll be in pain?"

"Excruciating."

"But—"

"But I will only have to endure it for a short time. Besides, it'll be easier for you to end my life if I'm in agony."

The Beast stirs, igniting a familiar hunger and reminding me of my vows. My mind focuses only on Nesy.

For her, I will endure the pain.

CHAPTER 28 - UNHOLY CHOICES

NESY

It's too late. There is no way out of this mess. This beautiful, perfect mess. Unless...

I walk to the sculpture. Mikayel and Azzaziel. An eternity of hatred between them. Mikayel's existence has always been about defeating evil.

Capturing Azzaziel.

I smile as the idea flirts with the edges of my thoughts. "I'm going to talk with the Council," I say to Aydan. "Work out a deal. Maybe if you help capture Azzaziel, Mik—"

Aydan crosses the courtyard in two steps, slipping his hands around my waist. "They'll never let me come back," he whispers. "I chose to fall. Anyone who is fallen does."

I tremble as his hot breath caresses my cheek. "But you didn't mean it. You're ready to change, right? They might understand." My voice is nothing more than a whisper. A thought. "They have to."

Aydan still has good in him.

I feel it in the way he touches me...*a moment of grace.*

Taste it on his lips...*a communion of souls.*

I have to get the Council to see him as I do. Show them the angel that still lives inside the demon.

I walk to our bench, my new mission clear. "I'm going to Celestium." The fierce determination of the Sentinal I am incrusts every word. "I'm going to convince them to offer you grace. Let you return to Celestium."

"No! They won't let you come back. They'll send another team. Nesy, please. Don't do this."

"I have to. I'm not going to sit here and send you to Abyss. I won't kill you. This isn't what being a Sentinal is about."

"This is exactly what being a Sentinal is. Slaying demons, capturing the UnHoly, and dealing with Azza."

"Not if the UnHoly is capable of redemption." I clench my jaw, my resolve absolute. "This is wrong, Aydan. It's just wrong. And I'm going to convince the Council."

"It's too late for my redemption. I loved a human."

"No. You loved an *angel.*"

He refuses to hear me.

"I twisted the minds of the humans I was bound to protect, Nesy. I made a deal with Azza. I let my rage consume me. And I've been paying the price ever since."

"And now you're willing to give all that up. You said so yourself. You won't feed. You won't do Azzaziel's bidding. You won't give into the Beast. You should be allowed a trial with the Council. It's only right."

"To you." Aydan takes my hand and kisses it. "I doubt Mikayel will see it that way."

"He understood when I told him about my feelings for you."

"Trust me, this isn't the same."

"It is the same. The exact same. I just need to convince Gabriel that this is the right thing to do. Then Mikayel will listen." I stare at my love. "I'll make him listen."

I pull my hand away, glancing back at the image of Mikayel. My plan's a long shot. But what choice do I have? I will not lose him again.

"I have to go." I walk to the gate. The sun sits high in the sky, a reminder of just how little time remains.

Aydan runs to me...*I wish he wouldn't.*

This is hard enough.

"Please don't do this. Not for me."

"Don't you see? I have no choice." I lean in and kiss his human face.

He refuses to release me and I fall into a ravenous kiss. Desperation, fear, and guilt riddle his lips.

"I'll be back," I say. "Trust me, this is our only chance." I slip from my human host, leaving her on the bench. Her skin is marred by battles she never should have fought. Another mistake I'm responsible for.

Aydan takes my hands in his. "I hope this works," he whispers.

"It will," I say. I focus my thoughts and forge open a portal.

Please work.

I slip out of the gateway, desperate to find Zane. The Mediator's central chamber is a large room adorned with images of angels appearing to humans. Emerald linens hang from the ceiling, softening the hard edges of the room.

I pace, pushing my thoughts out to my best friend. He has to find me, guide me.

"It is I you should be looking for, Sentinal. Not my counselors."

I know that voice anywhere. "Gabriel, sir." The words roll out too fast as I settle my nerves.

"What is it you seek?"

"Understanding, sir."

"A noble endeavor," he says, nodding. "Is there a particular type of wisdom you are pondering?"

"Yes, there is." I pause, searching for the courage I need. Can I really do this? I take a calming breath and stare into Gabriel's green eyes. I force out the only word in my thoughts. "Redemption."

Gabriel chuckles. "Redemption. Now that isn't something I expected to hear from a Sentinal. Warriors tend to deal only in absolutes." The laughter leaves his voice. His eyes pin me where I stand. "But then, I have only known of one other Sentinal to have loved another as you do."

Shoot. No secrets in Celestium. Forgot about that one.

Heat rises up through my cheeks.

"You thought I would not know? Ah child, everything the brethren of the Council know, I know. There are no secrets between us."

"Then you know why I'm here."

"I know you love the one you have vowed to vanquish. I know the idea of killing him pains you deeply." There is no malice in Gabriel's voice. Only concern, like a father to his child.

"Yes, it does." Saying the words out loud takes the breath from my lungs. I shove the feelings aside. I have only one shot at this.

It has to work.

"And I know you wish to speak to the Council about his redemption."

"Yes."

"You know the rules on such things?"

"I do."

"Then you know that I cannot grant what you ask, regardless of my personal feelings." Gabriel speaks softly with an unyielding firmness.

"But you *are* the Council. The others answer to you," I plead. He has to help me.

"No, young Sentinal, we answer to each other. No voice is greater than the others. Our rules were not made by us. They are in place to serve a specific purpose. I do not have the power to overturn them."

"They will listen to you, though. Mikayel will listen." Shameless desperation drips through my words.

"As he will listen to you. Have you told him what you feel?"

"No. But I know he knows."

"That is not the same," Gabriel says, the firmness returning to his voice. "You must speak with him directly. He will understand more than you think. Much more."

"Mikayel? No. He lives in a world of rules and order. He can never understand love. Or redemption." Anger seeps into my words.

"He listened before, did he not? Helped you find peace."

"Yes, but—"

"He will help you again. He understands in a way few can."

I think about Mikayel's past kindness. I owe him so much. But this? This is nothing he will ever be able to grasp. Without Gabriel's support, I'll fail. I know I will.

"Child, just because he is absolute in his resolve does not mean he has no idea of love. No, you must speak to him first. Then, if he wishes, you can speak to the Council."

I swallow back my tears. "There has to be another way."

"No. That is it how it must be."

Gabriel disappears before I can object further, Cass and Zane walking through his faded image.

"What are you doing here?" Cass asks. "Did you finish?"

"No. Not yet." I feel Zane's accusing glare slash through me. When did he get so darn judgmental? "I still have a day," I say.

"And why are you wasting it here?" Zane's contempt is palpable.

And getting on my last nerves.

"If you must know, I came to talk to you about Gabriel. But he found me first."

"Gabriel?" Zane asks.

"Yeah, I needed his advice about the Council."

"Why not go to Mikayel?" Cass asks.

"Gabriel was better suited for my questions. At least, I thought he was."

"Thought?" Zane furrows his brow.

"He is making me talk to Mikayel."

"Nesy, what are you planning?" Cass's words echo the concern I feel from Zane.

No point in hiding this from them. They're bound to find out sooner or later.

"I'm going to ask the Council to allow Aydan back into Celestium. Let him earn a position with us again."

"What?" Zane bellows. "No!"

"Yes, Zanethios." I match his anger, word for word.

I'm done listening to his lectures on duty. This time, *he's* wrong. And so is the Council. "He isn't what you think he is. He deserves another chance."

"He's killed angels."

"He was protecting himself."

"Was he protecting himself when he devoured the human girl's soul? Or the countless others he's killed over the years?"

My mind spins. Aydan stands for everything I hate, everything I've sworn to fight. But he also holds my heart. And I am forever connected to him.

There must be good in him somewhere. I wouldn't feel this way if there wasn't.

"Aydan has vowed not to feed again. He'll renounce Azzaziel and lead Mikayel to him." The words come out too fast. "He deserves a chance to make this right."

Cass places her arm across my shoulders. "It doesn't work that way, Nesy. Not for angels. There is no second chance for us. Not once the Council makes a decision. You know that."

"Yeah, I do. And it's wrong."

"We have choices humans don't. Everything we do is a choice. Our jobs, our friends, everything. Nothing happens by chance. Only by choice. You know this." Cass holds my gaze, trying to read my intentions, no doubt.

"And humans? They get second chances just because they don't understand the weight of their choices as we do? Because of destiny? Fate? It's not fair."

"Humans aren't ready for this type of freedom. Or for the responsibility that comes with pure choice. But we are. Our entire existence revolves around our decisions. Our duty to protect. You know this. Aydan knew this when he ignored his duty."

Not acceptable. Not to me.

"We deserve redemption, a second chance, just like humans." I wipe my damp eyes. "Aydan deserves this."

"Nesy."

"No!" I step out of Cass's reach and her suffocating sympathy. "I'm going to do this. You can help. Or not. Your *choice*."

I walk away from my friends and towards the Sentinal's tower.

Set high above Celestium, I can see my entire world from the windows of the Sentinal's chambers. Unlike the halls of the Anointed or the Mediators, the rooms are not adorned with images of angels or beautifully woven linens. Only swords. A tribute to the endless battle against evil and all those lost to Azzaziel and his UnHoly.

I walk across the wooden floor to Mikayel's private study. The door opens before I get a chance to knock.

Or breathe.

"Enter." Mikayel's voice is as it always is—hard and unyielding.

"Sir."

"You've not yet completed your task." Mikayel stares out of the arched windows, his back towards me.

"I have one more day."

"Yes, you do. But you are here instead. Why?" He turns to me, anger contouring the lines of his face. But not just anger, something else as well. Concern? Grief?

"You know why."

"And still, I ask." His expression darkens, along with the timbre of his voice. A lump settles in my throat. *You can do this. You can do this.*

I calm my thoughts and force out the words. "I came about Aydan." My resolve crumbles with every syllable, unable to withstand the intense stare of my master.

"And?" he asks.

Aydan's face forges into my thoughts. I have to do this. For him.

For us.

"I came to ask you and the Council to give him a chance at redemption. I want you to offer him grace."

"There is no redemption for any of the fallen." The bitterness in Mikayel's voice surprises me. I expect anger. Even disappointment.

But not this. Not…

Regret.

"He deserves this." The words escape my mouth too fast.

"You have strong opinions."

"I do."

"Why?" he asks. In a heartbeat he drills into my thoughts. My soul.

I allow him to see everything, hoping it will make a difference.

"I know Aydan," I plead. "He's ready to turn his back on Azzaziel. Renounce his life."

Mikayel retreats from my thoughts and for a brief moment a deep sadness grips my heart. Mikayel's sadness. I reach for it, trying to fathom any situation in which my master would harbor such strong emotions. Such anguish. But he retreats too quickly.

Walking back to the window, his body tightens and the familiar detachment returns.

I settle my heart and try again. "I think Aydan should come here and be offered a second chance."

"Why?" Mikayel's voice resumes its hard edge. "Because he's finally willing to forsake the Dark One? What about the four hundred years of killing he has done for him? Does that count for nothing?"

"No, but—"

"Or the members of my army he has killed?" Mikayel walks into the central chamber, waving his arms to the sword-encased walls. "Do your brethren deserve less from you than this fallen?"

"No," I say as I follow Mikayel. "It's—"

"And what of the choice he made with the Council? He could have stayed. Gabriel would have offered grace. But he *chose* to leave. Chose to fulfill a destiny with Azzaziel. None of that was forced upon him." Mikayel again faces me. Rage and disappointment mar his face. "Did he tell you that part when he brushed his lips on your human skin?"

I fume, frustration boiling into a cold, hard rage. My hands shake with anger as I ball them into fists by my side.

"Oh," he says. "You didn't realize how much I saw, did you?"

"That doesn't matter," I force through clenched teeth. "That isn't why I'm here."

"It matters to me." Mikayel nods towards the Sentinals guarding the outer doors of the chamber. They come and stand behind me.

This is really really bad.

"I know you can't understand this yet, but the UnHoly must be cast out. Regardless of your feelings for him, or of his feelings for you. Duty must come before love. Terrible things happen when we lose sight of that; things we can't undo."

I don't care what he thinks.

"Aydan is capable of redemption," I hiss. "We have to give it to him. *That* should be our duty. Not blind obedience to rules and retribution." The words are angry, rebellious.

And completely against my training.

"Enough! I will hear no more talk of this. You have clearly made *your* choice. Briathos, Zaapiel. You will see to the UnHoly." Mikayel turns away. "Nesayiel, you will stay here, confined to your quarters where you can contemplate that choice more fully."

My mind swims as his words continue. This can't be happening.

". . . when Aydan has been vanquished you can talk . . ."

Nonononono

". . . we will see what *your* future holds . . ."

My body stiffens as he raises a hand to dismiss me. I've messed everything up. There is no way out now.

Now way of warning Aydan.

Or saving him.

"Take her to her room," Mikayel orders. "And take care of the UnHoly."

The Sentinals nod, taking my arms. I wrestle against their hold. "No, Mikayel. Please. Don't do this. I have one more day."

"Take her now."

Zaapiel and Briathos tighten their grasp, dragging me from Mikayel's chambers.

"You don't have to do this. You're my brothers. Don't do this." My pleas fall on deaf ears as they toss me into the room, trapping me in a fate I won't accept.

I turn, locking eyes with Zaapiel. "Please. Don't—"

A portal opens, revealing the gardens, the statues of Mikayel. And Aydan. The Sentinals draw their swords and step into the portal. "No!" I scream as they disappear into the void.

CHAPTER 29 - REDEMPTION

AYDAN

I pace the gardens waiting for Nesy to return. She's been gone too long already. The sun streaks across the sky. There is so little time before Azza forces a choice I can't make.

One step. Another. And another. Each reminding me that she still isn't back. I can't take it anymore—can't stand not knowing.

Did she convince the Council?

—*Of course not, you are a Beast.*

Did she offend them in asking?

—*You know she did.*

Is she in trouble now?

—*Deep trouble.*

My mind folds in on itself as I reconcile the danger Nesy has placed herself in because of me.

Always because of me.

My pace increases with my agitation. I should've never let her go. Should've never started this so long ago.

My gaze catches her human form, asleep on the bench behind me. She looks peaceful. Angelic.

You have to be okay.

The Beast stirs as my mind wraps around my fear. It stabs at my heart, trying to shred my resolve.

I push it aside, focusing only on Nesy and all that she means to me. She was my past. She is my present.

But she can never be my future. Azza claimed that too long ago.

He will try to purge her from me. Torture me into forgetting about her and my love. I'll kill him before that happens. Kill me.

The Beast fights back, struggling against my intentions. *Kill me.* The words bounce off my thoughts. It is the only way to fix this. The Beast rams against my thoughts. My vows tug at me, reminding me of the impossibility of my death. Azza will never allow it, nor will the Beast. There is only one way.

Nesy.

It has to be Nesy.

I'll kill anyone else who tries, the rage more than I can control. But not her. I won't let the Beast touch her, no matter how intense the pain. She's the only one.

She must kill me.

Soon.

CHAPTER 30 – FRIENDSHIP TESTED

NESY

My voice bounces off the chamber walls as the Sentinals fade away. I run to the door, desperate. I can't leave. Mikayel's barrier is too strong. Impenetrable. I'm trapped, unable to warn Aydan.

I think of the Sentinals, Briathos and Zaapiel, charging after him. Best in their class, after me. Determined. Focused. Relentless. Everything I've been trained to be. Everything I was.

Before Aydan.

I pace in front of the door like a caged animal. I have to escape.

My heart slams against my chest, each beat tolling the end of Aydan's life.

The end of mine.

I scream out my frustration. What a mess everything has become—a mess I can't fix.

"I see Mikayel didn't like your suggestion." Zane stands at the threshold, his arms crossed over his chest, looking smug.

"Not at all."

"I'd say I told you so, but that seems a little harsh. Even for me." He stares at me, an impish twinkle in his eyes. "But I can offer you another way to fix this."

"Why would you do that? You agree with Mikayel."

"Yeah, I do. Your first duty is to Celestium. But Gabriel sent me. He told me what you two talked about and asked me to search my heart. He said I needed to come to my own opinions about your fate."

"Really?" I ask, my wings nervously twitching behind me. "And what did you decide?"

"I'm not ready to see my best friend cast out. Not over this. I think you should go back and fulfill your oath. Mikayel gave you three days. You have one left. Take care of this and the Council will forget everything. Don't, and you're as good as gone."

I release the breath I'm holding with a sigh. Zane never ceases to surprise me.

"So, you're going to help me escape?"

A slow smile streaks across his face. "Yeah. I'm going to help you."

I grab my sword and prepare to break through the barrier. All I can think about is getting to Aydan in time.

"Not like that," Zane laughs. "We aren't busting out of here. I have something better in mind. Another conversation with Mikayel. Don't blow it this time."

"Mikayel?"

"Just tell him you're ready to do your job. That's all he's looking for." Zane reaches his hand through the invisible barrier. "Come on."

"Are you sure this will work? Mikayel was pretty mad," I ask as we walk back to his study.

"It'll work. Just focus on finishing your job, okay?"

Mikayel waits in the chamber, stoic as always. "Gabriel says you are ready to be the Sentinal I expect?"

"I am."

"I'm not sure I can trust you now." There is a deep sorrow in Mikayel's eyes that takes me aback.

"Call off the other team" I say too fast. Maybe he is right not to trust me.

Zane throws me a cautioning look.

"Sir," I add. "I will do this, Mikayel. I will vanquish him as I've promised."

Mikayel draws a quick breath, considering every word. He has to believe me. I need him to trust me.

And I need to fulfill my oath. For Mikayel. For Aydan

For me.

"I will not call off the other team."

I open my mouth to protest as Zane grabs my hand and motions for me to quiet.

Mikayel squares his shoulders, every inch of sadness replaced by resolve. "You have a day. Nothing more. Do your job. No more talk of redemption. I will not have you ruin your life for that

UnHoly and the master he serves. Go and do what you must. I expect nothing less."

Once again images of the Abyss glint through my thoughts. I swallow it all down, ignoring the bitter taste my emotions leave in my mouth. "Fine," I acquiesce. "I'll finish this by your deadline."

"Thank you," Zane adds.

"Thank Gabriel." Mikayel turns away.

Zane raises his hands and forges open the portal. I step through, collapsing one world and entering the cathedral gardens.

I expect to see the other team, expect the battle to already be waged. But only Aydan appears before me, waiting.

"They let you leave," he says, scooping me into a strong embrace.

"Thanks to Zane."

Aydan nods at Zane.

Zane may be willing to help me, but Aydan will never be anything more than an Unholy in his eyes.

He ignores Aydan's appreciation and glares at me. "Don't make me regret this, Nes. Finish it. Now." He fades away, leaving me with Aydan.

And the burden of what I must do.

"What was that about?" Aydan asks.

"It doesn't matter," My throat is dry and the words scrape against my mouth. "The Council won't discuss your redemption."

He wraps his hands around my waist. "I didn't think they would."

"Actually, it's just Mikayel. I think the others would've listened. If only he wasn't so stubborn."

"Sounds like someone else I know." Clouds pass through Aydan's features. "Look, you tried and I appreciate it. But now you have to finish your task and send me to my death." Aydan frees his hold on me and drops to his knees. "Release me from my hell, Nesy. Please."

Tears burn my skin as they trickle down my face. I give him one last kiss, tasting his torment. I know he can taste mine.

"Please Nesy, do it. Before I change my mind." A single tear slithers down his cheek.

CHAPTER 31 – UNREQUITED CHANCES

NESY

There is nothing else to say. To do.

I wrap my fingers around the hilt of my sword as my wings unfurl behind me. "I love you, Aydan."

"I know," he says as he closes his eyes.

I whisper the words that will banish him to the Abyss, lift my sword to his chest and thrust it forward.

My own heart rips through my body. For a moment, I can't breathe. Can't think. Can't feel.

I watch the sword jab forward. Watch Aydan tighten his body, preparing for his end.

A barrier forms between us as Aydan flies away from me.

My body screams for air. My lungs fail and my mind swirls.

Aydan lands with a thud on the other side of the courtyard. He rushes for me, each step taking him further and further away.

I hear his screams. Feel my own.

My lungs struggle to draw a ragged breath—my final breath—as time seems to stop.

One second passes.

And another.

Confusion settles around me and I know I am dying. Until my lungs miraculously expand. Air fills my chest. My cells. My body. Along with the familiar scent of rotting flesh and ash. My stomach turns, threatening to empty. A warm foul stench spreads across my back.

"You know I can't let you do that, little Sentinal." Azza's voice fills me with rage.

"Azzaziel," I growl. I spin to face him, my sword level with his neck.

"You may want to rethink your actions."

"I doubt that," I spit.

My mind focuses sharply on Azza. Only Azza. His skeletal frame and bat-like wings fill my senses. I feel each tiny movement, anticipating his coming actions. Just as I've been trained to do.

Finally, I am the Sentinal again.

Aydan lifts from his human host and runs to the barrier. Over and over he slashes it with his claws. Nothing works. The invisible wall remains.

All manner of dark creatures pour from the corners of the courtyard. The fallen. The UnHoly. The Jinn. Demons in every size and shape. They nip the air around Aydan, digging their talons and claws into his skin.

I stare at my love, unable to save him from Azza's creatures. "What do you want, Azzaziel?"

"Your blood. And Mikayel's."

"That'll never happen," I say. "You're no match for him."

"Really? Is that what he tells his warriors now?"

My silence fills the space as I consider my options, Aydan's private battle always in my sight.

"Oh, I wouldn't try anything. You see, those creatures will do anything to keep Aydan from disrupting our little conversation." Azza's eyes dart from me to Aydan. "And they'll consume him if you try to hurt me in any way." His gaze settles on me. "I'm sure you wouldn't want that to happen."

Aydan continues to claw at the barrier between us. The creatures shred his arms, his legs. I cringe as his growls and shrieks split the night air. He kicks at them, throwing them off of his body. His eyes lock with mine as he fights against all that he is.

"Call them off," I whisper. My eyes narrow, focusing on Azza. "Call them off, and I'll hear you out."

The Dark One laughs. "You're trapped here. You'll do whatever I want. But, to show how accommodating I can be, I'll do what you ask." He nods again and the creatures retreat, slipping back into the dark crevices of the shadows. With a wave of Azza's hands, the wounds covering Aydan's body are gone.

I lower my sword in an act of submission.

I hope he buys it.

"Why am I here, Azzaziel? What do you want?"

"I think it's time you knew the truth about your boss."

I tighten my fingers around my weapon and look away. Like I'm going to believe anything *he* has to say.

"Mikayel and I were friends once. Did he tell you that? Best friends. Some would say brothers."

"I don't believe you. And what does that have to do with me or Aydan?"

"Patience, Sentinal. Patience." Azza circles me and continues his story. "We trained together. Served the Council before the Dark Times. That is, until he betrayed me."

I don't want to hear his lies. I turn and look at Aydan. The rage in his eyes matches my own.

Azza spins me around to face him. "Mikayel knows more about love than you think."

His words, lies, spark my memories. The pain in Mikayel's eyes when I talked of redemption. The grief I felt in his heart.

No, this isn't right. It can't be. Only lies. Azza's lies.

"I'm not listening to you. Now release me, before the army of Mikayel shows up."

"Not before I finish my story." His eyes harden and his voice reeks with impatience. "You see, Mikayel once loved another angel. Just like you."

I feel the color drain from my face. More lies.

But maybe…

"Oh yes," he says, drinking from my torment. "He loved a beautiful creature that served with us. Their love was forbidden by the Council. So he tried to choose duty over his feelings. He hid away his love for her. Let it torture and confuse him. He lost his edge, putting the rest of us at risk."

My heart pounds in my ears as I let his lie fill me. "Why are you telling me this?" I whisper.

"I couldn't let him destroy himself. Or risk destroying the whole of Celestium. So I found a way to release the angel's hold on him. I convinced her to let go of Mikayel. Renounce her vows. Choose mortality over him."

The words wrap me in temptation. I want them to be true. Want to be angry with someone other than myself.

"I took his love and forced her out of Celestium. But it didn't help. He threatened to follow her. Vowed to forsake everything…for her. I couldn't let this happen. Celestium needed him. So I went to her first. I found another way to release her hold on him."

"You killed her," I say.

"She killed herself."

Revulsion fills me as I glare at the Beast before me. I imagine Mikayel, broken by the death of his love.

Just like me.

"Mikayel didn't understand the sacrifices I made for him. He hated me for her. I saved him from himself and his foolish love. And yet he treated me like a monster." Azza stares into the empty space around him. "The Council stripped me of my grace, my immortality, everything. I was cast out to the Abyss."

"You deserved to be cast out."

Fire lights his molten eyes. A sardonic smile twitches on the corners of his mouth. "But I refused to be tossed aside. I found a different form of immortality. Through the souls of the worthless humans I used to protect. Imagine it, something so insignificant and frail was the key to another life for me. I drank their souls, fed off their torment and pain. And then I taught others to do the same and made my own army."

"You're a monster," I spit.

"I'm a survivor. And for that, I am persecuted." Azza's eyes glaze over as he turns away from me.

"Mikayel will defeat you."

"He's already tried. He's sent armies of Sentinals against me and they've failed. They've always failed."

I seize my chance and raise my sword to Azza's back.

"You can't defeat me, little Sentinel," he taunts. "Only Mikayel has the power to do that—him and his Sword of Truth."

"I'm sure I can hurt you, though." I lunge forward, slicing a long gash into his shoulder.

"You don't scare me, Sentinel," he howls. "Not one bit." He counters my next blow.

I block and counter, unleashing my anguish. Mikayel's anguish. The clash of our blades sends a flurry of sparks into the air.

"You'll be afraid when Mikayel shows up."

I spin out of Azza's attack.

"*If* he shows up." He lunges again, catching only air.

"He will. And when he does—"

"When he does, his precious Sentinals will be slain, your Aydan will be gone, and his nemesis will be nothing more than a cry on the wind."

I circle back around, leveling my sword at his neck.

I hear Aydan still clawing at the barrier.

I have to get to him.

Mikayel, I call. *Succurre.*

Aydan's image invades my thoughts. Pictures of his flesh burning at Azza's hands. His howls rip through the fragments of my mind, cracking the mask that holds back my emotions.

Azza presses into my sword. "If Mikayel comes, your precious Aydan will die. But not before he's tortured."

I look from Azza to the demons, enraged. I push the sword into his neck, breaking the skin. A stream of blood trickles down his demonic flesh.

Azza grabs the sword, letting it slice his hand. He growls as he pulls my weapon from me and clutches my arm. "There is another way," he says through clenched teeth. "We can help each other."

"There is nothing you could offer me that would make me help you."

"Mikayel has lied to you. He makes you suffer for a love he understands. He forces you to kill Aydan. And for what?" Azza watches as I swallow back my feelings. "To prove that love cannot exist for your kind? To follow a rule that has no meaning? To justify his own actions so long ago?"

I cannot listen to him. Cannot be seduced by the words I want to hear. I grab my dagger and ignore the heavy confusion sitting on my chest.

A smile glints through Azza's empty eyes. "I offer you a chance to stay with Aydan. I offer you...his life."

"I'll never work for you, Azzaziel. Never."

"Even if it is the only way to save Aydan?"

Temptation.

I would do anything to save him. Anything.

Azza's lip twitches. He knows I'm wavering, weak. "I want you to convince Aydan to take his oath to me. To bear the mark."

"And bind himself to you forever? Force him to forget who he really is? No!" The tension in my voice betrays my thoughts.

"Who he really is?" Azza laughs. "He is *my* UnHoly. He does *my* bidding. And you will make sure it stays that way. Or I will make sure he dies. By your hand. Or the others."

The other team. Oh no. I forgot about them. Death at their hands will be worse. Torturous, even.

Aydan asked me to do it. Me.

"The other team will be here soon. Aydan's weak. Hungry. He is no match for them. They will kill him swiftly. But not if you help me."

"You won't let them hurt him."

"You would rather me kill the other team?" Azza asks. "You're more like me than you realize."

The weight of my choices crashes through me, causing my legs to wobble. My mind betrays me as picture after picture confirm my fears.

Azza killing Zaapiel.

Aydan receiving the dark marks, forever bound to the Beast.

Mikayel casting me into the Abyss.

Every moment that passes fills me with anguish, confusion, rage. Aydan is right—the only solution is to end his life now. By my own hand.

Before Azzaziel can mark him. Before the other team arrives.

Before Mikayel sends his army.

I thrust my dagger into Azza's chest. "I am nothing like you. And I will never let Aydan complete those vows."

Azza screams as he wraps his spindly claws around my neck and squeezes. "You will regret those words, little Sentinel."

The air around me rattles. Deafening sounds—demonic shrieks, Azza's laughter, and Aydan's screams—fill my ears.

"No!" Aydan yells as I hear his claws finally rip through the protective barrier. "Let go of her."

Everything spins into focus when the invisible wall falls. Dark creatures flood the courtyard. Aydan rushes to my side.

"Or what?" Azza snaps. He tightens his grip around my throat. My skin sizzles from his touch. My lungs scream for air. I stiffen my neck against his hold.

Too late.

My mind begins to fade, my world darken.

I feel Aydan's arm swing around me. Feel the concrete as my body collides with it.

The second team of Sentinals arrives with swords drawn. They attack the dark creatures littering the space, forging a path to Azza. And Aydan.

Hands grab me from behind, pulling me from the battle.

"Let go," I mumble, barely conscious. I have to help Aydan. Protect him

"Nesy, it's us." The voice is familiar. Calming. "We have to get you out of here."

Cass.

I turn to the voice, feeling like I'm living inside a dream. A nightmare.

They pull me towards a vortex flanking the garden. They want to take me away.

No. Not now.

"I need to help Aydan! He's weak. He won't be able to fend them off. I'm not ready to lose him this way." A sob escapes. "I promised I would be the one. Me. I have to help him!" I try to wrestle myself free from their grasp.

Through tear-filled eyes, I see Aydan. He pushes away from the Sentinals, parries their blows.

The warriors are fierce, unleashing jabs and thrusts too numerous to count. They speak the words that will cast him into the eternal flames.

Dark creatures scream in horror as swords slice into their skin. The ground opens around the battlefield, sucking in the wounded demons.

Zaapiel takes the lead position—my position—in the attack. His war-hardened eyes never waver. He edges his way to Aydan, nicking his battle-worn skin.

Aydan clenches his jaw and backs away.

I watch in horror as Zaapiel corners Aydan against the sculpture of Mikayel. "Please," I say to my friends. "I have to help him!"

I yank free and run towards my love, my sword drawn. Years of training possess my thoughts. I raise the sword over my head, prepared to strike. "I don't want to do this, brother." I have so much more to say. Confessions of my love for Aydan. Anger at Mikayel for his impossible task. And blinding hatred for the one who started this so long ago—Azza. The words turn to ash in my mouth. My fingers tighten around my sword.

"Step down, Sentinal." Zaapiel's deep voice rattles the ground. "Mikayel—"

"Gave me until tomorrow," I interrupt. "I'm still in charge! You *will* yield to me!"

Zaapiel growls. "For now," He lowers his weapon and takes a step back.

LACRIMOSA

Chaos explodes around me as I try one last attempt to end Aydan's misery. I raise my sword and thrust it forward, mouthing the words that will seal my lover's fate. Azza forms through the chaos, sending me hurtling backwards. The sword drops from my hands, never piercing Aydan's heart. Never finishing my task.

Sentinals and dark creatures battle as a tempest swirls around me. Zane pulls me away. I retrieve my human host before Zane and Cass can force me into a portal. Demons strike the Sentinals and the vortex begins to close.

I hear Aydan yell.

See Briathos plunge a dagger into Aydan's shoulder.

"No!" I scream.

He slinks to the ground as Azza swoops into the fray.

The vortex pulls me away, Aydan and Zaapiel's screams the only thing I hear.

CHAPTER 32 - SEER

AYDAN

Nesy disappears as I fall. Safe.

But for how long? I have no idea what Azza plans for her, but I can guess. And I can't let him succeed.

The Beast growls, reminding me of my loyalty and gnawing away at my insides. He demands attention. I want to ignore him, overrule that aspect of me.

Impossible. He's too entrenched in my soul.

Azza's claws dig into my arm, pulling me to my feet. The sounds of war—metal on metal layered over the screams of the injured—pound in my ears. Instinct forces me to reengage, raise my sword. My arm trembles as the muscle tears from the strain. It's too much and my arm falls, unable to hold the weight of my weapon.

Angels and demons attack with one purpose. My death.

Should I acquiesce? It would be so easy now.

Azza answers for me, pushing me through the throng, perhaps to my end. Dark and murky shadows block the sun, throwing the courtyard into darkness. In the center of the eclipse, a portal. Azza pushes me through it and I fade into nothing.

Moments pass. Maybe longer. The swirling darkness erases all meaning of time. Something cold and hard shoves me forward. My knees grate across smooth wood as I slam into a floor.

I remember Azza and Nesy in vivid detail. The way he drove his knife into her. The silver color of her blood.

Vengeance clouds my judgment. I jump to my feet, my weapon in hand. The pain shoots up my arm as I engage my master.

Too long I've waited to exact my revenge.

Too long I've dreamed of his death.

He will pay for every ounce of agony and torment I posses, for every lost moment with Nesy. I point the sword at his cold heart.

"Put that away," Azza snarls.

"You attacked Nesy."

"And yet she lives. Do you want to make sure she stays that way? Or would you prefer I kill you first and have some fun with her before she dies?" Azza's fingers tap the hilt of his sword. His eyes narrow, pinning me. "Decide."

My heart clenches. I can't defeat him. Not until I receive the marks.

And it will be too late then—for either of us.

Rage stiffens my body and I withdraw.

For now.

"I thought you'd see it my way."

For the first time, I notice my familiar surroundings. The strange way the light plays off the stained glass windows. The echo of Azza's footsteps on the floor. The musty scent of the air.

He's brought me to the club.

Azza walks to the bar and digs his hands into the counter. "It is time for you to take your oath. Tonight."

My rage boils over. "No," I bark. "No more. I won't follow you."

Azza turns. "Did I say you had a choice?"

The weight of his stare crushes the air from the room.

"We have waited four hundred years for this. Four hundred years to find a Seer worthy of you. You will not waste this chance because of your misguided feeling for that Sentinal."

"And if I refuse?"

Azza is at my side in seconds. His foul stench curdles my stomach. "You will take your vows or I will feed you to the dark creatures myself."

His threat feeds my rage. And my fear. All I can think about is Nesy. What will he do to her if I refuse, if I end this now?

"If you die, Aydan, Nesy dies. If you try to join her, she dies. If she kills you, she dies. If—"

"You'll kill her if I don't do what you want. I get it." My mind whirls, trying to figure a way out.

"Good. You are taking your oath tonight. You'll drink the soul of the Seer, taste her blood, bear the marks. Under the sculpture of Mikayel, we will mock him and show all of Celestium who really holds the power." Azza's voice echoes through the empty club.

Torment circles around me, ignored. I've no time to wallow. No time to feel. "When I do this, will you guarantee Nesy's safety? Promise me you won't hurt her? Corrupt her?"

"You are in no position to bargain with me, boy. But, to show you how reasonable I can be, I will guarantee that I will not kill her."

"That isn't the same." What's he planning?

"That *is* my only offer. Take your oath as you have vowed to do, and I will not kill your lover."

I have to move, figure out the meaning behind his words. It's a trap, I know it is. But I have no choice.

Azza flashes pictures through my thoughts.

Nesy dying at Azza's hands

—*I'll kill you first.*

Dark creatures ending my life

—*not before I hurt you, Azza. Remember that.*

The Beast again reminds me of my oath, the bind that locks me to my master, whether I want it or not.

Refuse the Beast, refuse Azza, and Nesy dies a certain death.

Finish this, take my oath and bear the marks, and maybe there will be a way to keep her safe. One chance at ending this.

Maybe.

"Okay. Fine. I'll do it." The words stick in my throat as I choke on every syllable. The Beast awakens, as it will for an eternity.

An ominous glint flecks in Azza's eyes. "I knew you would," he hisses. "To start, you must feed. You are far too weak to go into battle. The Sentinals have alerted Mikayel by now. He will come and make his stand. He was never one to resist a fight.

"So I will brand you. And tempt him." A smile curls his lips.

Chills ripple across my skin as I taste my acrid rage.

Mikayel *will* come. He'll end this. End me.

Perfect.

"Tonight we will crush the Sentinals once and for all." Azza grows manic with every word.

"You promised Nesy wouldn't be hurt."

"I promised *I* would not hurt her."

His threat lingers in the air. "I will not let anyone hurt her. Not now. Not ever."

"And you cannot break your vows," Azza snaps. "But to ensure your loyalty, and guarantee your power, you will seal our deal with a blood oath."

"What? I've never had to—"

"You've never crossed me before. We have no trust between us. Not since you've decided that your love for a Sentinal means more than your vow to me. You will take a blood oath and bind yourself to your word or there is no deal and I will end Nesy's existence now."

Every muscle contracts with rage. My ragged breath feels like sandpaper against my throat. "Who?"

"You must make amends for the one you refused."

"Lori," I whisper.

"Yes. The Seer." A sadistic smile forms on Azza's face, moving from his lips to his eyes. "First you will taste her blood. Then you will drink her soul."

CHAPTER 33 - LIAR

AYDAN

I loved watching Elle and Lorelei together. It was the only time I saw Elle smile other than with me. They ran through the fields playing games or collecting flowers for their hair. More than once, I caught Lorelei hiding in the tall grass of the meadows while Elle and I kissed.

I knew Elle would never really leave her sister for me. No matter what she said she wanted so many years ago. Their bond was just too strong.

And now, I'm going to rip them apart. Permanently.

Nesy will never forgive this. Never understand why it has to be this way.

Maybe that's a good thing in the end.

Maybe her anger with me will keep her safe and enable her to do what she must.

I watch the auburn-haired girl sip her coffee, so alone and unaware. Where are the Guardians now? Why do they leave her unguarded?

Why do they make it so easy?

"Prove your words to me," Azza snarls, his feral gaze glued to Lori. "Bleed her."

I'm not ready for this.

"Here? No." I look around the crowded streets and turn to Azza. "I'll do what you demand, but not in the middle of the day. And definitely not in the middle of Chelsea."

"Fine. Then we'll take her back to the club."

"She won't go with us, not without a fight. And that would attract a lot of unwanted attention."

Azza faces me, his expression wild. "She hates me, not you. Not after your last visit with her. Not after you showed *compassion*. After you confessed your love for her sister." He spit the words at me, each one a dagger piercing my heart.

Lori's words that night replay in my mind. She knew my heart, saw the soul that still lives inside—the part worthy of Nesy.

"Of course," Azza says, interrupting my thoughts. "I could just take care of everything myself. Lori. You. Nesy." Azza's sadistic tone fuels my rage. "But then, our deal would be meaningless. As would my promises."

I release a frustrated sigh. "I get it. You don't have to threaten me. I know what you expect."

"And?"

"And I am prepared to do what you ask. I assume you'll hold up your end of our deal."

Satisfaction washes over Azza's features. "Of course," he says, the glacier tones chilling my dead soul.

Lori sits at a small table in the back of the corner coffee shop. I straddle a chair across from her, taking her by surprise. Her eyes widen and dart around the shop.

"Azza isn't here. It's only me." The lie rolls easily off of my tongue, as they always do.

"What do you want?" Panic fills her voice. I want to tell her everything is okay. Comfort her.

But that's one lie I won't say.

"Where's Nesy?" she asks. "Is she okay?"

Patrons walk around us, their chatter muting my thoughts. I focus on my story, choking on the details.

Fast. I have to say this fast. Get it over with before I can really grasp what I'm doing. Before I change my mind. "She's at the club. There was an accident. She asked me to find you." The words spill out, reeling her further into my web.

Every word poisons my soul, sealing my fate.

"The club? She wouldn't go there." Her lip quivers. I taste her fear. "Unless…Azza. She went after Azza."

"Yes. She was trying to protect you. Keep him from hurting you again." My stomach churns. The Beast grows. "Things went wrong. I managed to get her away from him. But—"

Lori hangs onto every syllable, barely breathing.

"Lori, she needs to see you. She…she may not survive." The words shred my throat. Tears fill my eyes. Real tears.

Torment over the betrayal I commit.

Rage for the murder I will perpetrate.

Misery for the one whose heart I just crushed.

A muffled scream draws my attention. No one seems to hear it but me. I look over Lori's shoulder, watching as Azza plunges a sword into a lone Guardian. A gasp escapes and my anguish grows, buffeting against my soul. Azza retreats into the shadows while the angel remains, bleeding on the hard asphalt.

Too much.

My body stiffens. I should run to the dying angel. Summon Raphael. Turn myself in.

I can't.

Those actions guarantee Nesy's death.

So, I focus back on Lori. "Will you come?" I ask, touching her arm. "Please? Before it's too late?" My face screams everything I can't say, urging her to comply.

"Of course, I'll come. She's my sister. I'd do anything for her."

"Thank you. Nesy said you are the only one who could help her now." I stare deeply in Lori's eyes and let her feel every ounce of my agony.

Her expression softens. "You must feel awful, caught in the middle of something so big. Unable to admit your true feelings for her." She takes my hand in hers. "I was wrong about you, Aydan. You haven't turned into a monster. Not really. I think you're more like the angel I met in Germany."

Her words kill me, stripping me from my hopes and confirming my fears.

I'm worse than a monster.

    I am the Beast.

    We walk to the club in silence as the sun arcs across the sky.

Fifteen hours until Mikayel's deadline.

    Azza's will come sooner.

        Much sooner.

CHAPTER 34 – TRUTHFUL LIE

NESY

Darkness shrouds me as I twist through space. I've never traveled this way as a human. The feeling is unnerving, like I've been squeezed through too tight a space. Breathing is hard. Moving, impossible.

"You should've let me help him," I shout into the pitch black that envelopes me. "You should've—"

Cass squeezes my hand, a reminder that I'm not alone. "It's okay, Nesy."

"Azryel's Wings, Cass. It is *not* okay."

The portal opens in the middle of my human bedroom. I fall onto my bed, weak. My mind sifts through the last images of Aydan. A sword protruding from his shoulders. Falling.

"I need to get back to Aydan. He is too weak to survive Zaapiel's attack."

"We know." Cass's eyes are gentle and understanding, a sharp contrast to Zane's ever-present condemnation.

"Then why didn't you let me protect him?"

"Nes, *Azzaziel* protects him," Zane blurts out. "Not you. *You are supposed to*—"

"Kill Aydan. Yeah, I got that message."

"Then you should've handled it."

"Zane, I know my job, all right? I tried to vanquish him. I really did."

"Then what happened? Hormones get in the way again?" The loathing in Zane's tone slaps across my face.

"Zanethios!" Cass says.

"Stay out of this, Cassiel. So Nes, what was it this time? True love? Attraction? The weather? What?" Anger radiates from his eyes. I've never seen him so angry. So disappointed. "I went to bat for you. Guaranteed your allegiance. If anything happens to the other team—"

"I know!" I yell. "Azzaziel got in the way this time. He stopped me before I could pierce Aydan's heart."

"Oh, Nesy," Cass says. "I'm so sorry."

"He trapped me in his own little world and tried to fill my head with lies about Mikayel, stories about him loving some angel. Azza said they were friends. He tried to justify his fall from grace."

Zane looks down, his features softening. Cass grabs my hand.

Their sympathy is too much.

"He asked me to join him. Offered Aydan's life in exchange for my loyalty. He said he'd spare more Sentinal lives if I joined him."

"What did you say?" Zane asks.

I can't believe he has to ask that question, after everything.

"What do you think?" I can't hide the anger in my voice. "I said no. And then I stabbed him."

"Good." Zane's relief, his smile, brings me no comfort.

"Look, Azza's deal isn't the problem. It's his plans for Aydan that worries me."

"Plans?" Zane asks, concerned.

"He going to bind Aydan to him. Brand him."

"He's figured out how to make Aydan his equal?" Cass asks.

"Yes." I fight back the image of Aydan bound to Azza for eternity. Panic creeps into my thoughts as I see my brethren fall at Aydan's hands. "He plans to do it soon, I think. He talked about waging war with Mikayel."

"War?" Cass asks. "We need to tell the Council."

"I know. He said he's made an army of UnHoly. If he marks Aydan—"

"We need to warn Mikayel," Zane urges.

"I tried to when I was with Azzaziel. But the other team showed up and, well, I don't know if Mikayel heard me."

"Then we need to go to Celestium. Now." Cass opens the portal.

"You two go. I need to stay and find out more about this branding. I have a really bad feeling that this may involve Lori, somehow." I back away from the portal.

"We'll be right back. Don't do anything stupid." Zane glares at me, a mixture of frustration and concern reflected in his eyes.

I wait for my friends to return, fighting back the urge to find my sister and make sure she's safe. I think of the old stories taught to me in Celestium. Azzaziel is why the Sentinal order exists now, why warriors were once again trained. He's the reason for angelic deaths. Him and his dark creatures. The story of his fall is required study in my world. They say he used to be one of the most favored of the angels. Until he disobeyed a direct order from the Council and killed a Guardian. A member of the Council. His story is meant as a lesson in obedience. The trial of Azzaziel and his condemnation to the Abyss.

But he didn't face the eternal flames. He found a way to cheat that fate. He connected himself to the oldest and darkest forms of evil, learning which souls would guarantee his immortality. Learning how to brand himself and become the Beast.

Bearing the marks of the Dark One revived an ancient rivalry with the Council. Mikayel, in particular, hates Azzaziel with a ferocity never before seen in Celestium. No one knows exactly why Mikayel is so enraged. Some believe that it's personal, that he and Azzaziel had a history. Maybe even a friendship.

Just like Azza said.

I compare Azza's lies to the stories of old. So similar. But, that's the way with lies, right? At least, the good ones. The believable ones.

I think of Aydan's fate to become the Beast and lose the decency I know still lives in his soul.

I can't let it happen. I won't.

I need answers, before things get any worse.

I pace the room, still waiting for my friends to come back. What's taking them so long?

All at once my body begins to shake as incessant thoughts explode inside. Voices, too many voices, all talking at once throughout my head.

One voice rises about the din...*Help me Nesy. Please. You have to help me. He'll kill me. He'll...*

Panic seizes my lungs as Lori continues her screams for help. Azza's hunting her.

Right now.

I run down the stairs of the brownstone apartment, unable to wait any longer. I search the crowded café-lined streets of Chelsea. Lori would be here. Somewhere. She has to be.

Centering my thoughts, I focus only on Lori, reaching for her. Dread seizes my body as adrenaline races through my veins. Azza will torture her. Kill her.

Not if I can help it.

I grab hold of the frantic emotions threatening me and attempt to forge a plan. Cass and Zane appear in front of me, their careworn expressions adding to my already fragile state.

"I can't find Lori," I say, unable to stand still. "You have to help me. I have a bad feeling about this."

Zane stops my pacing and swallows hard. "We found her Guardian."

My mind screeches to a halt. Pain rolls from my friends to me. "What happened?" I ask.

"He was...hurt."

Azryel's Wings, not again. "By whom?" I ask.

Zane holds my gaze while Cass grabs my other hand. This is bad. Really really bad.

"We think an UnHoly did it."

Nononono.

"Aydan?" I force the question out as I detach from the feelings raging through me.

"I don't think so. Whoever it was struck fast. They pierced the Guardian's armor." My world slips away as Zane continues to speak. "They figured out how to injure us, Nes. That's why Aydan could slice through your skin before. They know how to defeat us."

"Defeat us?" I can barely process the words. Our armor-skin has always protected us in battle. Made us invincible to their attacks.

"Yes, it's their blades. They can cut us. Kill us." Zane's face is hard, his jaw clenched.

"The Guardian's injuries were fatal," Cass says as she squeezes my hand.

My world closes tight around me. I can't stay here.

Yanking my hands free, I turn away from my friends. Everything is falling apart.

My brothers are dying...*all my fault.*

My sister is being hunted...*I caused this.*

Aydan is becoming a monster...*because of me.*

I have to find a way to make this right. "Did Raphael come for my brethren? Return him to Celestium?"

"Yes," Cass answers.

"There's more you need to know," Zane adds.

"What?"

"We asked the Guardian about the oath. The brand. We know Azzaziel's plans."

"Tell me," I order, afraid that my fears are right.

"He's going to mark Aydan's skin," Cass whispers.

"I know that part. What else?"

Zane's shoulders tighten.

Blazes, my fears are right. "Zane, tell me. Now."

"He has to drink the soul of a Seer. Lori."

My mind reels out of control. I push past my friends as Zane grabs my arm. "Let me go, Zane. I won't let them take her. Not

Lori. Not my sister." Tears pour down my face as I try to wrench my hands from Zane's firm grasp.

"It's too late, Nes. Azzaziel has her." Zane watches me closely.

"How do you know?" I manage to ask.

"The Guardian saw. Moments before he was struck."

Nonononono.

"And Aydan? Was he there?" In my heart, I already know the answer. But the words, I need to hear the words.

"Yes. He lured her to the club."

My body begins to shake as the ground trembles under my feet. My mind swims and nothing makes sense. I forget to breathe, to think, to stand.

My friends hold me up as my legs refuse to bear my weight.

Aydan. He betrayed all that we ever were to each other.

His promise to me.

His love for us.

Everything

"Nesy?" Cass reaches out for my heart.

"No, don't. This is all my fault. I never should have let that UnHoly live."

My tattered emotions fuse to my heart as my pain turns to bile in my stomach.

Maybe it's a big mistake? Maybe the Guardian was wrong.

No. I know the truth.

Aydan is the UnHoly, forever bound to Azza. Soon he would bear the marks and become the Beast. Whatever he used to be, he is what he is.

A monster.

"Nes, Aydan—"

"Died the minute he took Lori." I glare at my friends, my body cold. Rigid. The emotional wave is gone, replaced by a cold and fierce hatred. "I should have listened to you, Zane. I'm sorry."

"Don't think about that now," Zane says.

"You're right. I don't have time to feel anything. I messed this up. Just me. I trusted the wrong person." I take a deep breath, inhaling every ounce of rage, pain, torment. I'm going to the club. Lori isn't dying because of me."

CHAPTER 35 - TRIBULATIONS

AYDAN

I escort Lori into the deserted club through the alley. The dark hallway spills onto the main dance floor. The only light comes from the pulsating neon overhead. Music blares from the speakers, a strange mix of gothic rock that shakes the floorboards. Time has no meaning in this club. It seems late. Much too late.

My time is up.

"So, where is she?" Lori asks.

Candles light the old altar at the far end of the dance floor. The scene looks ominous. Lori's eyes widen. She begins to tremble and back away. "Aydan?" Her voice quivers. "What's going on? Where's Nesy?" Goosebumps erupt over her pale skin.

"I'm sorry, Lori." *I didn't have a choice.* I grab her arm and force her forward. "This is the only way I can save Nesy." A lone tear slithers down my cheek as the words sputter out.

Lori stiffens against my weak grasp, breaking free. She runs down the hall and pushes against the doors, pounding them until her fists swell. The doors refuse to budge.

She turns back to me, her face contorted with rage. "How could you?"

Smoke coils around her body. Bat-like creatures with black beaks and sharp claws emerge from the smoke. They push her, forcing her toward me. Toward the altar.

Lori's scream pierces my heart. The demon next to her clamps his clawed hand down on her mouth, nearly breaking her jaw. It nips the air next to her face.

"I wouldn't do that if I were you. My pets go a little crazy when they hear a scream." Azza steps from the dark recesses next to the altar, his black eyes ablaze. "I don't know how long I'll be able to control them."

He laughs as Lori screams again. The demon digs his claws into her face.

My mind snaps as her cheek bleeds. I swing my arm, colliding with the dark creature. I look at Lori, her eyes filled with the disgust I feel. I wipe the blood from her mouth, whispering "I'm sorry."

Azza's voice turns cold, menacing.

Dangerous.

"I told you not to scream," he says as he slithers next to Lori. He slaps her face and my blood boils. Another trickle of blood runs down the corners of her mouth.

I'll kill you, I think, careful not to act.

Yet.

"Now, now Aydan," Azza mocks, reading my intentions. "Your interference does not bode well for your trustworthiness."

Wait. I must wait.

"I think it's time you proved your loyalty, my apprentice. Bleed her."

The Beast screams within. And I can't move.

"Am I to assume our deal is off?" Azza's voice holds the threat I fear most.

I walk to Lori and stare into her eyes. With a finger, I catch the blood dripping from the cut on her mouth. I bring it to my lips. The coopery scent fills my senses. I lick the scant blood from my finger.

The Beast rages, begging for more.

I steel myself against every instinct I have to devour Lori in a single act. And take a step back. "Satisfied?" I ask.

"For now."

Azza slides next to Lori and brushes a clawed finger against her cheek. "I have big plans for you tonight."

Lori twists out of his grip and backs into a large post at the bar.

Azza follows. Grabbing her by her shirt, he dumps her onto the barstool and spins her to him. "I told you I'd be back. It's time to serve the same fate as your mother. But unlike her, you will not deny me your soul."

Lori spits in his face and runs.

LACRIMOSA

No! Don't! Fissures crack through my heart with each step she takes.

Stupid girl. Don't fight him. You can't win.

Azza catches her before she makes it past the dance floor. "So, you want to make this hard, do you? I like hard."

He throws her across the room. She collides with the marbled edge of the bar, opening a larger gash over her eye. In a flash, he's over her, pulling her to her feet again.

Too weak to move, too disgusted with myself, I weigh my options.

Rescue Lori

—condemn Nesy.

Kill Azza

—condemn Nesy.

Kill myself

—condemn Nesy.

There's no way out for me now. For Lori. I'm too weak, too broken. Every choice condemns the one I love. There's no way to prevent the agony of this night.

Azza squeezes Lori's jaw. "It's okay, little Seer. I like a challenge. It makes things so much more...interesting."

"Stop," I bellow, unable to watch any more of his sadistic fun. "You don't need to do this." I rush to Lori's side. "I took her blood. Bound myself to my word. I have no choice but to finish this now. You don't need to torture her."

Lori glares at me. Her hatred of me filters into my thoughts, mirroring my own. Weakening me.

"Oh, but I think I do. I'm enjoying this far too much to stop." I feel him pulling on my emotions, tasting every ounce of torment and anguish. "Oh yes," he whispers. "Much too much."

Azza wipes the blood from Lori's face and brings it to his mouth. "It doesn't have to be like this, Seer. I could make it almost pleasurable for you to die."

Lori turns away in defiance.

Azza grabs her chin and forces her to look at him. "What? You don't like this face?" Candlelight reflects off his skeletal frame, bathing him in a hideous glow. Terror reflects in Lori's eyes as a smile curls Azza's lips. He changes into the image of his human host. Black hair, hard jaw, pale skin. Only the markings down his neck and the inhuman, empty eyes remain.

The same eyes I'll have after tonight.

"Perhaps this is more to your taste." Azza says as he leans in and forces a kiss on her mouth.

Lori twists and writhes, pounding his chest.

The Beast pushes me forward. Begs me to finish her off now. I turn away, unable to stomach the image of Azza tasting Lori's soul. The image of what I must do.

Lori's muffled screams feed the Beast as I fight the urge to rip Azza to shreds and take Lori's soul for myself.

Azza releases a feral growl. I turn, surprised. Lori has clawed his face, leaving a bloody trail of scratches deep in his skin.

"You will pay for that one, Seer." Azza slams her against the post, knocking her head against the marble. She slumps to the ground, bleeding and unconscious.

The metallic scent of her blood beckons the dark creatures lurking in the shadows. They swarm around her body, consumed with their need to feed.

Her scent pulls on me as well. I strain against it, too weak to ignore the siren call of her soul. My hunger rips through me as I stare at her still unconscious body on the floor.

Azza holds the creatures back, a smile glinting in his eyes. "Are you ready to drink her soul?"

I tremble, unable to withstand the Beast. My legs move on their own toward her. My throats constricts. There is only one thing can quench the building thirst. Her soul.

"Yes, Aydan. Drink." Azza tempts.

My legs wobble as desperate hunger consumes me. I watch the way Lori's chest rises and falls with each breath.

The Beast urges me forward.

Drawing a deep breath, I lean down, kiss her forehead.

And walk away.

"I guess you get the first taste, my pets," Azza cackles.

I walk into the alley as the sounds of the dark creatures feasting on Lori's emotions, her suffering, fills my ears. My need for the Seer consumes my thoughts.

My body.

My soul.

CHAPTER 36 – FORSAKEN LOVE

NESY

I run towards the club, determined to save Lori. Kill Aydan. End this nightmare. The sun drops below the canopy of the buildings.

Too fast. Everything is happening too fast.

I want more time with Aydan. I need to make sure he's really a monster. My heart knows he can't be. Conflict paralyzes the whole of me. I don't want to kill Aydan, but he leaves me no choice. I must protect Lori. I must prevent the bond from taking place.

I must be the Sentinal I was trained to be, no matter the cost.

My heart seizes with every step. I can't breathe, can't think. I'm locked in turmoil as the truth—my truth—coils around me. I must kill Aydan.

And his death…

Will kill me.

My pace quickens. I push aside the feelings suffocating me. Mikayel's voice enters my thoughts. *Get this done, Sentinal. Now.* I cling to his words, letting them remind me of my true duty.

The Council.

Celestium.

Mikayel.

I cross the crowded streets with a new plan.

One: Pierce Aydan's heart.

Two: Cast him to the Abyss

Three : Take Lori and run.

Every move is choreographed to perfection in my mind. No hesitation. No opportunities for Azzaziel to interfere. No mistakes.

Not this time.

I slow to a walk as sweat streams down my brow. I'm ready. Reaching over my shoulder, I finger the sword hidden in its sheath. I long to feel its weight in my hand and breathe in its power.

Wielding a sword is second nature to me. Ever since Mikayel taught me how to use it, I've needed its power. Craved it the way this body craves air. And yet, today, the hilt of my sword feels foreign. There is no strength in it. No security.

Today it means nothing but death.

His death.

Only a few more blocks to go. I create a mental map of the club and begin to run again, desperate to save my sister.

Stop! Lori's voice rings through my mind. Burning sensations, mixed with the tearing of flesh from bone, spring to life in my thoughts. They consume me, searing my soul.

I stop running. My body buckles with pain. A sea of people swarm around me, almost trampling me. I can't move. And the nightmare unfolds in front of me.

Lori's living nightmare.

Something, someone, lifts Lori from the floor. Her lip is open and bleeding. She's barely conscious.

Azzaziel stands inches from her face. "Are you done fighting me yet?"

"Never," Lori says, her voice nothing more than a whisper.

"Then you leave me no choice." He rips his demonic hand across her flesh, opening new wounds.

The demons and other dark creatures crowd around him. Waiting. Azzaziel turns to the UnHoly standing guard at the doors.

"He wasn't lying." My voice floats off my tongue to no one in particular. I look at the pictures burning into my thoughts. The club, as crowded as any Saturday night. But not with humans. The UnHoly. Hundreds of them.

Azza's army.

Lori screams. It echoes through the club as the assembled mob cheers and screeches.

"String her up," the Dark One commands.

LACRIMOSA

Two of the UnHoly walk forward and bind her arms and legs. They hoist her up until her face is even with Azza's.

"Aydan will be back for you. He will drink your soul while my pets devour your flesh. You're the key we've been searching for. You will help us make Aydan more powerful than the angels. More powerful than his precious Nesy."

"Don't you dare say her name." Lori's voice cracks on the words.

"Oh, didn't I tell you? She's the reason you're here." Azza's sadistic laughs floats in the air as he walks away.

I pull myself from the nightmare. "You're not there," I say to the passing hordes. "Where are you?"

I replay the scene, searching for Aydan. Nothing.

Something's wrong.

This is different than I'd planned. Maybe Aydan can't do it. Maybe the Guardian was wrong. Zane is wrong.

Hope punctures my heart. None of it matters now. We're locked into a similar fate. He *will* kill my sister. He *will* receive the marks. He *will* become the Beast. His vows allow for nothing less.

No matter what our love might mean.

The club looms a block away, bathed in shadows. Night will be here soon and Azza will finish his ceremony.

Unless I stop it.

Adrenaline courses through me as my senses heighten. *Detach. Prepare. Commit.* I focus only on my creed as I walk the final steps to my end.

Standing in front of the old church-turned-club, I stare at the gargoyles adorning the top of the gothic bell tower. I rehearse the plan one last time, slowing each second down.

One shot. That's all I'll get to save Lori.

And kill Aydan.

I walk into the narrow corridor behind the church. Shadows dance across the stone walls as the sky turns fiery in its final moments before nightfall.

The back door opens. Demonic music cuts through the silent alley. I flatten myself against the darkness, desperate to remain invisible.

Aydan walks out, his human face ashen. His body trembles as he paces in front of the door, tensing and releasing his fists. Mumbling words I can't hear.

Anguish rolls off of him in waves. It slices through my warrior's shell. I edge closer to him, my body almost free from the shadows.

I want to run to him and comfort his broken soul.

I want to kill him for the misery he causes.

I take another step. And then another. His torment, his remorse compels me forward.

Aydan stops pacing and turns, staring into the shadows.

And into my eyes.

I freeze, my body barely shrouded.

"I'm sorry, Nesy." He whispers to the darkness hiding me. "I messed everything up. For you. For Lori." His voice catches on the last word.

A tear slides down his face.

"No Aydan, it's my fault," I whisper. "I let this happen. And now Lori, you, Mikayel's army—you will all pay the price for my selfishness." My vision blurs as tears overtake my eyes.

He stands so close.

"I have to do this," he says. "I know you can't understand. And you'll never be able to forgive me. But, it's the only way. There really is no other choice." His voice trails off.

I release a small gasp as I realize what he's preparing to do.

Aydan tenses, his eyes narrowing on me. I pull back into the shadows, barely breathing.

He takes a fragile step towards me. My heart rams against my chest and I'm certain he sees me.

Aydan pauses, shakes his head slightly and turns back towards the club. He stops at the door and takes a deep breath. Laying a hand on the handle, he pulls.

Lori's screams flood the alley.

And my world implodes under the weight of my anguish.

CHAPTER 37 - REQUIEM

AYDAN

My hopes fall away as I walk back into the club. Lori is strung up against the backdrop of the altar, the candles burned down to their ends. Her arms and legs are bound together. Pieces of flesh have been torn from her body. Bruises—angry, purple and red—color her face, her legs, her torso. My insides clench as I look at her, pain forever carved into her face.

The crowd has grown in the club; one big mob of the UnHoly. They clamor around the nearly dead Seer, hungry.

Azza strokes Lori's hair, caressing her. Bile churns in my throat as rage surges through me. I want to kill Azza.

Later.

Right now, all I can think about is Lori and the way her soul calls to me.

"Ah, you've come back," Azza mocks. "I knew you wouldn't be able to resist her. But just to make sure—" Azza rips his claws against her torso.

She screams. The sound reaches into my soul, pulling on the Beast. I can't control the need rushing through me. My breath comes in small, shallow gasps as my legs move against my will, bringing me closer to her.

"It's time to make good on your promises, Aydan. For Nesy's sake."

The sound of her name on his lips crushes me. I want to scream "No!" Tell him to forget his miserable plans.

I want to kill him where he stands.

"I know you want her. I can feel your body reaching for her." Azza whispers in my ear. "Do it, Aydan. Take her. Fulfill your destiny."

My body shakes.

I look into Lori's eyes, bloodied and red. She radiates agony. It passes from her to me, breaking my resolve. Unleashing the Beast.

I don't know how much longer I can hold back.

"Please," she whispers to me. "Kill me. I can't take anymore of this. Don't let him be the one."

"Quiet! We like our meals silent," Azza barks.

A cacophony of screeches erupts from the mob. They move closer, pressing in on me. I lock eyes with Lori, desperate to understand her unspoken words.

Does she really want me to do it? Kill her?

"Please," Lori says much louder this time. A final act of defiance.

I can't bear the torment I see in her eyes. All because of me. Because I was so weak so long ago.

Never again.

"Kill me," Lori mouths. "Please. For Nesy."

I move closer, my body next to hers.

"It's okay," she mouths, barely able to move her mouth. "I'm dead anyway."

Her body trembles in my arms.

"Do this," she says, choking on every word. "To save Nesy. You owe me that much." I owe her so much more.

Azza watches as I stand inches from her face, quivering.

"Let her down." I choke.

Azza nods his approval and the UnHoly release their hold on the ropes. She drops into my arms. Gently, I place her on the floor, cradling her broken body. My muscles tense. I don't know how to control the impending frenzy. Part of me doesn't want to.

She looks up at me with moist eyes. "Thank you," she whispers. She closes her eyes. "You're not like Azza. Remember that in the end. Remember."

I hear my master urging me, commanding me to drink her soul.

I can't refuse. She won't let me.

Carefully I place my trembling lips on hers. I taste the elixir of her life, feel her surrender to me. The sweet nectar fills my mouth, my body. I take her breath.

Her life.

Her soul.

"Lorelei!" Nesy's voice bounces throughout the hall.

I jerk towards the voice. No! Why are you here?

Nesy slices and hacks her way through the crowd straight for me.

I lay Lori on the ground and mouth a silent prayer. "Be at peace now. I'll find a way to protect Nesy. I promise." I stand, ready to face my fate.

Nesy barrels into me, lodging her sword deep into my flesh. Piercing my heart. White hot pain streaks across my body as I feel her anguish rip through me.

"Nesy. I—" I can't stand, my human body too weak. I slump to the ground as the UnHoly descend on her.

I must find a way to protect her.

Azza stands over me. "Release yourself. Or I will kill her myself."

I unleash a feral howl and step out of my human form. Hatred permeates every cell.

Hatred for the choices I've made.

Hatred for the master I will spend an eternity serving.

Unless...

"Get out of here Nesy," I yell, stronger now that I've released my form.

She doesn't listen. Holding her sword in one hand and a dagger in the other, she thrusts and jabs everything in her path. "You promised," she spits at me. "You swore you wouldn't feed. Promised you'd help keep her safe."

Two UnHoly fall as she continues her attack.

Azza watches. Amused. He raises a hand, stopping the UnHoly.

Leave Nesy, now.

"You're a good warrior, little Sentinal; that is, when you aren't ruled by your self-inflicted torment. But, you're wasting your time. The Seer is dead. And Aydan will receive his marks tonight. You're too late."

Nesy thrusts her blade toward me.

I want her to kill me. End my pain and torment. *...You die, she dies...* Azza's words remind me of everything. I duck and spin away from Nesy's attack.

"Are you not listening, Sentinal? He won't let you do that. It's too late. You've already lost." Azza's voice fills with malicious laughter.

"Is that true? You *want* to join him now?" she asks me.

"Yes," I lie.

Her eyes turn cold. Enraged.

Good.

"I won't let you." Again she lunges forwards. *"Divina virtute in infernum detrude daemones"* The condemning words ring through the club as she continues her attack.

"Nesy, stop."

"No!" she yells. "I *will* finish this. For my sister."

Her pain pours from her words, coating my skin. She lunges forward again. A blood curdling scream cuts through me. Nesy's eyes widen. A trickle of blood pours from the corners of her mouth and she falls to the ground.

Azza pulls his sword from her back. "That was getting tiresome."

Blood pools around Nesy's human body. "Why?" she chokes out as her eyes flutter and close.

Release, Nesy. Release. I repeat the words over and over, willing her to survive.

I charge at Azza, grabbing his arm. "You promised she wouldn't be hurt."

"I promised her *angelic* form wouldn't be hurt." He yanks his arm free. "And it isn't. Unless she chooses to die."

"Leave her alone, Azza. I fulfilled my oath. Now fulfill yours."

"You have not fulfilled yours yet, my apprentice." His voice rattles the walls of the club. The dark creatures cower. "But," he says, his voice dangerous. "I will let her go. *If* she can free herself from her form before it dies."

I bend down and cradle her. Her breath rattles and I know her human lungs have been punctured. "Let go, Nesy. Please. Free yourself." The words stick in my throat, along with my emotions. I can't bear watching her die. Not again. Flashes of Elle's broken body bombard my thoughts. "Baby, do this for me. Release yourself. Please." I push myself into her mind, her heart. Open myself up to her, leaving hidden my plans.

Nesy opens her eyes just as her human body takes one last gasp. I move away from her as she detaches from her human form. She floats through her remains, her angelic skin casting a blinding golden light around the room, illuminating the darkest recesses of the club. Her wings expand to their full height. She draws her sword and faces Azza.

"I am letting you leave, little Sentinel. This time." Azza stands inches from her face. "But if you interfere in any way with my plans for young Aydan, I will not be so kind again."

I tug on her arm. "Get out of here before he changes his mind."

She shoves me away, lifting her sword to Azza. "You'll never win."

I grab her arms more firmly and push her through the horde. She wrestles against my grasp. Azza laughs as I push her into the alley.

The wind ruffles her wings and sends a chill through me.

"So this is *your* choice then?" she asks. "Joining Azzaziel?" Her voice quivers with every word.

A vortex opens before I can respond. Her friends, the Mediator and the Anointed, step out.

"Yes," I say to all of them. "I've pledged myself to him. Taken a blood oath." My focus narrows on the angels. "I have no choice now."

Please work.

"I won't let this happen. I'll find a way to stop you." She rushes for me, stopped by the Anointed.

"Nesy, your shoulder. You're hurt." The Anointed pushes Nesy into the portal. "You have to let Raphael look at it. Now!"

Nesy takes one last look at me, resigned. A lone tear slides down her face, the only sign of her pain. "I wish I never met you, Aydan. Not in any life. I should've killed you that first night in the club."

"Yes. You should've." Every syllable sticks in my throat.

The portal closes and Nesy fades from view. My own eyes fill with tears. The Mediator steps forward, his dagger drawn.

"You don't need that," I say. "I'm not going to hurt either of you."

The Mediator stiffens and glares at me.

I don't blame him. I wouldn't trust me either.

After several moments, the angel stows his weapon. "What happened in there?"

"I threw everything away." My heart clenches. "I ended Lori's life." My hollow voice dies in the air around us.

The Anointed gasps.

"But, not because the Dark One bade you to." The Mediator continues to stare at me.

"No," I say. "How did you know that?"

"Lori *asked* you to help her. She wanted you to end her suffering and save Nesy somehow. You…you were merciful with her."

"I tried to be."

The Anointed furrows her brow. "I'm lost here. Zane, what's going on?"

"Search his heart, Cass. He didn't murder her. He saved her. He even helped her to find peace in the end."

I feel the Anointed enter my heart. She shuffles through my emotions. Everything I want to hide streams forward at her request.

My torment.

Lori's suffering.

Mercy.

I can't watch the pictures rushing past my sight. Can't feel these feelings again.

I throw her out of my heart and drink the feelings back down, choking on my own betrayal.

"Does she know?" Cass asks.

"No."

"You have to tell her." The Anointed again tries to enter my heart.

"No!" The force of my words surprises even me. "She can never find out. If she thinks I'm nothing more than a monster, she'll find a way to kill me. She'll call on the Sentinals. She'll tell Mikayel and he'll come and end this." My voice drops to a whisper. "He has to."

"You want him to kill you?" Zane asks.

"I need him to. Once I'm marked, I won't be able to control my need to inflict pain and suffering. Mikayel's sword is the only way now."

"And you would have Nesy hate you for eternity?" Zane voice holds a mixture of shock and confusion.

"Better her hatred than her death."

Footsteps resonate in the alley. I tense, worried. "You guys need to leave. I've already been gone too long."

"I was wrong about you, Aydan. Completely wrong. You *are* everything Nesy said you were." Zane opens a portal. "I'm sorry things have to end this way."

"You knew there was no other choice. Just make sure she calls on Mikayel. Make sure he comes with his army. He can't fail."

The angels step into the portal as I walk to the door. "Nesy can't find out about this or she'll change her mind and do something foolish. Promise me you won't tell her. Promise me you'll make sure she follows through with everything."

"I promise." Zane begins to close the gateway.

"Wait," I turn back to the angels. "When this is over, when I'm dead, tell her I loved her. I have always loved her."

"I will."

I watch them fade as Azza spills into the alley. "You weren't doing anything stupid, were you?"

I swallow my feelings. And face my fate.

CHAPTER 38 - PAINED VENGEANCE

NESY

I march into the empty Council chamber, shattering any tranquility around me. I can't control the emotions flowing through me. The rage.

My anger coils inside, consuming every ounce of love I hold for Aydan. Bathing me in his lies.

Why?

The question tosses, tosses, tosses in me. It doesn't make sense.

He promised he'd never feed again...*he killed Lori.*

Promised he'd refute his vow...*he's taking his marks.*

Promised he would love me....*he chose Azzaziel.*

Everything I trusted slips away as I feel the full weight of his betrayal. Gabriel and Mikayel walk into the hall, absorbed in their own conversation.

"Sirs," I interrupt. Anxiety flutters through my limbs.

"Nesayiel. Why are you here? You were not summoned." Concern replaces the smile on Gabriel's face.

"No, I—"

"Then you have finished your task?"

"No." The words fade from my mind. Along with my resolve. But not my rage. Never my rage.

"The Council is not in session. If you need to report something, speak with Mikayel."

I release my torment, letting it seep into the Council Elders.

"I suggest you control your emotions when you come here, Sentinal." Mikayel's eyes are as hard as ever. "I assume there is a reason you are here. Or, was my faith in you to finish this unfounded?"

"No more than my faith in you." The words escape too fast from my lips.

So much for staying calm.

Mikayel's eyes ignite. "What did you say to me?"

"Enough, Mikayel," Gabriel says. "This is not the time. I am certain your Sentinal came for a reason." He faces me, urging me to continue.

"Yes. I did."

"Well, what is it then?"

"It's Azzaziel. He's figured out how to brand Aydan. He's going to do it. Tonight."

"Brand...but he would need to have the soul of a Seer for that."

"He does. Aydan already drank her soul."

"The Seers are gone. Who did he find?" Gabriel's mind eases into mine.

I let him see every moment, feel every emotion.

"Oh. I see."

I look down. I never told them about Lorelei. Never mentioned a Seer. Another failure I'd have to live with.

Assuming I survived the night.

"The human girl?" Mikayel's voice hinted of a grief and anguish lurking beneath his façade.

Guess I'm not the only one pretending here.

"Yes," I whisper. "My sister. From Germany."

"How long have you known? Why did you not tell this Council?"

The weight of Mikayel's disappointment bears down on me. "It doesn't matter. Not now. All that matters is that we stop him. Before it's too late."

"So this is why you've come? So I can clean up your mess?"

Enough.

"No! I came so you can end this business with *your friend* once and for all. Before the rest of us have to pay the price," I fume. "Again."

"You will hold your tongue, Sentinal, or I will end this conversation now." Mikayel's voice echoes throughout the chamber.

I inhale my rage. For now. "Azzaziel wants a war. He wants vengeance on you. That's his sole motivation for branding Aydan. You must stop him. Bring the Sentinals. Prevent his sacrament before it's too late." I struggle to control my breathing. My emotions. "I've seen his army of UnHoly. He has thousands. Thousands. "We *must* do something."

Mikayel's eyes widen "Yes, we must. Brother," he says to Gabriel. "It looks like we are at war."

"It would appear we have little choice in the matter," Gabriel replies. "Take your Sentinals. Summon Sariel and the Guardians as well. You'll need all the help you can get."

Mikayel hardens. "They are not trained to fight the UnHoly."

"True. But they can protect the innocent. Humanity. As for the others, I will call Raphael. We fight with you, Mikayel. But not our divisions. Theirs is not the way of war. They will help those who survive."

Those who survive... The words nestle around my shattered heart. My brethren are going to die. All because of me. Because of my selfishness.

"Nesayiel." Mikayel's voice slices through my shame. "Nesayiel, I expect you to fight with us."

"I was counting on it," I say, ignoring my inability to control my emotions.

Gabriel stares at me. "Perhaps, Mikayel, it would be better if she did not."

"No, I can do this. I *need* to do this."

Emotional mess or not, I'm still a warrior.

Mikayel nods. "She understands her duty, Gabriel." He turns to me. "Be ready in an hour."

"There's one more thing," I say. I have to tell them everything now, something I should've done all along. "They know how to pierce our skin, get through our armor."

"We know. The minute we heard about Aydan slicing your arm, we knew. We will have extra protections. They may not be enough, so we will have to rely on our fighting skills. Azza's mob is no match for the Sentinals."

"Careful, Mikayel. Don't misjudge them. Azzaziel was trained just as you were." Gabriel's words bleed into my thoughts.

"Wait a minute. What? The stories are true? He *was* trained with you? You really were..." I can barely form the words. "Friends?"

"That is not your concern." Again I see guilt pass through Mikayel's eyes.

My cold rage explodes. "Azryel's Wings, it isn't!"

"That's enough." Mikayel booms.

"No! Tell me the truth! Were you friends?"

"Nesayiel, go prepare for battle." Gabriel's voice quiets my mind instantly.

Darn Mediators.

"Mikayel, you have a war to prepare for. We will deal with her concerns later."

He lied. Mikayel lied to me.

And Azzaziel—he told the truth.

My mind can't reconcile my thoughts. I walk to my room, confused.

Enraged.

There is nothing glamorous about war, or its preparations. Not donning the heavy uniform, dark leather that stands out against the golden hues of my pale skin. Nor mentally preparing for death.

It's been more than four centuries since the last conflict with Azzaziel. He and a small army tried to invade Celestium that time. The war lasted three minutes. And the Dark One ran, defeated.

This time would be different.

This time he had an army of thousands.

The time he had an equal. Aydan.

I grab the whetstone and sharpen my sword and dagger. Each stroke caresses my anger, fueling it. Mikayel's conversations rise to the surface of my thoughts. I felt his torment, his guilt, his shame. The old stories were true. Azzaziel's stories were true.

Mikayel knew about love and the choices I face. He knew who Aydan was, knew about my love. He knew everything.

And he refused to help me.

"I brought the new armor," Mikayel says as he appears at my door, his eyes sad. "Let me help you put it on."

The golden breastplate matches my skin. Mikayel's sword, the symbol of the Sentinals, adorns the front.

Mikayel helps me fasten the armor around my body. "We should talk."

"I have nothing to say to you."

"Nesayiel—"

"No. You lied to me." There is so much anger in my words, anger I have no intention of controlling. "You told me *I* was the problem, that my feelings for Aydan were the problem. You made me feel ashamed. And all the while, you knew exactly what I was battling inside."

"What did Azzaziel tell you?"

"He said you fell in love with an angel. A Guardian. You betrayed your orders to end the relationship. He said you put everyone at risk."

Mikayel's shame is palpable. His emotions—anger and guilt—pass through his expressions until he becomes stoic.

"So it's true, then? Everything Azzaziel told me was true?"

Deny it. Deny it. Deny it.

"Yes, it's true."

Disappointment washes through me. Azza, the Dark One, the embodiment of evil—he's the honest one? Mikayel, everything I aspire to be…

I can't finish the thought, can't conceive of a world where my mentor lies. Everything I thought I knew rains down as my illusions are shattered.

"Why didn't you tell me? Why were you so…hard on me?" I can't stop the pain seeping into my words as my body shutters.

He stares at me, the same hard expression on his face. "To keep you from making the same mistakes."

"What mistakes, Mikayel? Loving him?"

Tell me the truth, Mikayel. Tell me.

"No!" He yells. His voice betrays the anguish he tries to hide. "Risking lives to satisfy that love. I'm certain Azza didn't tell you the whole story."

"He told me enough."

"Did he tell you what her death did to me? What my choices condemned me to? I live with the burden of her death. Her torture. Me. Azza may have committed the crimes, but it was my fault. And now we are locked in an endless war because of my own selfishness." Mikayel's wings ruffle as he opens and shuts his fists, his body stiff. "I did not want you, my best Sentinal, to repeat my mistakes." Mikayel whispers. "I couldn't let you live my life of shame. I care too much to let that happen to you." His face softens. "You remind me too much of *her*."

"There were other options, Mikayel. Aydan still has good in him. I can feel it. You could have shown mercy. Offered redemption. Gabriel would have agreed if you asked." I don't care about Mikayel's excuses. I stand, stoic and stiff. Exactly like my master.

"Things are seldom as easy as you make them out to be."

"You stole the only hope I had. The only hope he had. And we will all pay the price for it now. He has turned to Azza. He will become like Azza. Everything that was good will be—"

"I know." Mikayel looks broken—as broken as I feel.

"And you did nothing to stop it. *You,* the only other Sentinal to understand love, chose to turn your back on him. On me." I turn away, unwilling to see the pain my words inflict. "Did you know about our past?"

Say no. Say no. Say no.

"I suspected after you failed at the club that first night."

My world spins to a halt as his words stab at my heart. "You should have helped me then." My voice cracks as my wings twitch nervously behind me. So much betrayal. So much pain. "You should have warned me," I whisper as my legs buckle. "Prepared me for this."

"The Council believed—"

"What? All of you knew? The whole Council?"

Mikayel sucks in a deep breath and hides behind his warrior façade. "None of that matters at this point."

It matters to me. Anger and pain weld together as the walls to my chamber close in around me. I pace, desperate to escape the feelings that threaten to undo me. I grab my sword, allowing its weight to focus my thoughts. I swing it once, twice, three times. The movement centers my mind.

"Azza must be stopped," Mikayel says as I swing the sword once again. "Before Aydan can join his ranks."

"At least we agree on that." I thrust the air in front of me.

"I want you to fight at my side, Nesayiel. But, I need to know you will do what I ask of you. No matter what I order."

I stop and stow my weapon. "I have never disobeyed you on the battlefield."

"You have never faced off with your lover, either."

His words flatten me. "You already condemned him to death the minute you refused my request for redemption. He means nothing to me now." A lie, I know, but one I have to believe in if I'm to do what I must.

"Promise me, Nesayiel. You must follow every order. If I command you to leave, you leave. Otherwise, you must stay here with your friends."

"I'm not staying here. No way. This is as much my fight as it is yours. He killed Lorelei, my human sister. And now he's prepared to join Azzaziel. I will not let him twist into a replica of the Dark One."

"This cannot be about vengeance."

"Why not? It's about vengeance with you. It always has been."

"Because, Sentinal, it will cloud your judgment. Trust me." The authority in Mikayel's voice stops me. "If you are only going to seek vengeance, I will forbid it. It has to be about something more."

I shroud my feelings, becoming the Sentinal Mikayel trained me to be. "Vengeance is no more my cause than it is yours. I will do anything you command of me."

Mikayel drills into my thoughts. I allow him to see the torment and betrayal, see the pain he has inflicted—pain as deep as that inflicted by any of the UnHoly.

Mikayel's face echoes my feelings, passing from agony to anger to detachment. "So you agree to my terms? You will follow every command?"

"I know my duty." I say, my detachment matching his.

"Then, we leave in ten minutes."

The tears fall as soon as I'm alone, stinging my cheeks. Betrayed. Again. And not just by Mikayel, but the whole Council.

Their silence condemned me to this fate. Condemned Aydan to his death.

Their silence killed my sister.

My stomach clenches as I swallow everything down.

My guilt.

Mikayel's lies.

Aydan's betrayal.

Lorelei's sacrifice.

I don't have time for this. Don't have time to wallow in my useless emotions. So I focus my energy elsewhere.

On Lori...*They'll pay for your death, my sister. I promise.*

On Aydan...*You betrayed me for the last time.*

On Azzaziel...*One way or another, your reign ends tonight.*

Fastening my gauntlets and strapping on my weapons, I walk to the Great Hall, ready for war.

And my sweet vengeance.

CHAPTER 39 - MARKED

AYDAN

I emerge from the shadows into the church courtyard. Mikayel's statute looms in front of me, holding the Sword of Truth. Soon it will be the only thing that can kill me. *Make him come, Nesy. Make him finish this.* The words bring little comfort.

I look around the gardens. Four days since I met Nesy—again. Two days since I knew who she was. One day since I promised myself to her.

It feels like a century.

She hates me now. Hates what I'll become.

So do I.

"A few more things before we can proceed." Azza places a hand on my shoulder, sending a shiver down my spine.

Shadows coil around the courtyard as the UnHoly file in around us.

I've never seen so many dark creatures assembled in one place. I wasn't part of the last battle with Celestium. From what I was told, that one ended in defeat. Based on the mob mustered here now, things will be different.

Deadly.

"Tonight is the night we've waited centuries for," Azza bellows. "Tonight, we will end the Council's rule and crush their army. We know how to penetrate their skin, how to end their lives." Azza's voice bleeds through the ranks of UnHoly. They scream, their hatred palpable.

My stomach twists with disgust. *I'm sorry, Nesy.*

"Tonight," Azza continues. "I will forge another Dark One as I unleash the Beast. Aydan is more than my apprentice now. Tonight, he becomes my equal. One more that cannot die at the hands of the Sentinal. One more to secure our victory over Mikayel and his army." Azza catches my eye and smiles.

The crowd erupts in a burst of anticipation.

"Aydan is no ordinary UnHoly. He was trained by me for one purpose. To bring down the Sentinals once and for all."

More cries erupt from the mob.

"And he has done a brilliant job. He confused the one meant to destroy him. Convinced her to betray her orders."

Azza's words slap me to attention.

I did confuse her

—*and she confused me.*

Profess my love for her

—*I will always love her.*

Tempt her

—*was that always your plan, Azza?*

"Tonight he binds himself to me. He will bear the marks and eliminate the last of his ties to Celestium. None but Mikayel will be able to harm him." Azza's voice drops to a whisper. "And Mikayel will not live through the night."

The horde goes wild with excitement. They throw rocks at the statue of Mikayel, breaking off pieces of stone from his wings, his body, his face.

What have I done?

What have I done?

I close my eyes and do the only thing I can think of—something I haven't done since leaving Celestium.

I pray.

"*Succurre mihi, Mikayel. Defendere Celestium. Divina virtute in infernum detrude daemones.* Help me, Mikayel. Defend Celestium and cast Azza into the Abyss. End his reign." My whisper pulls me into a strange place deep inside my memories. A place before my fall.

Fresh scents invade my thoughts—a combination of sunshine and vanilla. Celestium. The younger version of me accepts my role as a Watcher, taking an oath to protect humanity from the likes of Azza.

So much has happened since then. So many broken promises and shattered vows. And yet, as the ancient prayer lingers on my tongue, a part of me feels like I never really left Celestium. Never entered the nightmare that now defines me.

A symphony of screams from the UnHoly fills my senses as the last of the prayer fades away. Azza pulls me close, the foul stench of his breath hard against my cheek. "You will not betray me now with your little prayers, Aydan. You will take your oath and wear the brand."

Although his words are barely audible, they scream through my thoughts. My life is what I've made it.

A Living hell.

"I am yours, Master."

Azza wears a sadistic smile as fire erupts on the ground next to me. A stone pedestal springs up from the flames. Six weapons lay on the altar. One for each of the marks I am to bear.

Azza picks up the weapon closest to him—his own dagger. He places it into the blue-orange center of the fire and turns it until it glows red-hot.

"Almost time, Aydan. Almost time. When the ceremony is complete, you will forget all about your warrior angel. And any hope you still harbor of living in Celestium."

I stare into the abyss of Azza's eyes. "You'll keep your agreement about Nesy? You won't hurt her if she returns?"

"I will not be the one to harm her as long as she does not interfere. But if she tries to stop me in any way, I will end her life with one swift stroke."

Her name feeds my torment. "And you will instruct your UnHoly to not harm her?"

"*Your* UnHoly. Once the ceremony is complete, they will serve you as well."

I don't want followers.

    I don't want to rule.

        I only want her safety.

"You didn't answer the question."

"You heard all I will say. Now, will you take your marks? Or does Nesy die?"

For a second time, I pray. The prayer offers little comfort. Images of my life as the Beast churn my disgust.

A moment passes

    —there is no way out.

And another

    —I chose this fate centuries ago.

Azza's grips my shoulder and squeezes. "Well?"

"Let's get this over with," I say, eyeing the red-hot dagger in Azza's hands.

My heart pounds too loud in my ears as I drop to my knees, the concrete grinding into my skin. I can hear the blood thrumming through Azza's veins, hear the wind moving through the air. I tilt back my head in submission, ready to end my life.

The dagger twirls in Azza's hands. He draws the hot blade across my skin, carving the long Celtic symbol down my neck. The mark extends from my jaw to my collarbone in an intricate pattern of knots that blend into my flesh.

Blinding pain streams through me. I grind my teeth, refusing to acquiesce to the feeling of the blade slicing through me. Every loop, every line, brings more torment. Putrid scents invade my nostrils as I hear my flesh sizzle.

Azza chants in the ancient language, releasing the Beast. His voice filters through me. Each word flares the agony caused by the mark, fusing it to my skin. Syllable by syllable, cut by cut, Azza forms the loops and knots of the first mark.

I squeeze my eyes shut, enduring each hate-filled moment.

I will not break.

Seconds click by until Azza finishes the first rite. My torment ebbs with the withdrawal of his dagger. My nausea passes. As my mind clears, I know…

I will never be the same.

"The first of six has been placed," Azza says to the crowd. "Each mark is to be made by a different tool, each representing a different bond. One to me and one the UnHoly. One for the clans of dark creatures. One for the crimes of Celestium, one for the sins of mankind. And the final mark as a commitment to freeing our brothers in the Abyss. When Aydan has received all six marks, when we have beaten the Sentinals, we will free those trapped in the eternal flames."

The mob roars with excitement.

"We will never be subject to the Council's twisted version of justice again."

More screams erupt around me. My mind twists around the sounds. I may have survived the first mark, but I doubt I can stay conscious for the rest. Nesy floods my awareness—the scent of her hair, the curve of her face, the blue of her eyes.

    My salvation.

    I must stay alive, if only to keep her safe.

    "Ready for your next mark?" Azza's breath quivers the hair on my cheek. "That one was nothing compared to the rest."

    I paint a picture of her in my mind.

    Help me, Nesy.

    Azza grabs the next tool of my torture, the fang of a werewolf. "I've been saving this one just for you. Ever since you killed my pet in Germany." He dips the fang into a vial of smoldering violet liquid. Drops fall to the ground, scorching the concrete next to me.

    He loops the second mark through the first, creating a maze of crisscrossing patterns. It feels like liquid fire against my skin. A growl escapes my lips. I look at Azza and grind my teeth. Again, I think of Nesy. Picture the way she looked the first night at the club. Blond hair cascading over her shoulders, endless black leather boots, eyes I can lose myself in.

    If only.

    My master continues to carve the pattern in my skin. I cling to the image in my mind. Clawing my own skin, I fight back the nausea welling inside. Lightning streaks across my vision.

    I will not scream.

I will not scream.

My skin hisses as Azza forms the mark. He chants, sending a fresh wave of agony through me.

Seconds last for hours as Azza replenishes the smoldering liquid on the fang. Each gash burns its way through the outer layers of my skin and into my soul.

He carves a third, deeper mark with the fang. The violet liquid drips down my neck as the mark is carved, leaving its own trail of pain. And I know…

This is death.

Time has no meaning to me now. The UnHoly groan, scream, cheer as the mark is finished. But Azza does not pause; he begins the next line immediately. His tool, a dagger stolen from the Guardian he killed on the streets of Chelsea, is coated in angelic blood. It feels like acid pouring into my raw flesh. Fiery agony fills every cell. I have to stay conscious, keep myself from dying.

But nothing makes sense. Not the muffled sounds of the UnHoly. Nor the ancient chant spoken by Azza.

I try to focus on Nesy. Try to keep from losing my mind.

Not possible.

Azza loops the fourth mark through the first three, weaving it wide across my neck. Each knot strips a piece of Nesy from me. I pull on to the vanishing memories, desperate to hold onto her.

A scream erupts from somewhere outside of me. Tears overflow my eyes. "Nesy!" Her name rips across my lips, scorching every part of me.

Azza smiles down at me as my defenses crack. Everything I am—everything that is good or merciful, everything that belongs to Nesy—falls away. Wave after wave of nausea rolls over me. My soul shreds to pieces.

Along with my memories of Nesy. Of our love.

"Let go of her and this will be easier."

"Never," I utter.

"Suit yourself. But you won't survive the sacrament if you don't let go. And if you die, I will be sure to torture your love before I end her life."

Azza grabs a crude human knife from the stone alter. "Do you know what this is?"

I can't process the words.

"The knife of Akedah. Soaked in the blood I drained from the dregs of humanity. With it, I will end your ties to Celestium. And your lover." Azza dips the knife into his concoction and places it against a new part of my neck. Starting near my ear, he loops the fifth mark into the others, weaving and knotting each connection.

The human blood eats away what's left of my flesh as my soul absorbs every torment. I scream, white-hot pain searing my senses. I search my heart for Nesy, for us. I need her love. "Nesy, help me." The words escape my mouth before I can stop them.

Azza's maniacal laugh slaps me. "Too late for that. I doubt her sword could hurt you much now."

He continues the fifth mark, my torture nearly complete. Flashes of my past stream in front of me, only to fade.

Every touch.

Every kiss.

Every moment.

Forever gone.

I bite down on my hand, desperate to stop screaming.

The mark continues.

I cling to the passing images, pushing against my own anguish.

I can't let her go.

Let myself go.

My mind closes in on itself as the last knot of the fifth mark is finished.

"Nesy!" My scream ends as Azza lifts the knife.

"You're stronger than I thought. But this last one will break you. And then, you will belong to me. For all eternity."

"Mark me, Azza." My voice is raw. Barely audible. "I will still never belong to you."

He howls as he slaps his hand hard against my face. I fall, my skin angry and my flesh raw. Azza lifts the final torturous tool—his own angelic sword from before his fall. He slashes his forearm, coating the metal with his demonic blood.

The final mark begins. And my mind turns black.

LACRIMOSA

I walk through the city streets as the evening fog hugs the ground. I move through the mist, confused. She is near. Somewhere just out of reach.

I search through the tangled jungle of metal and concrete. "Nesy, my love. I need you."

"I'm here, Aydan."

I turn toward her voice. Her image emerges from the fog. Magnificent golden skin, cascading hair that shines like the sun. Penetrating blue eyes. She carries no signs of battle. No wounds from Azza's sword, no scars of any kind.

I run to her. Embrace her. She pulls back and cups my face. "I love you, Aydan. I'll always love you." She kisses me gently.

I need her. Hunger for her.

I pull her flat against me and deepen the kiss.

She struggles against my embrace. I want to stop. Must stop.

The frenzy is too great.

I drink from her soul, unleashing the Beast.

I can't stop.

Every last drop drains into me.

Until she is gone.

And I am forever…

Damned.

"No!" I scream as I wake.

Azza smiles. And begins the final mark.

CHAPTER 40 – ARMAGEDDON WAGED

NESY

The Great Hall is full by the time I arrive. Zaapiel nods at me, his cold eyes sending shivers down my spine. He and a handful of Sentinals are locked in conversation with Mikayel. About me, no doubt.

"Wow. You Sentinals always look so impressive in uniform." Zane materializes next to me, Cass two steps behind him. "When do you leave?" he asks.

"Anytime now."

"I don't think you should go," Cass says as she pulls me away from the crowd and into one of the interior corridors. Zane follows close behind, looking angry. No not angry, worried maybe.

"Cass, stop." Zane says, his eyes darting from Cass to me.

"No, I have to say this. Nesy, it's a trap. Azzaziel's using Aydan as bait. He's going to kill you."

Yeah, no kidding.

"He can try."

"I'm being serious, Nesayiel."

"And so am I. Cassiel, I'm not planning on tangling with Azzaziel. I'll let Mikayel take care of him. I want Aydan. I'm going to do what I should have done four days ago. If I happen to kill a few more UnHoly along the way, all the better." Anticipation wells up through me, mixing with my torment. "They're going to pay for what they did to Lorelei. What *he* did."

Zane shifts uncomfortably, his wings stretching behind him. "Not that I'm unhappy that you are back to acting like the cocky Sentinal again, but something about this doesn't add up." His worried expression deepens. "Since when were you willing to let go of your feelings for Aydan?"

He knows me too well.

"Since he decided that Azzaziel was his last hope." My face hardens with the words. "Since he killed my sister."

"Nesy," Cass says as Zane grabs her arm.

I ignore Cass's words. "Aydan made his choice. We both did. The difference is I thought about someone other than myself when I made mine."

"Aydan isn't the bad guy you think he is," Cass says in hushed tones. "He *wants* Mikayel and the army to come down. Wants—"

"Cassiel," Zane warns "Don't."

"You made the promise, Zane. Not me. Nesy deserves to know the truth. I won't let her go on thinking—"

"Guys, I'm standing right here. Stop talking about me like I'm not. Tell me what's going on or get out of my way. I have an army to join—some demonic butt to kick."

"Fine," Zane says, releasing a deep sigh. "Aydan didn't kill Lori for Azza."

"I saw him do it. And I don't care what he thinks his reasons were. It doesn't matter now."

"Nes, listen to me. He did it to save her, to end her suffering. She begged him to kill her and save you. He did it for her. He committed a selfless act. On his own." Zane stares at me, the weight of his words a yoke around my neck.

"So what? Am I supposed to be impressed by that?" My voice cracks and my stupid tears return.

I am so tired of crying over him

"He let you believe the lie so you would tell Mikayel. Ensure his death."

Like that makes a difference.

"He never planned on joining Azza. He's only doing this to protect you. Save you." Zane stares through me.

Dangit.

"It doesn't matter now," I lie. "Lorelei is still dead because of him. Aydan still belongs to the Dark One." The words strengthen my resolve. "His intentions don't matter now. It's too late."

"It *does* matter. Do you know what Azza will do to him?" Cass asks

"Yes. He'll receive the marks. Be branded for eternity."

"And those marks will strip everything away, Nesy. Everything. His feelings for you, his mercy for Lori, his memories. All of it. When Azzaziel's finished, Aydan will be nothing but a killer."

Cassiel's words cut through my warrior's shell. Bitter acid fills my mouth as everything I hope, every crazy fantasy I still have, ends.

I can't let him do this. Not for me.

"I have to stop him," I whisper.

"That's what Azzaziel is counting on. He wants you dead. You and Mikayel." Cass puts her hand on my shoulder.

"What am I supposed to do? Let Azzaziel strip Aydan's soul away? Let Mikayel kill him?"

Yes, that's exactly what I'm supposed to do.

"What if Mikayel fails?" I ask. "What if Aydan is bound to Azzaziel forever, another Dark One we can't fully defeat?" I pace in front of my friends, trying to ferret out a solution. "I can't let that happen. I have to get there first—before Aydan receives the marks. While he still remembers who I am."

War trumpets blare through the city.

I'm out of time.

"Guys, I need you." I swallow hard, forcing out my question. "Will you help me end this? The right way?"

"We've been ordered to stay," Cass says. "Help with the wounded."

"I know, but I can't do this without you; I can't fight off all of the demons, the UnHoly and stop Azzaziel all by myself. I need help."

Zane and Cass share a glance before looking at me.

I knew I could count on them.

I look into the Great Hall one last time. Mikayel catches my gaze.

Blazes!

His eyes widen as he recognizes my intent.

I open a portal in the narrow corridor.

"Nesayiel. Wait!" Mikayel pushes Zaapiel away and runs to me.

"I'm sorry," I whisper. "I have to do this." The portal closes as Mikayel fades away, concern marring every feature.

CHAPTER 41 – CHAOS INTERRUPTED

NESY

Aydan's voice fills my soul as I whirl through the darkness. He screams my name. His anguish rips a hole through my soul. I reach for Zane's arms as my legs buckle under Aydan's grief.

"Nes, what is it? What's wrong?"

"It's already started." I say, gasping. "He's being branded. Now."

More waves of torment roll into me. *...I love you...* Aydan's words float through my mind. A farewell. I draw my sword. "I need to stop this before Azzaziel finishes."

Cass and Zane draw their daggers.

"You guys get Aydan. Get him away if you can. I'll deal with the Dark One."

"Nesy, no." Concern paints Cass's face.

"There aren't any other options. Mikayel will be here soon. I just have to distract Azzaziel long enough for you to get Aydan away."

The vortex opens next the statue of Mikayel. I hear Aydan's screams before I can see anything.

The courtyard has changed, transformed from the intimate setting where Aydan and I professed our love into a battlefield. Uninvited fear bubbles through me. Fear for Aydan. For my brethren. For everything. I tighten my grip on my sword and spring from the void.

The wind ripples my wings, causing chills to erupt down my spine. Azza's putrid scent mixed with the smell of scorching flesh, burns my nostrils. My mind goes dark as instinct replaces thought. In one swift move, I swing my sword, striping the angelic sword from Azzaziel. "Get him. Now!" I scream to Cass and Zane. They pull Aydan away from the crude stone alter.

Aydan rises to his full height, his eyes clouded. Lifeless. He swings at Cass, sending her dagger flying.

"It's too late, little Sentinal," Azza laughs. "He has already forgotten you."

I refuse to believe Azza's lies, no matter how much my heart knows the truth.

I *am* too late.

"Get him out of here, guys. Invade his head, his heart, whatever you have to. Just get him out of here."

Aydan growls and swings again at my friends. They turn and run into the crowd of dark creatures, Aydan in close pursuit.

"You condemned them both to death when you brought them here. Hope you can live with that. For the few minutes you live." Azza's foul breath coats my skin.

I lunge toward him. He spins, narrowly missing my blade. Several UnHoly rush toward me.

"No," Azza commands. The dark creatures stop. "She's all mine." Azza draws his sword and circles me.

Game on.

"I suppose I should thank you for interrupting our little party," he taunts.

I match his movements, step by step.

"With your arrival, I can kill you myself. And make Aydan watch. A little incentive to ensure he finishes his rites."

I thrust forward, catching Azza's side. He growls. Counters. His sword slices the skin on my arm and my silver blood trickles from the wound.

"Shame about that skin of yours," he sneers. "Looks like we can penetrate it now."

"Just like I can slice yours." I lodge my blade deep into his thigh, ripping a long gash across his leg.

His scream rattles the concrete. "You'll pay for that, Sentinal. You *and* Aydan."

Our weapons clash in a shower of sparks as we match each blow, each trust. The scraping of our blades split the night air. Dark creatures circle us, watching. Waiting. They bite the air with their sharp beaks, hissing. I block it all out, thinking only of Azza. And his death.

"You can't beat me." Azza crows. The crowd's excitement grows to a feverish pitch, leaking into my thoughts.

Their screams taunt me and I wonder if Cass and Zane's screams are amongst them. I force out the images that spring to life—images of Aydan killing my friends.

No. Focus, Nesy. Focus.

I shake away my fear in less than a heartbeat and attack Azza. "Maybe not," I taunt. "But I can certainly hurt you." I attack again. And again.

Azza parries. He swings around, lodging his sword into my back, slicing through the muscle.

My mind explodes in an inferno. Agonizing pain grips me, engulfing my senses as I crash to the ground. My sword clatters on the concrete, echoing around me.

I gasp for air.

Azza wraps his spindly fingers around the hilt of my sword, raising it over his head.

Mikayel! I scream through my thoughts.

Terror seizes every muscle as my skin registers the whooshing air of Azza's blade coming toward me.

I roll away on instinct, my mind too lost to the pain to think.

The ground shakes and the courtyard erupts in a field of chaos. Vortexes open throughout the battlefield. Sentinals pour from every opening, poised to strike.

The scene distracts Azza for a moment and I grab my dagger, throwing it at him. "You won't win this, Azza. Not now. Not ever."

He ducks. But not fast enough. It lodges into his shoulder.

"Attack," he screams as he drops my sword.

I inhale the pain, the torment, the grief. Pushing myself up, I swallow back the agony exploding across my back and retrieve my sword. *He will pay...for everything.*

Two beasts land on my back, sending blinding light across my vision. My senses go into overload as I growl, and spin, throwing the creatures off. An Unholy, tall with the same bat-like wings and same foul stench, rushes toward me.

"*Vicis morior.* Time to die," I whisper, disposing of him with a single thrust.

I turn, looking for Azza. Gone. He's faded into the horde.

Coward.

More demons close the distance around me. I hack my way through them, ignoring the clawing and snapping of talons and beaks. I focus on one thought, one goal. *Aydan.* I must find Aydan.

I reach out for his heart.

Nothing. I feel…

Nothing.

Are you already dead?

CHAPTER 42 - MALEDICTION

AYDAN

My mind is not my own. It's wild, violent.

I attack the angels, desperate for their blood. But something holds me back, keeping me from killing them outright.

Pointless.

I will destroy them. I will kill them all.

I attack with my sword. Rip at them with my claws. Nothing but their death can stop me now. I chase them through the mayhem, my excitement, my need, growing with every step.

"Zane. This isn't working." I know her voice, remember it from my life before. Cassiel. Her fear urges me forward.

"I know, Cass. Just try to keep from getting hurt. I'll push into his thoughts again."

Zane.

I know them both.

Not that I care.

Kill them

—*No.*

Do it now

—*Stop.*

My hand rips across Cass's back. Her scream floods my ears as her torment flows through my senses, feeding me.

More.

I need more.

A voice, not my own, floods my thoughts...*Stop. This isn't who you are...It isn't too late...Please. For Nesy...*The words tumble through the recesses of my mind, tugging on something deep.

Stop

—*Keep attacking.*

Let them go

—*Kill them now.*

Agony explodes up my spine, setting my blood on fire. My need coils around my torment, suffocating me.

"Zane. Do something." Cass pleads. The gash on her back sizzles.

"I am. It isn't working." Zane dodges my blade.

I corner them against the stone walls of the cathedral.

Must.

Kill.

Now.

The stones reflect the crimson glow emanating from my marks.

"Cass, you try. Go into his heart. Try to—"

I strike Zane, ending his words and sending him to his knees.

You're mine.

Something—someone—floods my heart. Cassiel. She showers me with memories best forgotten.

Love for an angel

—Nesy.

Mercy for a human

—Lori

"Get out," I yell through gritted teeth. I pin her with my glare, stealing her air. The color drains from her face. She grabs at her throat, unable to breathe. Her eyes widen with fright. I shove her against the stone wall, and tear her from my heart. Her eyes roll back into her head as she collapses to the ground.

"Aydan. The marks aren't complete. You can fight your way back."

Zane's words mean nothing to me. I raise my sword to strike.

My thoughts blur.

My mind goes blank.

My hand opens against my will, sending my sword crashing to the ground as my thoughts explode in a burst of emotion. Hunger. Guilt. Torment. Love.

Each feeling is a distraction. The Beast screams as the feelings attach themselves to every part of me. I scarcely notice the ground shaking. Or the Sentinals pouring into the courtyard. They close in around me. And chaos descends.

Demon against Guardian.

UnHoly against Sentinal.

Fear, despair, and death rage as the battle drones on. It feeds me, focusing my efforts. Making me strong.

Zane dives for me, his fingers wrapped around his meager dagger. I strip his weapon from him with a flick of my hand, sending him hurtling to the ground.

The Sentinals descend on me. "I knew I should have finished this before," the leader says.

Zaapiel. His name is Zaapiel.

How do I know this?

I engage the Sentinal. We spar, the sound of our blades lost amidst the battle sounds circulating around us. We circle and strike, a fatal dance to the death. Zaapiel's rage fills the air and coats my tongue.

I want more. I hook his dagger and slice through his arm.

Got you now, little warrior.

Zaapiel counters, thrusting his sword into my flesh. My mind swirls as I stare at the sword protruding from my chest and stumble. I'm hurt, but not dead.

Not by a long shot.

Grabbing the hilt with both hands, I yank it free with a feral scream.

"You will pay for that Sentinal," I snarl, my words sounding more like a growl.

I lunge forward, digging my claws into Zaapiel's throat. His flesh sizzles. He slides to the ground next to Cass and Zane, blood oozing from his wound. His pain feeds me. His torment fills the empty spaces inside.

I lift the Sentinal by the throat. His eyes are cold. Hard. He tries to speak. Garbled sounds replace his words.

Cass and Zane rise.

They slam into my mind. Take over my heart.

Emotions ebb and flow for a moment. Until I block the intrusion and throw them from me.

"That won't work, little angels. Not anymore." I bring Zaapiel within inches of my face.

Time to feed.

I bring my lips to the Sentinal's mouth as a familiar voice screams in my head.

Killing me.

CHAPTER 43 - LIBERA ME

NESY

"No," I scream, watching Aydan across the courtyard.

He will destroy all of you, Azza taunts, his voice resonating deep within my thoughts.

"He's not yours yet." I push through the throng of dark creatures. "Stop, Aydan," I yell at the Beast before me. "This isn't you."

The sound of breaking stone and metal pulls my attention to the statue of Mikayel. Pieces of stone fall away as the sculpture comes to life, turning into my master. "Go," he says. "Tend to your friends. I will find Azzaziel."

I run for Aydan, desperate to stop him. His death-lust radiates through me.

"Aydan! No!" I scream as his lips cover Zaapiel's mouth. "Remember who you are."

I barrel into Aydan, slamming him into the stone wall and pinning him with Zaapiel's sword. He's stronger now, so much stronger. I shove the sword against his throat, staring into his lifeless face. "Zane, Cass. Get Zaap out of here. Now!"

"But—" Cass moves to help me.

"Do it now!" My voice booms off the stones as I push the sword harder against my love.

Zane grabs Cass. They take Zaapiel and disappear through a portal, their actions only a blur. I stare into Aydan's hard face as he growls at me. His beautiful amber eyes are gone, replaced by the empty black orbs of the Beast.

Just like Azza's

"You're too late, Sentinal. Your Aydan is gone."

His voice fills me with fear. Gone are the musical notes that filled me with love yesterday, replaced by something so sinister it rattles my core.

My gaze travels down his face and neck, counting the angry tangles of lines that crisscross and knot across his flesh. One.

Two.

Three.

Four.

Five...

Only five completed patterns.

There's still hope.

"You're not lost, Aydan. You're still here, trapped somewhere inside of yourself. I can feel it."

Chaos swirls around us as the sounds of battle increase. Screams mix with metal and the swoosh of portals and gateways opening. Aydan wrestles against my sword. Wrapping a hand around the blade, he shoves hard, slicing a large gash. He continues to push, slamming the blade into my chest. The blow rolls off my breastplate as I spin away. "Aydan. It's me."

I parry and block his onslaught of blows, unable to counter. "Stop this. You aren't lost. I can still feel your heart. I know you're in there. Our love still lives in you."

I step back and duck, his blade a mere inch overhead. "Please, Aydan. Stop."

He growls and attacks again. Blow after blow. Thrust after thrust. Relentless.

I block every attack, retreating into the shadows. He advances, nothing but desperation in his black eyes.

"I love you Aydan," I say, pleading. "Still."

He refuses to abate the onslaught of his hits. Every parry I make, every counter I strike, seals our fate.

Maybe I am too late.

Please, I scream into his thoughts. *You aren't like him. You have a choice. Don't do this.*

He waivers. His hungry expression turns to anguish. "Come back to me, Aydan. Love me."

He stops and I knock the sword from his hand. His eyes widen with recognition. The black orbs begin to change, lighten, as amber irises fleck through the dark circles.

Every jagged line of color brings me hope. "Aydan?" His name scrapes across my lips as my heart clenches.

"Nesy." He chokes. "Wh—?"

His knees buckle. He lowers his head and I watch the color drain from his face.

"Sshh," I say as I grab his arms. "Don't try to talk. You're weak." I bear his weight and steady him.

I feel him melt into my arms. A silhouette forms in the darkness, accompanied by the unwanted stench of death.

"He is far from weak, little Sentinal." Azza emerges from the shadows, armed with a Sentinal's sword.

Releasing Aydan, I raise my sword. Azzaziel is not claiming Aydan now, not while I'm still alive.

Azza raises the Sentinal's sword to Aydan's neck. The blade drips with the same black liquid oozing from the Dark One's wounds. Our eyes lock.

"I won't let you finish that mark," I say as I circle towards him.

"And Aydan won't let you prevent it." He counters. "He knows what will happen to you if he doesn't complete the sacrament."

"Don't listen, Aydan. You don't have to do this." I edge forward, glancing between the sword at Aydan's neck and his eyes. *I love you,* I whisper into his thoughts.

Nodding imperceptibly to Aydan, I swing a large arc over his head, slicing into Azza's flesh.

The move catches him off guard. He stumbles back and drops the sword. Aydan reaches for my arm and smiles. His eyes lighten even further.

"Let's end this," I say.

Together.

The UnHoly swarm around Aydan and me, weapons swinging in every direction. We slash through them together and push the mob back into the shadows.

Azza retreats from our blows. I dive for him, carving new gashes into his skin.

He parries. Attacks. Slashing into my armor, he batters me. His blows are strong—but not as strong as they once were.

Azza and I circle and lunge with deliberate precision. The force of each blow rattles the ground, sending tiny tremors up my arm. I advance, steering Azza away from Aydan and back to the broken statue of Mikayel. New gashes appear on his thighs, his shoulders, his chest.

He counters every blow, searing his own trail of lacerations along my flesh. But every blow costs him a little.

He's growing weaker.

I double my efforts, ignoring the pain and fatigue coating my cells. I can think of nothing but Azza and the vengeance I crave.

"You won't win." He attacks, colliding with my breastplate. "You won't save Aydan."

"I already have." I swing, landing a hard blow across his heart. Every moment of torment, every ounce of vengeance is poured into that blow. Azza crumbles, falling to his knees at my feet. His weapon falls from his hands as confusion paints his expression.

I kick the weapon far from his reach. I don't care that I can't kill him, don't care about anything other than unleashing the fury I've felt for so long. Gripping my sword with two hands I stand over him, the blade positioned over his heart. I stare into his cold lifeless eyes. Vengeance is mine at last.

"This is for Aydan," I whisper, plunging the sword deep into Azza's chest and pinning him to the ground.

His screams echo through the courtyard. Thick, black blood scorches the pavement as Azza falls back, his empty eyes still open.

CHAPTER 44 - RUIN

AYDAN

I charge into the UnHoly descending on me, striking at everything in my path. My mind is sharp, determined. My own.

The marks on my neck flare to life and scorch my soul. I drink my anguish, allowing it to sharpen my senses.

Nesy screams in the distance, locked in battle with my master. Their swords clash, each stroke filling me with dread. He will not let this pass. He will kill her.

Unless I kill him first.

A loud scream fills the courtyard, burning into the Beast. Pain rips through the marks seared on my neck and for a moment I can't breathe, consumed with the same agony I felt earlier this night. Nesy has pinned my master. He is immobile.

For now.

Good.

I expect to feel relief. Hope. Satisfaction. Anything but the fear suffocating me as the UnHoly horde pulls back. A large gateway opens in front of me, lined with Sentinals. Fifty. Maybe more.

My death has arrived.

    Finally.

The Sentinals pour in around me, swords drawn. I back away, blocking the initial attack. Blades roll off my shoulders, slicing the air around me.

    There are too many. I can't fend them off.

    I don't want to.

They rip open every wound, every scar, slicing new gashes over my body. The marks on my neck burn with crimson heat. I taste death in the air. My death. It floods my senses and nourishes my soul. It strengthens me.

The Sentinals continue their attack. Their blades lodge deeply into my flesh. Black liquid oozes from every wound, scorching the ground as it pours from me. I counter and block the attacks out of instinct.

I need to hold on. Make certain Nesy is safe. My hunger flares to life, the scent of my own blood, my death, urging the Beast inside.

    Fight back

        —I will not kill.

    Feed from them

        —I will not nourish you.

A feral scream rips through me as I push the Beast aside.

    For now.

I parry the relentless volley of blows, refusing to counter. I will not submit to Azza. I will not be the Beast. The brands eclipse every thought, searing my hope.

Feed on them

—no.

Fulfill your destiny

—never.

Obey.

The Beast growls as my body lunges forward. I counter the raging attack of the Sentinals.

Yes.

Thrust into the angels before me.

Good.

No.

Nesy, think of Nesy.

Blades whirl around me. For a moment time stops and my mind clears, illuminating what I must do—the only choice left to make. Inhaling a deep breath, I open my arms, allowing my sword to drop to the ground. The Sentinals thrust forward, piercing my shoulders, my arms, my chest. I sink to my knees, embracing my death.

My one chance.

The earth begins to shake.

"Stop!" Mikayel steps from a vortex opening next to me. His voice booms over the battle, stopping the attack.

Yes yes yes.

Shadows mix with the fog cowering along the ground. It grows, darkening everything in its path. The UnHoly run toward the smoke and darkness.

"Go after the UnHoly. Don't let them escape." Mikayel's order rings throughout the ranks. They swarm the shadows. Screams bounce off the mist and gloom.

I look up at Mikayel. End this, please. End me. "You need to kill me. It's the only way."

"I know," he says.

"Thank you."

Mikayel raises the Sword of Truth and mouths a silent prayer.

CHAPTER 45 – MY KYRIE

NESY

The Sentinals chase the dark creatures into the encroaching fog. I watch as they lose them in the black emptiness, listening to their cries of frustration. My sword remains planted in Azza's chest. I call Mikayel, but my voice dies around me.

Not good.

I will always love you, Nesy. Remember me... The words replay in an endless loop through my mind. I feel Aydan's love. His pain.

His resolve.

No!

A small sound floats from Azza's mouth. "You still lose, Sentinal," he spits. "You still lose." A malicious smile flashes across his face as he chokes on his own laughter.

I drive my blade deeper into his chest. Black liquid trickles from his mouth. His face drains of color. Rotting flesh falls from his bones.

That ought to shut him up.

Again Aydan's voice finds my heart.

Where are you?

I step over Azza, ignoring the breathless laughter emanating from his nearly dead mouth.

I'm coming, Aydan. Wait.

I search through the murky fog surrounding me. A valley of mist clears in front of me revealing my own personal horror—Aydan on his knees; Mikayel pointing the Sword of Truth at his chest.

"No!" I yell across the expanse. "Stop." My legs refuse to respond, pinning me where I stand.

Stand down, Sentinal. Mikayel's words slam into me, mixing with Azza's incessant laughter.

I can't do this.

I take one more step forward as the weight of Aydan's torment crashes over me, mixing with my own. My gaze meets his, tears trickling down our cheeks.

"Goodbye," he silently mouths.

Run...*it's too late.*

Stop him...*Aydan wants this.*

Mikayel will do what I can't. And Aydan will finally find peace.

I stare at Mikayel and nod. His eyes widen, sadness replaced with a feral rage.

Aydan opens his mouth, clamoring to his feet.

Blinding pain explodes through my body, my stomach, my chest.

My heart.

I look down as a sea of nausea envelops me. Hot sticky wetness mats against my skin, coating my armor. A dagger lodges under my breastplate. Blood fills my throat, covering my tongue and lips.

Azza stands beside me, his eyes locked with Aydan. He yanks the blade through my flesh.

A fresh wave of agony overtakes me. I fall, my body convulsing, flashes of my life streaming around me. Moments with Adam. With Aydan.

The feel of his touch on my skin.

The sound of his voice in my ears.

And the look of love in his eyes.

My body folds in on itself as everything turns black.

Aydan's voice fades from my mind.

And my thoughts…

End.

CHAPTER 46 - DIVINITY

AYDAN

"Nesy!" I scream, pushing away from Mikayel. The Akedah knife lies at my feet. I hurl it at my master, cursing him. The knife whirls through the air, lodging in his neck.

Azza howls in agony and pulls out the blade.

Nesy slinks to the ground, silver blood pouring from her mouth, her chest. It soaks through her armor. Coming. Coming. Coming.

Rage explodes the brand on my neck. *You'll pay for this, Azza.*

You'll pay for everything.

I barrel into Azza, thrusting my sword into the open wound on his chest. He growls and tosses me aside.

Not this time.

A snarl rips across my lips. The marks blaze against my skin. I hunger for Azza. For his death.

It's a hunger I'm more than willing to feed.

I push back into him, clawing his skin with my taloned fingers. Feeding off his rage.

Azza wraps his hands around my throat and squeezes.

"I'm too strong for you now. You should've killed me before you marked me as your equal." I'm blind with fury for the Beast that is Azza. The Beast I've become.

I wrench myself free from Azza's grasp and rip open his skin.

Mikayel's strong hand stops me from shredding Azza. I wrestle against his hold, desperate to do what I should've done so long ago.

A shadow coils around Azza. I reach for him as he begins to fade.

"No," Mikayel says. "Tend to Nesy. She needs you. Get her to Celestium before it's too late. Get her to the healers, to Raphael." Mikayel chokes on the last words, his battle worn features marred by a lone tear slithering down his face.

Nesy.

I look at the tattered body of my love.

Nesy. Not you. Never you.

It was supposed to be me.

Me.

Tears overwhelm me as my rage gives way to sorrow.

"I'll go after Azza. You help Nesy." Mikayel places a gentle hand on my shoulder. "Take her home." He disappears after Azza, fading into the darkness as a scream echoes in the fog.

Kill him Mikayel. Kill him for me.

For Nesy.

I bend down and cradle her broken body. Her eyes flutter open for a moment. "Aydan," she rattles.

"Sshh, love. Don't try to speak." I can't stop the tears, the pain, the rage.

"Did I stop him? Before the last mark—did I stop him?"

"Yes, you did great."

Nesy's eyes roll back in her head.

I hold her, knowing she won't survive. Fighting my need to end her life, still. I strain against the Beast and carry her to a portal.

Cass and Zane run to me, their bodies and faces bruised. Battered. By me. Grief blankets their expressions as they look from Nesy to me. I shake my head and feel our hearts shatter.

For Nesy.

"We'll take you to Celestium." Cass takes my arm. "To the healers."

Nesy groans with every step.

"I'm sorry if this hurts, love." I can barely speak. "I have to get you home. I promised Mikayel."

Her eyes snap open. "Aydan," she forces through gritted teeth.

"Shhh, it's okay." Zane caresses her forehead, calming her.

"Aydan. Listen to me," Nesy whispers. "I need you to remember who you are, okay? In case I don't make it." Her face shows the agony she feels.

The agony calling me to feed.

"You are an angel, Aydan. My angel. Not some monster for Azzaziel. Remember." Her voice fades. Her eyes close. "Tell Mikayel. You are still an ang—" She stops and her head rolls to the side.

My world rains down on me as my knees begin to shake.

Her beauty

—gone.

Her love

—taken.

Her life

—over.

"Stay with me, Nesy. We're almost home, baby. Please, stay with me." The words shake as my voice cracks.

I can't stand.

Can't breathe.

Zane takes my arms, bearing some of the load I carry.

"We have to go. Close the portal," I manage to choke out. "Now!"

The spaces close in around us, Nesy's limp body in my arms.

CHAPTER 47 - OBLIVION

AYDAN

The Council chamber is different than I remember. Smaller and less foreboding. I pace, too anxious to do anything else.

Please be okay. Please be okay.

Anxiety seeps through me as I wait for news on Nesy.

Images of Azza's dagger slicing into her replay in my mind. I lean against the wall, unable to stop the ocean of grief pounding into me. Pieces of my soul shatter around me as I slide down the wall. Agony fills the darkest recesses. I can't breathe, drowning in the weight of my pain.

Nothing matters without her.

Nothing.

I pull my legs to my chest, burying my head in my hands. I should push away these feelings, be strong.

But I don't want to.

I deserve every moment of this torment. Every ounce of agony.

Moments pass, or maybe hours, until the storm finally ebbs. I draw a ragged breath and open my eyes. The sun casts ominous shadows across the large hall.

My mind wanders, flipping through the last few days.

Azza caused this. All of it.

Azza and me.

The marks on my neck burn as my wings—so different from what they once were—shift and twitch. I stare at the black skin stretched over bone, reminders of what I truly am.

You're an angel, Aydan. You're my angel....

Nesy's words chastise my vengeance. Revenge got me into this mess.

Revenge caused her death.

—is she really dead?

I have to find a way to control my fury.

For her.

The Council doors open. Gabriel walks into the large chamber, his robes casting emerald beams into the shadows.

"Where's Mikayel?" Tell me he's killed Azza. Please.

"He has not returned from the battlefield. Raphael is with Nesy."

My heart stops for a moment. Is she okay? Is there a chance?

Compassion sweeps across Gabriel's face. "We do not yet know her fate. The wounds appear fatal. Raphael is trying everything he can. There may still be hope."

"If there's anything I can do." My voice fades. "I will gladly give my soul for hers. Anything."

"I know." Gabriel places his hand on my shoulder. My grief abates in an instant.

But not my shame.

Never my shame.

My brand ignites, reminding me of what I am now; what I will always be.

"What is it?" Gabriel asks.

"I won't become like Azza."

"You have shown compassion, mercy. Those are not the traits of the Beast."

"Yes, but if I stay here, the marks will change me. And if I go to the eternal flames of the Abyss, I will still be a monster. Azza will come looking for me and finish what he has started."

"What are you asking of me?"

"I—" The sound dies on my tongue. I inhale my fear and ignore the rage seething inside. "I need you to kill me. I need Mikayel to use his sword and end this. Permanently."

"And if Nesy were to survive, is that still what you would want?" Gabriel stares through me, waiting.

My heart and mind open up to him. My torment continues to slam against my soul, a sharp contrast to the peace Gabriel offers.

But there can be no peace for me. No peace for the Beast.

"I won't be like Azza. And if I live, I can be nothing else." My mind is set.

There is no other choice for me. Not now.

Gabriel nods. Silent.

A moment passes. And another. Finally Gabriel looks at me. "The Council will consider your request. Wait for us in the antechamber. This is not something I am willing to decide without the others."

They have to agree. One way or another I'm ending my life.

The antechamber is small, adorned with nothing more than a few oversized chairs and small tables. The walls are decorated with reliefs of the Council members. I stare at the picture of Mikayel.

Where are you?

The brand on my neck smolders, an eternal reminder of what I am. Each moment that clicks by increases my rage—my lust for revenge. My need for death.

Each moment brings me closer to the Beast.

I focus on Nesy. She loved me, believed in me. She saved me once.

Will you save me again? Can you?

My thoughts fade and fill with hatred, stoking a rage impossible to contain. I can't live like this. I sit back on the large chair, closing my eyes. Sleep comes quickly. As do the dreams…

"Aydan. Where are you?" Nesy's voice calls through the thick forest.

Lost in the maze of trees and shrubs, I follow her voice, unable to catch it. I break into a clearing.

LACRIMOSA

Azza stands before me, Nesy's sword in his hands. "Time for your final mark." He swoops down and grabs my neck. "I will take her from you forever. Force you to feed off her soul." Azza takes the sword and carves into my skin.

Screams fill the small chamber as I bolt upright. Sweat beads down my brow. Zane and Cass stand before me, their faces ashen.

"It was just a dream," Cass says. "A nightmare."

"Azza." I shake away the dream, pushing aside the constant urgings of the brand. "How's Nesy?"

Cass avoids my glance. I look to Zane. The pain in his eyes answers my question. "Is she—?" I can't say the words.

"Raphael has done everything he can. She's gone."

My heart slams my ribs and stops. The marks on my neck explode, aching to be satiated.

Everything I was

—*gone.*

Everything I loved

—*taken.*

"I'm so sorry," Zane says. His voice is gentle, so much like Gabriel's. "There was nothing you could've done."

"There are so many other choices I could have made. So many." My thoughts simmer with anger.

And vengeance.

Again Nesy's words filter into my mind, pushing back the Beast.

For now.

Gabriel walks into the antechamber, solemn. "We are ready for you, Aydan."

"What's he talking about? Ready for what?" Cass looks from Zane to Aydan. "Zane?"

"You asked them to kill you, didn't you?" Zane's gaze penetrates my mind.

I turn and walk away, praying for my miracle.

Sariel and Raphael are locked in tight conversation, tears in their eyes. I meet Raphael's gaze. He nods at me and looks away. Mikayel's face is battle worn, his clothes covered in the blood of the UnHoly.

Have you finished this? Is Azza gone now?

I watch as Mikayel clenches his jaw. His rage matches my own. Gabriel motions for me to sit.

I wave him off. I want answers. Need them. "What did you decide?" I ask.

"I think it is time for you to go with Mikayel." A sad smile touches Gabriel's lips.

Finally, and end to this nightmare. "Thank you," I say, nodding to the Council members.

"Thank you, Aydan, for returning Nesayiel to her home. And for your sacrifices." Mikayel's voice cracks. "You have taught us a lot about the nature of redemption. And love."

"You have Nesy to thank for that." I drop my head, drinking in the torment that will not subside.

Never subside.

Mikayel and I leave through the antechamber. I look at Cass and Zane, mouthing a silent goodbye.

At last.

CHAPTER 48 – CHOSEN

AYDAN

Puget Sound, Washington, January

I climb the short trail behind my apartment, eager to reach the summit and outrun my dreams. My nightmares.

They're always the same. A shapeless girl. An endless fight. Hideous creatures. Angels.

And demons.

The nightmares torment me every night, as they have for the three months since leaving Celestium. My mind drifts to my last days in that place. I should have died. I wanted to die.

I still do…

Mikayel walks with me to the Sentinals' chamber

"Did you kill Azza? Is he gone?"

"No." The sadness in Mikayel's voice is overwhelming.

LACRIMOSA

"And will you kill me now?"

"I cannot."

"You must," I beg. "It's the only way. I won't be able to hold back the monster I am. Not for long. Not without Nesy."

"You aren't a monster."

"You know I am."

The memory clears as I reach the top of the hill. The fog rolls off the Sound. Snow blankets the ground around me. I watch the light waves caress the water. Whales crest the surface.

Why are they here?

The frigid January wind rips through the trees and my cells. I pull my jacket close around me and tighten my scarf. Drawing a deep breath, I look across the Sound. Everything is so different here. Green and open. Nothing like the tangled mass of buildings I called home for so long. The air smells of pine, reminding of things I long to forget.

Germany.

Her.

I've tried to detach, forget. But she won't let me. She visits my dreams and hides in the shadows of every waking moment. Even now, on the crest behind my home, I hear her voice on the wind.

I release another breath and hike back down the hill. My body, this experience, are foreign. I sense nothing but my own skin. Hear nothing but my own thoughts. I feel none of the connection I've shared with the dark creatures. No thoughts of rage or lust.

No visions of angels.

No ravenous hunger.

Nothing.

The change leaves an empty hole inside that cannot be filled. I feel alone, abandoned. I walk back into the large apartment and stare at the leather journal waiting for me on the table. The soft brown binding and crisp blank pages call to me, unleashing even more memories.

I can't quiet the noise of my own thoughts.

Or my feelings…

"You may find being human far worse than being the Beast you fear." Gabriel probes my mind again.

"I doubt that."

"Tell me, are you upset with your judgment? Your sentence?"

"No," I answer. "Just confused. Why can't Mikayel just kill me? Why would you want to make me mortal?"

"We will not kill any creature capable of mercy. Compassion."

"But——"

"And we cannot let you live in our world. Or in the Abyss. If you are with us, Azzaziel will surely find you. He will awaken the Beast and eventually it will consume you. Being mortal seems the best alternative in this situation."

"What if I can't resist the marks?"

"Resisting that part of your nature will take all of your strength, yes. But it is not impossible."

I stare at my feet. Still confused. Still afraid.

"Don't fear who you are, Aydan. Those marks on your neck do not have to define you. You have a lifetime to master your nature. Just remember your true essence."

"And what is that, sir?"

"You must discover that as well."

"And if I can't, what then? If the marks consume me, how am I to resist?"

"I brought this for you. It may help" Gabriel hands a small leather book to me.

"What's it for?"

"Your thoughts. Fears. Anything. Many humans find it a helpful way to remember."

"Remember?"

"Their nature. I will see you at the end of that life, when you again face the Council and await your judgment." Gabriel walks away.

"If I return," I whisper, the weight of the book heavy in my hands.

I stroke the leather binding and place it back on the table unopened. Always unopened.

CHAPTER 49 - REBIRTH

AYDAN

The new semester starts and I must resume a normal life. Go to class, meet people. An unfamiliar fear rattles through me. I drown under the loneliness that now defines me. I walk up the steps of my new school, anxiety an ever-present part of my new body. Stealing a glance at my reflection in the glass door, I see myself. Just as tall, just as lean, with skin the color of tea. My hair naturally dark, curling at the ends. My eyes look inhuman—black orbs colored with streaks of amber.

A black turtleneck and heavy scarf hide the remainder of my shame. The top of the brand peeks out from under the scarf. My hands instinctively move to the black marks. They no longer burn, no longer control me.

But for how long?

Trepidation tosses my stomach as acid swirls up my throat, coating my tongue. I pretend I'm fine. Pretend my life is fine.

If only.

Registration takes moments, Gabriel made sure of that. I get my books and walk to class. Every shadow whispers to me. Azza is out there. Somewhere. He will seek his revenge.

He always does.

How can I fight what I can't see? What I can't sense? Will the angels who sent me here protect me? Can they? How long will this mortal life last? Not long, I think. Too many questions I can never answer.

Staring at the schedule, I read the name. Aydan Johnson. Just like before. I walk into European History. The teacher assigns me a seat at an empty table.

Good.

No one to bother me. No one to voice the things I cannot say. I think about the past Gabriel has constructed for me. A broken home with parents long dead. The tragedy of that story mirrors my own.

School passes in a blur, one class into the next. One day into the next. There has to be more to this life. More than the loneliness I can't seem to escape.

Another month passes. And then another. I have no friends. Speak to no one. Azza will send spies to tempt me. Demons dressed up as friends.

I trust no one.

My dreams have turned into waking memories. Images of Nesy are permanently burned into my thoughts. I see every detail of her face painted in the landscape around me. I feel her touch on my skin whenever the wind blows.

And I remember how it felt when she died in my arms.

The scenes of that time repeat over and over in a never-ending loop, constant reminders of the Beast I was.

The Beast I may still be.

I'd accepted my judgment without question. Agreed to live a mortal life. I didn't know my memories would come with me; didn't know I'd relive them every day.

Death would have been more merciful.

The leather journal still sits on my table, dust collecting on the cover. I grab it, again caressing the binding. *Use this to remember who you are.* Gabriel's words repeat in Nesy's voice.

Remember who you are...

A lone tear slithers down my cheek.

Can I do this?

I open the book, looking at the white linen of the pages. They call to me, begging to be written on. I have nothing left to lose now. The pen gripped tightly in my hand, I begin to write...

I didn't know being human would hurt so much. I feel so cut off. All of the time. And yet, my emotions consume me constantly.

The words pour onto the pages as I write my last confessions.

Forbidden love for a human who was an angel.

Fear of the Master who was the Beast.

Hatred for the angel who craved revenge.

Hatred for me.

I empty my soul into the book, one page at a time, until the sun sets.

Tired and vacant, I sleep a dreamless sleep.

At last.

CHAPTER 50 - HOPE

AYDAN

The day starts as every other, except somehow I am less afraid. Hopeful, even. I walk into class and sit at my no-longer-empty table. Books and notebooks spill over the desk. A notebook is open to pages of careless doodles. Pictures of wings. Angels and demons.

I can't help but look at the drawings. Can't help but remember that life.

A girl slides into the seat and cleans up the mess. She's tall and lean. Shoulder-length black hair arranges itself into sharp angles around her face. Her pale skin looks almost translucent. Dark glasses cover her eyes. She ignores me completely and continues to shove her things into the bag.

"Hey," I say, curious.

She nods and goes back to her books. The teacher begins a familiar lecture. Central Germany. 1500's.

Why do teachers always want to discuss these legends?

A chuckle escapes as I remember the countless times I've heard this lecture. And how different the legends are from the truth.

The girl removes her sunglasses and furrows her brow. "Something funny?"

Her voice sounds like music. My heart stops as I look into her now visible eyes. Blue. Deep blue. Her gaze penetrates my soul and for a moment I can't breathe.

She smiles. "Well? What's so funny?"

I force myself to breathe in and out. In and out.

You died. I felt you die.

She looks at me, expecting an answer.

I breathe in and out. In and out.

It can't be you.

"Um," I manage to choke out. "Nothing."

She smiles again, awakening something deep inside. I lean in and catch her scent—vanilla, lavender and sunshine.

"So, what's your name?" she whispers.

My mouth refuses to work.

"I said, what's your name?"

Her eyes are so blue. So familiar.

"Aydan."

"Nice. It suits you," she says. "I'm Vanessa. Most people just call me—"

"Nesy," I finish.

"Actually, I was going to say Nessa. But Nesy works. I like it."

I smile, lost in the endless blue ocean of her eyes. Maybe I will be okay in this life now.

With her.

ACKNOWLEDGEMENTS:

Writing this book was a journey within a journey. Countless moments of hope; countless moments of despair. Fortunately, I had many amazing people keeping me focused and helping me pursue this elusive endeavor:

To Heather McCorkle and the team at Compass Press ~ WOW, just wow. Your constant belief in the words on the page kept me going in the most difficult of times. Thank you for trusting that I could see this through and deliver a story as powerful as the one you saw in the raw words.

The earliest readers of the story ~ Elana Johnson and Michelle McLean. You two witnessed the birth of this story. You helped me find it and shape it. Told me when it sucked, helped me find Nesy's voice. I am forever grateful in ways I will never be able to fully express.

My early Betas ~ Laura Diamond, Amanda Bonilla, Julie Butcher, Danyelle Leafty. You watched me query, watched me fail, and helped me retool the story into something more…so much more.

My later Betas ~ Ali Cross, LK Gardner-Griffie, Heather McCorkle. You all convinced me that this was worth being published. You understood Nesy and Aydan, and helped me keep my promises to them.

My teen readers ~ Fabiana Fonseca, Delaney Jures, Rebecca Lewis. Your belief that this story would happen helped in ways I can't begin to explain. You helped me find a voice, a title, so many little things. THANK YOU! And yes, I am giving you three a copy of the book. I promise!

To the online community of writers, bloggers, readers and friends ~ all of you helped me navigate through the hazards and scale the mountain. Thank you for the support, the fellowship and the friendship. Thank you for reading my prequel and encouraging me to write more. I am truly more because of all of you.

And finally, to the foundation of my life ~ my husband, my children, my sister-in-law and my brothers-in-law, my dad and my mom. Your sacrifices, your confidence, your support of both my coffee and music habits…without all of you, this book would still be collecting dust on my hard drive.

CPSIA information can be obtained at www.ICGtesting.com
Printed in the USA
BVOW030934010213

312121BV00001B/5/P

9 780984 786367